Watch for other titles from
Dagger Books and
Paul Mohrbacher

www.secondwindpublishing.com

THE

MAGIC

FAULT

To Mike — one of my favorite character!

BY

PAUL MOHRBACHER

Paul Mohrbacher

Dagger Books
Published by Second Wind Publishing, LLC.
Kernersville, NC
Second Printing, 2012

Dagger Books
Second Wind Publishing, LLC
931-B South Main Street, Box 145
Kernersville, NC 27284

First Dagger Books edition published January 2010.
Dagger Books, Running Angel, and all production design are
trademarks of Second Wind Publishing, used under license.

For information regarding bulk purchases of this book, digital
purchase and special discounts, please contact the publisher at
www.secondwindpublishing.com

Cover design by Stacy Castanedo
Cover art: Detail, Michelangelo, *Last Judgment*, fresco, Sistine
Chapel, Vatican, Rome
Author Photo: Andrea Cole Photography

Manufactured in the United States of America
ISBN-13: 978-1-935171-54-6

Author's Notes

Historians love using the present tense in talking about the past. "Abigail Adams sits down to write a letter to her husband." "Lincoln dresses to go to the theatre." Words have magical qualities, and the present tense is a way of summoning the past, as one would a ghost.

The Shroud of Turin, whether it is authentic or not, urges the viewer to make the death of Jesus present. "They wrap his body in a shroud." The experience reanimates the past: "They wrap his body in *this* shroud."

This is a story about people who take the reanimation literally — something that touched Christ's skin must still have power of its own. Wasn't its original role in a miracle alleged to have been healing the skin of someone who had Hansen's disease — leprosy? How far might its power extend today? To the end of the earth?

The Separation Between East and West

In the 4th Century CE, the Emperor Constantine moved the capital of the Roman Empire from Rome to Byzantium, an ancient city at the eastern edge of the empire. He renamed it Constantinople, and established it as a more congenial center for the Christian Church toward which he was increasingly drawn. So began the rivalry between Rome and Constantinople, with the Pope and traditional authority in Rome, and the Emperor and a more freewheeling theology in Constantinople.

For the next six centuries the Eastern and Western Churches chafed with one other and traded accusations about orthodoxy and papal supremacy, but kept the Christian church as one. It was not until the year 1054 that a final split took place, when diplomats from Rome excommunicated church leadership in Constantinople. This break was not perceived as a schism, but a separation — one that still stands today.

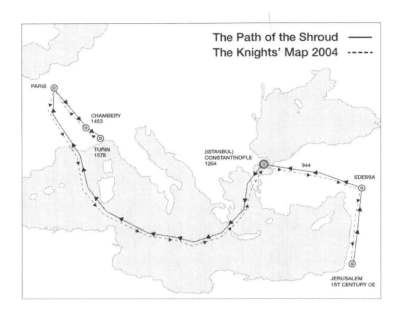

The Path of the Shroud —————
The Knights' Map 2004 - - - - -

PARIS

CHAMBERY
1453

TURIN
1578

(ISTANBUL)
CONSTANTINOPLE
1204

944

EDESSA

JERUSALEM
1ST CENTURY CE

The tradition is that Thaddeus, the disciple who replaced Judas, was sent from Jerusalem to evangelize Edessa, a city in modern-day Turkey. Carrying a cloth image of the face of Christ, he worked miracles, including healing the king of Edessa of his leprosy. In the second century CE the cloth went underground along with the local persecuted Christians and was lost until the sixth century.

Muslim forces took control of the city in the 7th century. In the 10th century, a Christian delegation from Constantinople purchased the image from Edessa. The church in Constantinople displayed it from time to time until the 4th crusade in 1204. Crusaders looted Constantinople and brought the image to France. What today we know as the Shroud was displayed in different cities and towns, until it was transferred to Turin in the 16th century.

In 1898, investigators used a camera to discover that the sketchy set of markings on the cloth was a photographic negative. A controversial radiocarbon dating in 1988 concluded that the Shroud was produced somewhere between 1260 and 1390 C.E.

In 2004, the fictional Knight Precursors of Christ the King set out to reverse history.

Acknowledgements

I'm grateful to Mary Logue, who edited a very early kitchen-sink version of the story; Francis Leonesi in Paris, for insights on matters French and Italian; Jacob Chizzo in Istanbul, for being my virtual guide to that ancient city; my agent Dawn Dowdle for her support and professionalism; and Second Wind Publishers for accepting *The Magic Fault*.

My interest in writing this story began through my wife, Ruth Murphy, who led me to Turin and the Piedmont region for the Slow Food Movement's *Salone del Gusto*. As in life and love, one thing led to another.

Paul Mohrbacher
www.magicfault.com

THE MAGIC FAULT

Mea culpa, mea culpa, mea maxima culpa.

Through my fault, through my fault, through my most grievous fault.

From the Confession of Sins in the Roman Catholic Tridentine Mass

O felix culpa quae talem et tantum meruit habere redemptorem.
O happy fault which received as its reward so great and so good a
redeemer.
From the Holy Saturday service of the Roman Catholic liturgy

Poena potest demi, culpa perennis erit.
The punishment can be remitted; the fault will be everlasting.
Ovid, Letters from Pontus, I, 1, 64

CHAPTER 1

Why — on the one day he had been out of his office in six months — had the security system malfunctioned? After a grueling six-hour trade show in Milan, the chief of security sat in his office in the cavernous basement of Turin's Saint John the Baptist Cathedral. Eager to head home for a glass of Alverno before supper, he hunched over the computer. He was bewildered by two words on the screen: *Backup System.*

Had there been a power loss earlier in the day? He sat there, puzzled. He picked up the phone and punched the number of the remote monitoring service. The person on duty nonchalantly assured him, *"Niente."* *Niente* was his daily bread; with that assurance, he could go home satisfied; without it, he could not go home.

He stared at the enormous computer console and clicked on the master control program icon. *Backup software has temporarily overridden the primary software program. Click here to reinstate the primary operational system.*

What was that all about? Who had engineered the override? Why? He shuddered and instinctively looked behind him. He was alone in the church, he knew. But he sensed a presence, another intellect at work here. Never had the complex system balked. An override was an intentional act, not a misfire.

Never in his career had he opened the safe on the wall of his office. He stood and shuffled over to it. He dialed the code, tugged at the door, took out a ring of keys and removed the cover of a small metal case. He reached in. He had never touched the *ultima chiave* before, the key to the great stone case. He removed it gently, trembling. He went back to the console panel, entered a code and saw the emergency icon appear on the screen. He clicked on it. The entire security system of the Cathedral of Saint John the Baptist became disarmed.

Immediately the phone rang. *"Niente,"* he muttered to the operator.

He placed the key in his pocket. It was dark in the hallway outside the control center. He turned on a bank of lights leading to the elevator. He quickened his steps, entered the elevator and punched the button. Slow — the old mechanism creaked. When the door opened, he stood directly outside the security door of the Savoy Chapel. The Chapel of the Holy Shroud, *la Sacra Sindone,* the burial cloth of Christ.

The jangle of the keys rang out in the empty church. He opened the door. A single security lamp flickered on a darkened wall. He went to a control board and brought up the spotlights. The Shroud's display case looked intact. He felt the presence again, the alien spirit. He could not stop shuddering. His hand withdrew the *ultima chiave* from his pocket; he dropped the key, retrieved it and inserted it clumsily into the keyhole of the cover panel. He lifted the panel.

The cloth lay there. *Che beatifico!* He fitted a pair of white gloves lying nearby over his hands and carefully lifted the top fold of *la Sindone.*

Santa Madonna! Where was the backing cloth of raw linen? He felt deeper, frantically pulling more and more of the material out of the case. No backing, anywhere. He studied the more obvious body imprints on the fabric. Authentic, but he had never been an expert. And there was no backing. The true *Sindone* had just been outfitted with a new raw linen backing. This was not *la Sindone* — it was gone.

His watch showed 3:30. He fumbled for his cell phone, punched in a set of numbers and waited, heart pounding against his ribs. He scarcely heard the archbishop's hello. He gasped, his voice caught in his throat. *"Pronto"* sounded again at the other end. He found just enough oxygen to whisper.

"Buon giorno, monsignòre. I'm sorry to bother you. *La Sindone.* It is not here. I'm sorry. Yes — Gone."

CHAPTER 2

At 6:30, in Piazza Della Republica, not far from the cathedral, a black limousine pulled up to where Tom Ueland stood waiting, a backpack at his feet. He tossed it onto the backseat and surveyed his driver. *"Parla Inglese?"*

"Dude, I own *Inglese!*" shouted the chubby driver, turning to size up the American and looking offended by the question. "Why else would Archbishop Tucci designate my fleet as his official carrier for important visitors? Welcome to Torino."

"I have an appointment with him in fifteen minutes."

"Amico, I know, I know. But you've got your work cut out for you." The driver rolled the Fiat into traffic. "Listen to this radio!" It was talk radio, Italian style. The talk jock was screaming at one of his callers.

"I can't follow it. What are they saying?" Tom leaned forward.

"Everybody's got the answer. It was the Jews. The Muslims. The Taliban. Al Quaeda. Atheists. Right-wing Christians. Madonna. Walt Disney. You name it, a screwball believes it."

"Believes what?" Tom hung over the back of Tony's seat.

"Who the two guys work for — the ones who took the Holy Shroud five hours ago, man. It's *kaputt,* out of here. The biggest thing to hit this town since World War Two. That's why you're here, right?"

"I was at the cathedral five hours ago." Startled, Tom leaned back.

"You got to be kidding."

"I'm not kidding. Just me and a bunch of Italian tourist ladies."

"My man, you are not playing a game, right?" The driver pulled the limo over to the curb, checked his fare log, slung his arm over the back of the seat and stared at the American. "You're Tom Ueland, right?"

"My name's Tom Ueland. What's yours?"

"Antonio Palmitessa. But my business name is Tony Mezzo Soprano. Call me Tony."

"Tony Mezzo Soprano. OK, why not?"

Tony smiled into the mirror. "You like it? I have a patent pending."

1

"I like it. What's going on?"

"The Holy Shroud, kept under security like you never saw, part of Torino for four hundred years — poof! Gone. Stolen. *Rubato.* Just five hours ago — my man, the cops are looking for you. A tall, light-haired guy in his thirties. You are a suspect."

"Whoa, wait a minute. What do you mean, a suspect? Everything was OK at the church."

"No, everything was not OK!" Tony's retort caromed off the dashboard. He was back in traffic, both hands waving. He caught the wheel just in time to avoid clipping a Vespa and dumping its rider, a pert young helmeted woman with long legs gracefully poised on the floor board. Tony waved at her. She crooked her arm at him, fist tight.

Tony turned up the radio. "Here, listen, the archbishop's statement to the press. I'll translate for you." The deep, quivering voice of the archbishop resonated across the airwaves. Tony mimicked the voice artfully: "We are in great distress, great sorrow; how unbelievable it is that someone would carry out the shameful theft of one of our church's most revered relics. We pray that those responsible for this act will return *la Sindone* to the faithful immediately — fat chance," said Tony — "We will cooperate with the government in the investigation of this terrible loss. To all who have been comforted and strengthened in their faith by *la Sindone*, we share your profound grief." Tony turned to Tom. "You, of course, would say, 'We feel your pain.' Right? This is a very big story, OK?"

"Turn around. The cathedral — take me there."

"Listen. Did you act suspicious when you were there? Giovanni said you were taking notes, acting funny."

"Who's Giovanni?"

Tony maneuvered his squat short body sideways, one eye on the road, one on Tom. "He was your tour guide today. He knows that place like his own home. Giovanni was guiding you and those old ladies from the south today. He saw you. He saw the two guys. Some of the women saw four guys. Chiara, another volunteer lady at the church, saw seven. She's blind as a bat, getting battier by the day, and she always makes things out to be bigger than they are. Oh, yeah, there's La Prostrata; she saw ten thousand virgins."

"Who?"

"La Prostrata. The crazy lady. She crawls on her hands and

2

knees up to the shrine, where Giovanni has to pick her up and take her outside and calls me to take her home. Giovanni said there were two, that's it. They even saluted him when they were leaving; turned and saluted him." He raised his hand to his brow.

"He saw two guys besides me. He saw them take it? He thinks I took it?"

"You were in his group. The two guys came in like they were going to fix something. Electricians. In and out. Bandits."

"I never saw a thing. So where is Giovanni?"

"Why do you need to know? With the cops, he is a prime witness. The tourist ladies have been released to go home to Naples. You can be damn sure they are going to be in hot demand on TV. Giovanni and the volunteer lady, they are under protection. So how many were there?"

"I told you I didn't see anybody. I was taking notes." Tom saw the spire of the cathedral a few blocks ahead. Traffic was gridlocked and the police were routing cars away from the church. A line of TV trucks was a block long. "You believe me, right?"

"Parla Italiano?"

"Lo parlo poco. Capisco un po."

Again, the rearview mirror squint. "Tom Ueland, eh, my new American buddy, the VIP who had an appointment with Archbishop Tucci — why not believe you? Right? You were taking notes — but you don't understand Italian?"

"Right. Absolutely."

"Did you know there was a prayer note? That's still a secret. Left in the stonework around the holy water font. You write it?"

"Listen Mezzo Soprano, I was going to see the priest at his invitation; I set up the appointment two weeks ago. It's pure coincidence I was in that church today." Tom took a business card from his billfold. "What did the note say?"

Tony peeled off a business card from a little box stuck to the dashboard and handed it to Tom. Mezzo Soprano Private Limo and Taxi Services. "I am trusting you, *amico.* Here is what it said, translated from the Italian. 'Not stolen. Borrowed. To be returned after it protects us from the coming catastrophe in the land of its origin, birthplace...' I can't translate the last word."

"Could it be 'provenance'?" Tom moved toward the door; the limousine was blocking cars behind; horns blared in unison. A tram was trying to squeeze by. Tony turned to chat. He owned the road.

"Sounds good to me. 'In the land of its provenance.' Here is what I think, Tom; *la Sindone* is being Fedexed to Jerusalem inside a shipment of Gucci suits, and the guys are terrorists and are going to hold it for ransom until the church pays millions for it. They are trying to use it to get the church into the Israeli-Palestinian thing. Take my word; Tony Mezzo Soprano knows what he's talking about." A deep breath. "Unless you have another angle."

In no way would the priest want to see him now. "Let me out here."

"I am trusting you to go right to the cops. If you don't, I will tell them you stiffed me and bolted. And I've got you on video."

Tom scribbled a phone number on a business card and laid it on the front seatback. He jumped out and handed Tony some Euros. He could feel the driver's eyes memorizing his every feature.

"You have the archbishop's phone number?" he asked Tony.

"His secretary's number." Tony scribbled a number on another card and handed it to him. "*Amico*, we will stay in touch, OK? *Ci vediamo.*" It was a warning. He edged the limo back into traffic, his eyes still peering out the rearview mirror. Tom saw him pick up a cell phone. Either another fare — or the police. Who was this guy and how did he know so much about this crime?

Via XX Settembre was the street name and it led directly to the cathedral. All his senses were bristling — he was sweating through his button-down shirt and cotton jacket. It was a lot warmer than Minnesota in October. What was happening back there at the college right now in the 2004 fall semester? Monday morning classes. His students both happy and disappointed they were taking history from a clueless first-year teacher.

This chat with the archbishop was supposed to be just a spirited session on magical thinking, a painless expense write-off. Now he was a suspect in the theft of the church's holiest relic. He broke out in a sweat, stepped off a curb and felt himself free-falling off one of life's slippery turns.

CHAPTER 3

He took a deep breath and plowed into a crowd of 5,000 people. The police cordon was a block away, Turin's finest, outfitted in helmets and truncheons. Somebody up ahead had figured out a way to let the crowds pass single file in front of the *Duomo*. He was abruptly jostled into the line, tugged toward the square three blocks ahead that had been almost empty two hours ago. As the silent crowd snaked along, he caught a glimpse of the cavernous Piazza Castello to the east, with its regal palazzos towering over an even larger throng of citizens.

An hour later, Tom stood in the church square. Police surrounded the church entry and shaved down the single-file line into a solemn procession that kept winding back and forth like an airport check-in queue. He tried to take in the enormous diversity of faces: teenagers out on a lark from school, mothers with kids in strollers, old men and women with rosaries held tight and scapulars hung around their necks, nuns and priests, some Milan-fashion-show models on heels that had to be six inches long and the width of a pencil, elegantly dressed and manicured men with hair the cast of pewter.

He watched the cops' eyes; did they already have his description? Tony's video? With his 6'2" height, his angular profile and his Nordic features, Tom stood out. He hunched down. He wished Rachel were here; that would wait until tonight. Should he call the U.S. Consulate? No; stay with the crowd. Watch what was happening. *This* was history.

At the front of the line, he gawked at the façade of the *Duomo*, looming in front of him like the judgment seat of God almighty. On the steps, a priest in purple vestments was slowly blessing the crowd with a stone tablet that bore the image of a bearded man. The face of the Shroud. A young mother with jet black hair, tears streaking her cheeks, rocked in her arms drowsy twin girls. Rolling the infant in her right arm into her left where the twin slept, she made the sign of the cross along with the throng — tourists, pilgrims, mourning widows, skeptics, agnostics, nonbelievers. Knowing he fit in there somewhere, Tom blessed himself.

The line continued past the church on pavement that led under a brick archway. What lay beyond was a medium-size piazza that emptied out into a mammoth one. The line flowed into the thick, churning crowd in Piazza Castello. It was an immense urban space, rivaling anything he had seen in Europe. Ahead, two enormous equestrian statues bestrode the entry to the piazza: Castor and Pollux. The Green Guide had not prepared him for their Hollywood-epic dramatic perch in the center of the piazza.

Under the twins' stern gaze, the police formed a massive cordon around the perimeter of the square. Whenever someone in the crowd felt the urge to stand on a bench or retaining wall and start screaming, the police closed in. Tom caught enough Italian to know what they were screaming about. The fists told the story. Scapegoats, suspects, conspirators were being called out: Communists. Arabs, Jews, Evangelicals, the Russians, the French, the Brits, Berlusconi, even the pope. Everyone but the mafia. He was waiting for someone to finger him, "There's the American who stole the Shroud!" Flags stuck on souvenir stands floated precariously above the jostling heads: everywhere grizzled vendors were hawking posters of the Holy Shroud, postcards of the Holy Shroud, pieces of cloth with the image of the bearded face, imprinted cups, glasses, calendars, pencils, pens, cocktail napkins, cocktail tumblers.

The movements of the crowd surged and receded chaotically. Tom felt that given the right ingredients, the currents might unite into a mighty wave, a tsunami of human emotion battering down the police cordon and the palazzos and elegant edifices that lined the square. The men: were they feeling guilty over having fallen away from the church? The women: were they protesting a sacrilege? Or was everybody just enraged over this insult to their national pride? You could read all kinds of emotions on these faces, none that he could quite identify with, except that he — the suspect — felt safe. Not like in the States, where every other wacko in a crowd could be packing a Smith and Wesson.

He pushed his way to the far end of the piazza and reached an intersection where he had to brave a lineup of Nascar wannabes edging defiantly into the pedestrian crosswalk, their horns honking in support of whatever was going on, their feet light on the brakes as they anticipated the green. Once across, he found a sidewalk sheltered under an ancient portico. At the corner, seeing more crowds ahead, he turned right and walked toward a stunning glass-enclosed arcade. "Teatro Cinema Nuovo Romano" read the text over the entryway. Bordering it was a coffee house, "Baratti et Milano." He recognized it as one of the "must-see" destinations in the guidebooks. He ordered a cappuccino and savored it. He scribbled notes. Then it was time.

Glad he had brought along a special chip for his cell phone, glad he had remembered the cell phone which he had almost left on the dresser at home when he was packing, he punched in Rachel Cohen's number. Voice mail. "Rachel, Tom. You won't believe this. It's about the Shroud; it's been stolen. I am under suspicion for being an accomplice. Son of a bitch. I'm turning myself in. I still hope to see you in an hour. Later."

Next he called the number Tony had given him and told him where to get in touch with Rachel. Half an hour later, taking a deep breath, he punched in the phone number of the archbishop of Turin.

"Pronto." The voice appeared to be that of the priest's secretary — but the church probably had an entire crew handling the phone calls.

Tom cleared his throat, hoping the person understood English. "My name is Tom Ueland. I had an appointment with the archbishop; but I'm also the person you are looking for. Can you have the police come to this coffee shop — Baratti et Milano. No sirens — please."

CHAPTER 4

As dusk fell over the *autostrada*, nearing the Alpine border with France, a white van sped off an exit and tore down a country road. A mile or two later, it swerved off the road and pulled into a dirt track leading to an abandoned farm. It stopped behind the farm, out of sight of the occasional truck rumbling down the road.

Two men emerged from inside: Sidonius — tall, muscular and thin; and Trophimus — shorter, but equally gaunt. The third man, almost skeletal in sweatshirt and running pants, sporting a handsome forked beard, watched them. Jean Baptiste, they called him. The two had followed his every direction during the theft as he sat in the van outside the cathedral. They followed his commands now.

"Remove the ENEL uniforms. Fold them. Bury them with the banner in a hole. Attach the new banner to the side of the car." The uniforms were swiftly removed and folded. From the rear of the van Trophimus gathered up a crumpled gelatin banner bearing the letters ENEL, the national electric company. Sidonius dug a hole in the dirt next to a fence. They pushed the banner and the two sets of uniforms into the hole and quickly covered it. They unrolled a red gelatin banner and pressed its adhesive side against the panels of the van. *"Maranatha Università"* was inscribed on the banner. Headlights from a passing car caught the banner's glossy surface; they crouched; the car went on.

He was satisfied they had not been seen. "Change to the monogrammed warm-up pants and jerseys." They changed swiftly.

They rejoined the bearded man inside. The van returned to the road, but not in the direction of the *autostrada*. It took the Alpine route; minutes later it began its ascent into the night.

Gazing out at the starry evening sky, Jean Baptiste began chanting poetry. The language was Provençal. The poem was Mistral's *Miréio,* written in 1859. The others listened as the highway rose higher and higher into the Alps. They gazed at the valleys dropping away below them.

"The sovereign word, that man remembereth not,
Is, 'Death is Life'; and happy is the lot

The Magic Fault

Of the meek soul and simple, — he who fares
Quietly heavenward, wafted by soft airs;
And lily-white forsakes this low abode,
Where men have stoned the very saints of God.
And if, Miréio, thou couldst see before thee,
As we from empyrean heights of glory,
This world; and what a sad and foolish thing
Is all its passion for the perishing,
Its churchyard terrors — then, O lambkin sweet,
Mayhap thou wouldst for death and pardon bleat!
Hast thou, then, seen contentment anywhere
On earth? Is the rich blest, who softly lies,
And in his haughty heart his God denies,
And cares not for his fellowman at all?"

CHAPTER 5

Giovanni Palmitessa, head tour guide of the Cathedral of Saint John the Baptist, rubbed the firefighter lapel pin in the palm of his hand. Its finish had worn through. He was worn out. After being questioned for hours, he was ready for bed. He had been allowed to call only his brother Vittorio and given just enough time to tell him what the coming days would be like. He would be sequestered under round-the-clock protection. Food would be brought to him by an approved vendor. There was to be no contact with the media — not that he objected to that restriction, for he was no admirer of Berlusconi. The only concession to being a free Italian male: he was allowed to pick the restaurant that would provide his meals.

That choice was easy: Vittorio's Trattoria di Gianna. His nephew Tony would show up at his door shortly — under the custody of a beefy security guard — with a steaming package of *risotto al funghi*. It would be a simple matter to slip him the note he'd just written.

"Vittorio, these bastards are killing me. I have been grilled like a piece of chicken. I feel like they suspect me! As if I had never saved la Sindone in the fire seven years ago, put my life in danger for the holy cloth. Led those damn tours day after day for the last seven years. They're telling me I know the place inside out and upside down and did I ever have any contact with these two and why do Chiara and the pious ladies from the south say there were more than the two people I saw? Damn their arrogant asses! Brutte bestie.

"And let me tell you, Vittorio my brother, those two guys were insiders. They were the ones who knew the place upside down and inside out, that's for sure. I bet they were defrocked priests. And that American guy on the tour, taking notes — definitely an accomplice. Get in touch with somebody who can help me; I want to sell the rights to my story to that moviemaker from Modena. Or what's his name, Martino Scorsese. Make sure you put extra parmigiano in a package with the order and none of that shit wine from Friuli you got a deal on."

He eased himself down on the narrow bed, removed his shoes, and slid out of his pants. On the dresser lay his rumpled tie, still knotted. He looked at it. He always wore a tie when not in uniform, but he never untied it at night. The knot stayed tied, just like a marriage, he used to tell his skeptical wife. Never trust yourself in the morning to do it right; leave it tied overnight. It was a trick he had learned as a young altar boy at the cathedral over 50 years ago. Mornings could be brutal. Exploding out of a deep sleep with just five minutes to go before mass started, Mama banging on the door. "Giovanni! Giovanni! *Adesso!*" No time to knot a tie; he just left it loosened on the dresser the night before, then yanked it over his head while he bounded down the steps, crouching to ward off the back of his mother's hand. Once in the street, hike up the knot, run the three blocks to the church.

And then the shock of being knocked on the head once again, this time by the priest. "Giovanni Palmitessa, *ancora in ritardo!*" He would breathlessly button the cassock, wriggle into the freshly nun-pressed and starched surplice and then — as if he had been keeping silent serene vigil overnight before the altar — lead the priest in stately slow procession into the sanctuary before the handful of widows and the nuns, arranged in their pews for the 7 a.m. mass.

Tonight, the ancient smell of incense and candles rushed again through his brain. He lay back on the pillows. He was going to make something out of this whole scandal. He was the cowboy who was going to help the sheriff put the bad guys in jail, like on American TV. For sure he would put the handcuffs on that American stooge in his tour group. Smiling over his good fortune from his approaching fame, the TV appearances, the movie rights, he dozed off.

CHAPTER 6

Two immaculately black-and-white-uniformed officers escorted Tom from the coffee shop to the backseat of a squad car and whisked him, sirens blaring, to the headquarters of the Turin police force. In a stifling small room whose most memorable feature was a camera perched like a motionless raven on the wall, two unsmiling men in suits grilled him for what seemed like hours. Tom's line, "I had an appointment with the archbishop," was met with knowing, disbelieving glances. His alibi for being in Turin, likewise suspicious. His whereabouts after the cathedral before calling Tony — did he have witnesses? Well, maybe...

The next stop: Giovanni Palmitessa's room, for identification. Inside the lobby of an adjacent building that looked as cheerless as his guards, the police delivered Tom to an elevator manned by a giant in civilian dress, easily 6'6", with a size-17 neck and a bulky torso under a hot-looking black coat and white shirt. There was another person on the elevator — Tony Mezzo Soprano, toting an aromatic package of risotto al funghi and a bottle of wine. Neither Tom nor Tony pretended to know the other.

"*Il risotto non è fresco.*" The big cop was sniffing.

"*Invece è molto fresco.*" Tony shot back.

A few awkward deep breaths passed in stony stillness before the door opened. Tom found himself walking alongside Tony, staring down a hallway with cheap prints on either side — countryside scenes, rivers, mountains, fishermen, families on a picnic, baskets overflowing with meats, fruits, bread, wine.

He thought of Rachel in the *Salone del Gusto*, surrounded by food, getting ready for opening day Wednesday. He felt a twinge of guilt — here he was, entangled in a raging international incident. Would he see her tonight? Or would he be quarantined as soon as he stepped inside the door — that door, up ahead, the one guarded by two bigger guys. The two stepped aside as the elevator big guy knocked once on the door, opened it and led Tom and Tony in. "*Conversazione vietata! Fate presto!*" The big guy crossed his arms and watched. The door shut behind him.

Giovanni Palmitessa lay on the bed in his underwear. On a dresser nearby was his tie, loosened, but knotted — the first thing

Tom noticed when he averted his eyes from the nearly naked gentleman. Tony stood by the man's bed.

"Tom, this is Giovanni. He's my uncle; I forgot to tell you."

Giovanni opened his eyes, sized up Tom. "That's the guy!" he shouted in Italian. *"Mi porti pure."* He motioned Tony to set the package down on the dresser. He wanted to question Tom himself. *"Parla Italiano?"*

"No he doesn't," Tony deflected it. He slipped Giovanni's note into his pocket.

Giovanni scrambled out of bed and stood tall, all 5'8" of him, dignified even in his underwear. Nose chest-high to Tom, he was backing him to the wall, when the big guy yelled "Time's up." Turning his back on the cop, Giovanni feigned nonchalance. He motioned toward the wine bottle and wiggled his thumb like a corkscrew.

"Andiamo," hissed the big guy, who hooked his fat thumb toward the door. Giovanni grabbed a corkscrew off the dresser.

"Andiamo!" and the big guy was not kidding; he grabbed Tony and Tom's arms and squeezed hard. Giovanni would have to open his own vino. Tom and Tony marched out, prodded by the big guy. Giovanni ran right up to the door, only to be stiff-armed by the big guy's bigger guys who shoved him back inside and slammed the door in his face. Tom could hear Giovanni yell, "Scorsese!" Giovanni knew what he wanted, all right.

The big guy stopped at the door of another room, slammed a key into the lock and opened the door. In one motion the cop pushed Tom inside, lifted Tony off his feet by his shirt and shut the door. His first night in Turin. Tom Ueland in one room, Giovanni Palmitessa next door. No 9 p.m. supper with Rachel tonight.

CHAPTER 7

Rachel Cohen, back at her hotel at 8 p.m., turned on the hot water for a bath and undressed half-listening to her hotel phone messages. The bath was the balm she needed. It had been a good day setting up for the *Salone del Gusto*; she was engrossed in the activity, the people, the cause, the camaraderie.

A most glorious day — chatting with tanned farmers and all the growers and distributors of delectable foods. Italian pecorino cheese from the provinces of Teramo and L'Aquila. Smoked wild salmon from County Cork. Wines from the Loire Valley. Exquisite chocolate from Ecuador. Basmati rice from the foothills of the Himalayas in India, lemons from Sicily and the incredible verdure of the south of Italy — melons from near Palermo, oranges from the heel of Italy, tomatoes from Naples. She had dined at a banquet without eating, just absorbing a tingling sense of satisfaction. As they say in the movement, better than sex.

She dozed off in the tub. At 20 minutes to 9, she recovered, dried herself and dressed. At 9 she was in the elevator. She didn't know if she could eat supper, she was so smitten by the food she had only sampled or gazed at; she had put eating on the very back burner. Even Tom was only occasionally a flicker on her mind's eye. But the *Salone del Gusto* had slowly generated a feeling of utter sensuality in her and she was eager to see him.

The doors opened to the lobby — no Tom. She checked her cell phone messages. She listened wide-mouthed to Tom's brief goodbye from the coffeehouse. A pudgy man, 30-ish, who looked as though he slept in his car, approached her. "Rachel Cohen, I bet." Not a question, more like a pickup routine. "My name is Tony Palmitessa. Tom Ueland is in custody. Would you join me in the bar for an espresso? He's a suspect — for now."

CHAPTER 8

Just then, in the middle of the night, the van crested the Mount Cenis Pass between France and Italy. "We are among the last vehicles over this venerable Alpine pass before winter. We have liberated the Lord's Holy Shroud. We are returning it to His tomb so He may rise again! Listen for His voice: We are very near the judgment seat of Christ," the bearded leader shouted. "Heaven is ours! Those below are doomed!"

Hours later, the van entered Chambéry, in the heart of the French Alps. Inside, two metallic suitcases lay under the rear seat. Atop them, a rifle glistened in the moonlight. The bearded one placed a hand on one of the cases and inscribed the sign of the cross.

"Sainte-Chapelle in Chambéry!" he shouted.

A cell phone rang. Retrieving it from his pocket, he looked at the number.

"What could the doubting Thomas want now? Of course we have *la Sindone*, oh man of little faith!"

He spoke tersely to the caller without greeting him. "Soon enough you will be able to touch the cloth that covered the Lord's body. We cannot speak now." He snapped the phone shut. The three men flung open the doors of the van.

The French city of Chambéry was asleep in darkness. The white van was parked outside the old castle of the Dukes of Savoy. Even in the darkness one could easily find the castle, which stood out among the surrounding hills and mountains of the French Alps. At the end of the castle's north wing Jean Baptiste saw the Gothic Sainte-Chapelle, and he reflected on the stained glass and the artist Vicario's paintings that it held within. He chuckled and spoke calmly to his two brother monks. "Will anyone in this city of fifty-five thousand see three men wearing sweat suits, unloading molded suitcases from their vehicle then entering by a hidden door into the castle's north wing — no one!"

Once inside, the leader and the two acolytes pulled white robes from the other suitcase and swiftly placed them over their heads, letting the hems drop to the floor. The bearded man directed the others to unroll the Shroud carefully. It was a ritual they had practiced often. The two stood at either end of the cloth's 14-foot

15

expanse; the leader lighted a small piece of charcoal, placed it in a censer's tiny thurible and sprinkled incense out of a glass jar over the charcoal. The scent filled the chapel; inhaling it, the leader processed around the Shroud, swinging the censer. The leader bowed deeply and then, slowly, spreading his arms straight out, began to chant in the Provençal tongue.

"We begin the great journey to return the Shroud to its home. Amen." At each "Amen," the others shouted the word again.

"We dedicate our lives to carrying out this sacred trust. Amen!

"He who redeemed us from Adam's sin without our help will not save us from our own without our help! The cosmos and its hidden truths must bow down before the simple truth: Jesus Christ lives, and at His name every knee should bend. Before His burial cloth, every heart should confess the simple truth: He shall return! *Maranatha!* Come Lord Jesus!"

The pores of the precious fabric drank in the pollen of Chambéry. The three men inhaled the incense and looked to the heavens above.

***

Halfway through his early-morning rounds, the elderly security guard sensed something was wrong. It was barely dawn, long before the civil servants would arrive at the prefecture of Chambéry to begin their day's work of greasing the wheels of French civility. Someone was inside the old castle, somewhere. He could smell it — incense. A strange scent coming from the heart of local government offices. Had there been a service? In the Sainte-Chapelle? Was his lifetime of Sunday mornings in dark churches that reeked with burnt incense overpowering his grasp of what went on in a government building?

La Sainte-Chapelle. *Mon dieu.* Yes, the scent was stronger as he limped quietly into the north wing of the prefecture. The ache in his bad hip flared up. He opened the doors to the chapel.

There was a blur of movement in the apse, under the stained glass window and the paintings. He blinked. He could not believe his eyes. The Holy Shroud, which had been kept in this chapel 400 years ago, was hanging there in front of him, held up by hooded men on either side. And kneeling before it was a third man, his arms outstretched. The three were dressed identically in long robes.

16

He stood transfixed. The kneeling man stood, turned and looked at him. He seemed to be returning from a trance, his eyes glassy.

The old man felt his gaze; it turned cold, stony, menacing. He trembled.

"Now you can dismiss your servant, O Lord," the guard shouted, quoting old Simon of the gospel. "My eyes have seen the salvation which you have prepared for all the nations to see." He turned around and started to limp back to the door.

At that moment, a rope tightened around his torso from behind. The old man twisted and turned and tried to push off his attacker. The man with glazed eyes now raised them toward heaven as he pulled the rope ends tauter. The man spoke.

"Old man, if you will be Simon, you will obey us. We have vowed to find the true Shroud. We have come here to reverence a replica of it in this chapel where it once was displayed. If you break the prayer chain — forged by the thousands of faithful who are united to us — if you disclose what you have seen, you will frustrate our purpose. You will stand against all the saints of God and on the side of the forces of Lucifer. And you will die a painful and accursed death and suffer eternal damnation in the deepest regions of hell." His eyes blazing, the man released the rope, and the guard, struggling for breath, fell to the floor.

***

Minutes later, a white van sped out of the castle complex, the sun just showing above a blood-red horizon. The van left the city and headed north. Inside, the lingering scents of incense and beeswax mixed with the sounds of three men chanting Psalm 51.

"Miserere mei Deus secundum magnam misericordiam tuam et secundum multitudinem miserationum tuarum dele iniquitatem meam. Have mercy on me, O God, according to thy great mercy. And according to the multitude of thy tender mercies blot out my iniquity.

"Amplius lava me ab iniquitate mea et a peccato meo munda me. Wash me yet more from my iniquity and cleanse me from my sin."

The cell phone had not stopped ringing since they returned to the van. And again the leader ignored it. The other two looked at him nervously, and he finally spoke.

"We have been kind to the old fool. Be rid of your scruples. The burial Shroud of the Lord of Hosts is finally at the center of our life together. Nothing else matters. In all things — all, even our most grievous faults — may God be glorified."

CHAPTER 9

A groggy suspect awoke to a knock on his door. It had been a long night; no telephone, no cell phone, no TV. Tom had lain awake much of the night, alone with memories of others in his family tree who had been detained by the law. An immigrant great-grandfather in North Dakota, plowing the prairie into fields of wheat, enraged at the grain company monopolies in Minneapolis, starting a farmers' grain co-op, becoming a socialist. Tom's grandfather, moving to Saint Paul to run a co-op grain elevator, jailed in union strikes, working to elect Floyd B. Olson, Minnesota's socialist governor in the 30s. His grandmother, arrested in suffragette protests. His parents, card-carrying Vietnam protesters, jailed many times. And now him.

Him? A liberal whose idea of activism was a subscription to *Mother Jones Magazine*, he was single, thirty-six, in love with research and teaching, satisfied with pointing out history's never-ending parallels. Satisfied, until now.

He was here, in this city, in this country, on his way to something called the 2004 *Salone del Gusto* in a convention center called the Lingotto Fiere. Professor Ueland was not one to be alone in a European city without protective cover: a coterie of fellow historians, a schedule, speaking fees if he was lucky, a career-enhancing agenda of research, or, at the very least, a tax write-off of part of the trip. This time, he was following somebody to an event described as "A fair and a market of quality food and beverages from all over the world."

Rachel Cohen had busted the academic routine he had perfected during sabbaticals in past years. This trip had little protective cover. This trip was all about Rachel Cohen. The agitator. The World Trade Organization protests in Seattle. She had been tear-gassed and clubbed by the Seattle cops as she led a protest against Monsanto. In the Left's strange ladder to fame, she parlayed the incident into back-to-back college speaking gigs: "The Corporatization of the Seed: How biotechnology is taking ownership of the food supply."

He heard about the lecture and recommended it to the department of concerts and lectures at the private college where he taught; because of a scheduling conflict, the lecture was moved to a nearby community college. That was 10 months ago, in the dead of a Minnesota winter. The students turned out, but the lecture was a dud and the relationship would never have gone anywhere if he had not written a piece on it for the *Pioneer Press*, the local newspaper. He was not happy with her performance, and the piece was not complimentary. He described this intense woman haranguing the students about food politics and the World Trade Organization and then asking for questions, getting a few and scolding the students for not being engaged.

"And why so few questions?" he asked the reader. "Because many of these kids enrolled in community college after failing to find a job, or because their parents had barely scraped together enough money to make them the first generation in the family to go to college, or because they were trying to get off welfare. They had other, more immediate, concerns than food biodiversity," he had written. "When is America's left going to learn how to embrace America's young outsiders, its disaffected and uncommitted young people? This is not the sixties, folks."

Rachel was sent a copy and e-mailed its author. Thus began a correspondence that started from her side with "Dear esteemed tweed-jacketed history professor: You teachers are all the same. Join the real world, jerk." And from his, "Dear Rad-Lib, know your audience, Ms. Cohen; this is not Harvard. Get a real job." Gradually the exchanges — secretly awaited by both — cooled down to pleasantries and requests for lunch the next time she was between flights in Saint Paul. And then more e-mails. And then she got a real job, traveling the world representing a Turkish family exporting organic olives and olive oil to the USA.

The real job was a real hindrance to their meetings — her shuttling between Turkey, Europe and New York; him in lockdown, teaching courses in European and Minnesota history at the college. When his sabbatical semester started, he chose Turin, where she would be spending a week in October for the 2004 *Salone del Gusto*. It was one Italian city he had never been to.

"Liquid Gold: the Treasures of Turkey's Olive Groves" was the title of her workshop. Over the past months she had weaned him off his supply of non-organic olives and olive oils made in the USA to the Turkish small-farm brands she represented.

Cultural history was his thing. Food was — well, it just was. But here they were, together in the same city for the first time in two months, for a food convention reputed to attract over 100,000 adherents. He was skeptical. He was intrigued. And he was in police custody.

He never would have been in that church yesterday if not for one other person. A month earlier, he had received a letter from the archbishop of Turin, a priest named Michael Tucci. Tucci had read an article on magical thinking in the *New York Times* arts section. In the article, Tom had been quoted as an authority on the topic. He summarized the Historian Norman Cantor's insights into medieval behavior during the Black Plague of the 14th Century: Christians blamed the Jews for the plague. "Scapegoating is magical thinking," Tom wrote. "And it goes on today. We blame the 'other' for everything wrong in our lives. Religious extremists are often the worst offenders."

The priest wrote that he was deeply fascinated by the topic and invited him to Turin. Tom wrote back he'd be there in a month. Yesterday was to be the day for the meeting. Tom had decided to check out the famed Shroud of Turin relic first.

Now it looked as though he might not get to see the priest. Next stop: The U.S. consulate in Turin, if there was one. And he needed a lawyer.

Another knock on the door; the big guy barged in and spoke actually using nouns and verbs. "The archbishop of Turin wants to see you."

Tom looked at his watch — 7 a.m. The cop had brought him a shaving kit, a cappuccino and a bag of fresh bread and rolls. "Get dressed, please, and I will be back in thirty minutes." "Please" meant something for sure — he was cleared.

"It's about time. Is it a trial, the inquisition, what the hell is going on?"

The big cop had undergone a personality change from the night before. He even looked smaller. "The archbishop will meet you in the *Duomo*. The scene of the crime. Then of course, if all goes well, you are free to go about your business in Torino."

CHAPTER 10

It took Tom just minutes to shower, shave, dress. Downstairs, his guard released him to the same two still-crisply-uniformed policemen in their squad car.

Lights flashing, the car bore down on the *Duomo*. The same crowds were still there, a little smaller, and the same cordon of cops was keeping them at a distance, today further away than yesterday. A large black sedan, engine running, pulled out of a small side street and wheeled around as the squad car approached. Tom's driver followed the sedan into a park behind the cathedral, then another side street, which led to another street and then to another, until Tom saw the backside of the cathedral come into view, the side opposite the one he walked past yesterday. The two cars pulled up to a door that was totally fenced off from the public, not a soul in sight. They were near a palace. The two cops scrambled out, opened Tom's door and stood at attention.

Tom crawled out of the backseat and the first thing that struck him was how the church and the palace seemed to be one big building. Church and State, united. The black sedan's doors were open. Coming on fast were two large men, with bulging Roman collars around their necks. Priests. They looked as though they could break his neck as well as baptize him. They stopped five feet from Tom, turned around toward the door, walked back and went inside without looking back at him. The police motioned for Tom to follow them. He entered the building and for a moment saw nothing in the dark interior. He was standing in a large room; perhaps it was where the priests put on their vestments, or maybe a library. It smelled of incense. The vesting area, he bet.

"Prego! Come in." A man in his 70s sat behind a long table, looking directly at him. He wore a black suit, a gold chain crossing his black vest. The two priests stood on either side of him; he waved them to stand further away and motioned to Tom to take the vacant chair on the opposite side of the table. Tom got a good look at him as the priest barked something in Italian to the two husky clerics. Wonderful full gray hair, brushed neatly and not a strand out of place. Lean, a good-looking man, furrows plowing across his forehead, sharp features, an aquiline nose. He tapped his fingers

lightly on the table, smiled at Tom, stood and reached across the table to shake his hand.

"I am Father Tucci." He held out both arms. "What a strange fate — You come to Torino to consult with me and you get arrested. Please. I apologize for what you had to put up with since yesterday."

"It's been exciting, I've got to say. I simply wanted to see the Shroud before I saw you. Then the fun started."

"It has been an ordeal for all of us. Sit and be comfortable in the finest folding chair Italy can offer. I would have seen you at my office in my residence so we could have shared some coffee. But under the circumstances, it seemed better to meet here. You have a promise of coffee from me another time."

Tom watched the priest watching him and mentally frisking him — like Tony. "Thank you, sir. You have a lot on your mind today."

"Yes, true." He arched an eyebrow at "sir." "You are not Catholic."

"I come from a Midwestern American Lutheran family, with roots in Norway. Raised in Minnesota. Umhh, should I call you 'pastor'?"

"'Pastor' is fine. Shepherd sounding. So you have not seen your friend at the *Salone del Gusto* yet?"

So he knew about Rachel. Tony, of course. "No." He felt Tucci's laser gaze cut through him.

"Your friend will be disappointed, yes? She will ask, 'What kind of church is this that can throw people in jail?'"

"Oh yes, she will ask, but right now she's busy at the *Salone.*"

"Ah, *bene, bene.* It's the one event I really love to attend. I have a feeling the church would be healthier if it followed the precepts of the Slow Food Movement with one-tenth the attention it pays to the Gospel." He smiled, winked and looked like he just wanted to put his feet up on the desk, light a cigarette, order a beer and talk about the good Italian cooking of his childhood. "She is Italian?"

"American. Born in Istanbul, though."

"The most beautiful city in the world!" The priest's face lit up. "And the spiritual mother of all Christianity as a world religion. The Roman church is an orphan, cut off from her."

"She's Jewish."

"Exactly. Judaism, Islam, Christianity. I tell you, she is the city of God."

"My friend Rachel is Jewish, I mean. She says it is the most cosmopolitan city in the world."

"*É vero!* I love her dearly." The archbishop sighed, coughed. "Forgive the tangent. People never tell an archbishop to shut up. Please be assured I am not accusing you..."

"Look, Pastor, I know you're not. But I think the police were convinced they had the accomplice."

The old man, still studying him, spoke slowly. "Giovanni wanted us to know three things: posing as employees of the national electric company these two men saluted him, they blessed themselves with holy water and they shook the water off their hands. The first would indicate they were Italian, the second Catholic and the third — fallen-away Catholics? Practicing Catholics wipe the holy water on their clothes. I will tell you, frankly, there are no clues to why they did this; but I believe it may be thanks to magical thinking — what we were going to discuss."

His host stood. The two priests whirled to attention. "Come with me, Signor Ueland. I want to take you back to the scene of the crime." The two husky hockey types sailed into wing positions alongside him. "I apologize, I have not introduced my secretaries. This is Father Raffaelo and this is Father Roberto." Tom forgot immediately who was who.

The retinue marched into the main body of the church. Here he was, a total outsider and still possibly the criminal, accompanied by the archbishop of Turin. "Do not cross" yellow tapes were draped everywhere. The heat generated by huge floodlights on poles was stifling. More than a dozen men and women, some in police uniforms, some in white lab coats, some in business suits and dresses, whispered and chattered intensely. They all stopped what they were doing. "Don't stop," said the priest, with a smile. They all looked busy, but they were watching.

"You are aware, Signor Ueland, that there were several witnesses here at the time of the crime, including yourself. But it is Giovanni's recollections that I am interested in. You have stated you saw no one because you were listening to Giovanni. He stood here" — Tucci pointed to an "X" taped to the floor of the church — "and was talking to you and the tour group at the side chapel when he saw the two enter the church — oh, sorry, the Shroud chapel is directly behind us." Tom turned and peered into the chapel interior. The cover of the Shroud case stood open. "Yes, the two were standing over here when they saluted him. Would you mind standing where they stood, and I will remain here where Giovanni saw them. We will see what the background shows. If you please."

Tom walked the few feet over to the double X mark on the floor and turned to face Tucci. The two priests were in the way, and he could not see beyond them. Tucci shooed them off and they dutifully shuffled out of the sightline.

"*Allora,* Signor Ueland, what is behind me?" asked the priest. A hush fell over the multiple conversations going on around him. Tom squinted at the sanctuary. Directly behind Tucci, perhaps 30 feet away, was the high altar of the *Duomo*.

"I see the altar behind you." Tom spoke quietly. He made a smart salute toward the archbishop.

"And if you were to salute this chapel — say this plate glass window near which I am standing — would you have to turn a bit or would you keep your feet planted where they are?"

"I would stay right where I am. It all is in the same general direction: you, the altar and the window. I would not have to turn." Tom was about to salute again, but the silence in the nave paralyzed him. He was sweating like a man caught in the act. Was the salute exercise under the lights and the scrutiny of investigators meant to break him down?

If so, it was working.

CHAPTER 11

"Grazie, Signor Ueland. I wanted you to see the situation from our thieves' perspective. Let's go back to our table. I don't want to keep you from your friend." Side by side Tucci and he marched back into the vesting room, followed by Father Roberto and Father Raffaelo. Who was who? Fiddle Dee Dee and Fiddle Dee Dum, Tom decided. He was still sweating. He sat down opposite Tucci, who folded his hands in the clerical tent so familiar to Tom from his own minister's conduct during confirmation class. "So tell me your thoughts on the salute." Tom relaxed slightly.

"Maybe the salute meant they were knights of some exotic order. Or they just wanted to assure the old man they were public servants too. The Holy Water meant they felt they were doing God's work. I don't know what the shaking off of the drips of water meant. That they had a big job ahead of them?"

Tom felt out of his league talking Catholic customs. "How about the usual suspects, the Knights Templar? Some believe the military salute dates back to the days of knighthood, when the knight lifted his visor — 'I'm a friend, not a foe.' Could it be…"

"Listen, my friend, I believe this repugnant act was done by a new movement within the Catholic community. It's political theater. They want to pressure the church into taking political stands — between Israel and Palestine, or against Islam in Europe. They are computer savvy; look at the way they compromised our security systems. We are checking into the vendors who sold us these systems. One would think that such inside knowledge had to come from the manufacturers or the maintenance technicians. People had to know someone who knew someone. But that inquiry is merely into the 'how.' It is the 'why' of this bizarre act. What would move somebody to plan and carry out such madness?"

Tom frowned. "You've left out the obvious suspects." The archbishop leaned forward. "I mean the people you trust, the people who have the keys, the code. Your security chief. The national electric company. An insider crime, done for money on behalf of a wealthy — angry — religious fanatic."

Tucci smiled. "I think your President Bush once said of Mr. Putin of Russia, 'I looked into his eyes and saw his soul.' Or something like that. I am quite sure he later regretted saying it. No, I have met with the one man who has total knowledge of the security system, the key keeper, you might say. It was he who reported the theft to me yesterday. He is shattered. I have seen his soul. He is not involved — however — the thieves knew his schedule; the one day he has been away from the cathedral in months."

"Could he have mistakenly given away the secret? Put the combination in an e-mail that some hacker crashed? And his wife — could she have mindlessly told a caller he would not be at the church Monday?" Tom was feeling more comfortable now with the priest.

"We are combing all computer files as we speak. So far, nothing. And ENEL, the national electric company, assures me that all of its Torino employees are accounted for; none was here. And his good wife: tight-lipped." Tucci's hands flexed in tandem and he looked as though he wanted a cigarette. Tom decided to let the priest know he knew the contents of the prayer note; he recited it.

"'Not stolen. Borrowed. To be returned after it protects us from the coming catastrophe in the land of its provenance.'" Tom studied the furrows on the priest's forehead. They appeared and spread rapidly; he was either impressed or displeased that Tom knew about the note.

"Antonio told you, I suppose; he knows things days before I do. We are running tests on the phrasing, looking for parallels. As you can imagine, there are thousands. I think it is the message of some deranged soul who believes that the size of the coming catastrophe is so huge that it can only be averted by *la Sindone*. A Middle East conflagration, for instance." The priest rose; the two Fathers Fiddle jumped to attention. "You have things to do; I have kept you; we will meet again."

"Archbishop, a question; where did you learn your English? I can't believe this town. Mr. Palmitessa's nephew is fluent in street jargon, and you are fluent in the language of diplomacy." The priest motioned to him to sit down.

"Google my vita," Tucci said slyly. "Can I call you Tom?" Tom nodded. "Born in Montepulciano, raised in Italian seminaries, I was apostolic delegate to the USA for fifteen years. Everyone used to laugh at my English for the first five years. I would preach at American seminaries and when I finished I would say to the seminarians, 'Piss on your fathers and piss on your mothers.' And what I meant to say, of course, was 'Peace on your fathers and peace on your mothers.' But after ten years, I could pass for a native. No more pissing around."

Tom grinned; this cleric is real, he thought. "Pastor, listen, I have read one book on the Shroud. I am aware of its historical connection with the Templars and the devastation of Constantinople." Tom leaned back. "Magical thinking. I hope I don't offend you, Pastor."

"I hope you do. That's why I invited you to talk to me a few weeks ago."

Assured, Tom leaned forward in his chair. "There is a thin line between religious belief and magical thinking. We all have our little ways, those little rituals like wearing charms or saying prayers to a saint to influence the outcome of a big deal. But we always come back across the line; we 'come to our senses.' I think these guys crossed the line and are not coming back. They believe carrying out their mission will force God's hand in their favor, somehow. In their hands, the Shroud is a bomb. An amulet with great power. The theft is not a matter of possession. It is a matter of obsession. In the hands of compulsive obsessive people, magical thinking is a lifeline to power when they have no power. And a very dangerous one."

The furrows multiplied and deepened, and the facial expression seemed more pensive as the priest searched for words. "The message says more to me about possession than obsession; 'Not stolen. Borrowed. To be returned after it protects us from the coming catastrophe in the land of its provenance.'"

Tom rested his arms on the table, his face close to the priest's. "Why are you so intimately involved in this investigation? Why aren't you with the pope or somebody, planning strategy for damage control, all the usual pro forma procedures? And why did you want to talk to me about magical thinking in the first place?"

"I thought you might offer some insights. *Credo...*" The prelate spoke slowly, softly, looking at his two priests. "I believe that this act has everything to do with the madness that is a byproduct of religion. I have been a diplomat all over the world. The clash of civilizations is the clash of religions. Religions inspire their followers to commit acts of cruelty or delusion in the name of a god whose will and purpose are known to them alone. This theft is one of these delusional acts. And — I regret to say — we are one of those religions."

"That was my point about Norman Cantor, Pastor."

"The *Times* article quite intrigued me, Tom..."

"Magic usually has a strong element of blame in it; witchcraft, the inquisition. So today radical Muslims blame the Christian West for their ills — and want to kill infidels. And perhaps your thieves blame the entire world."

The priest pointed to the cross that was half-hidden under his coat lapel. "Most of my colleagues in the church do not like this kind of talk; they like scapegoats: materialism, liberalism, anti-clericalism, Islam; it's part of the strategy we employ. Of course people find ways to counter the strategy with their own tactics for survival — look at our thieves? As you see, I find it difficult to think like my peers. I like thinking — how do you say — outside the box."

The archbishop extended his arm downward like a guillotine strike and smiled. "The box that collects the head. The inquisitory spirit lives!" He laughed and leaned back in his chair. "You remind me of an old friend, now dead; he and I had many deep conversations about magical thinking. He wrote brilliantly about it: possession by devils, that kind of thing." The priest seemed lost in remembrance. He stood. "I have enjoyed our conversation. You should come to the diocesan headquarters at 11; our press office is giving the media a basic course on the Shroud. You are welcome to stop by my residence afterwards — it's just next door — for the promised coffee. More magic talk."

Tom stood and reached across the table to shake the priest's hand. "If I can pull Rachel away from the *Salone.*"

"Yes, bring your friend!" The priest waved to his acolytes. "Fathers, see Signor Ueland to his car. *Arrivederci,* Tom!" He shook Tom's hand and waved him off. The Fathers Fiddle strode athletically ahead of Tom and led him to a waiting cab. Fiddle Dee Dee opened the back door and Fiddle Dee Dum closed it.

"You lucked out," announced a waiting Tony. "Those two bozos hit me up for a big tip the last time they held the door for the archbishop. Isn't he a sweet guy, that man?"

"Yeah, a sweet, complex guy. He's not a big shot, I mean, a cardinal, right?" Tom leaned forward.

"He should be," Tony stressed each syllable. "When *Numero Uno* croaks down in Rome, this man should be in the running to be the next pope. But those old conservatives will take over the conclave and end up picking a conservative attack dog. I am laying odds two to one."

"You trust him?"

"Him alone, out of the whole bunch of them. One hundred percent."

"You trust me?"

"Maybe fifty-one percent."

"Where are you taking me?"

"To my uncle's bar. You have a date with your friend for coffee. Welcome back to being a free man."

"Wrong," Tom shot back. "I think I'm digging a hole for myself deeper into this mystery."

CHAPTER 12

And there she was, surrounded by a few small jars of olive oil. Trattoria di Gianna's adjoining bar was full, upstairs and downstairs, front and back, and Rachel was waving to people — it had been recommended by the Slow Food Movement as *the* place to be in Turin.

He had been watching a coterie of Greeks hovering near her table where she sat alone. No slouches on olives, they had been grilling her in a mix of Greek, Turkish and English. He watched the Greek men drowsily basking in her "wine-dark" beauty as they ambled away. The olive oil and her skin tone were almost a match. She was radiant in her white blouse and purple peasant skirt but pouted when she saw him.

"If there are fifty ways to leave your lover, you have invented a fifty-first. Get arrested."

"Hey, how's it going?" He gave her a nonchalant greeting and kissed her cheek.

"I'm OK; you're not. I always thought you might quit being a college professor, throw off the ball and chain of tenure, leave behind the intramural faculty backbiting, hit the road into real estate or hedge funds. This, however, is ridiculous — you, a religious kleptomaniac. Both sides," she instructed. He kissed her other cheek. "Enough about you. I'm coming off the most intoxicating day of my thirty-five years of life. I am in love with food and the people who grow it!" She took his hands across the table and squeezed.

Tom grinned. "You are surrounded by people with their hands in dirt. You are in touch with the earth, the simple human act of growing and eating food. I on the other hand spent the last twenty-four hours with people grieving over a crime against the supernatural, consumed by a relic that is all about leaving behind the earth — way behind. You have to meet Giovanni."

"Who's Giovanni?"

"You really want the details?"

"Come on, tell me the story. The Shroud is not on my radar screen, as you might imagine. Jews are not big fans of the crucifixion."

"This is a really big deal for the Italians. I can't think of anything

31

like it in the States. Maybe the Declaration of Independence getting ripped off. The city is angry and the rest of the country too, not to mention about a billion people around the world who have put some kind of faith in it."

"How did you find out you were a wanted man?"

"Yesterday, I made the acquaintance of a cabby, a certain Tony…" He paused, realizing how ridiculous this was going to sound. "…a certain Tony Mezzo Soprano."

"Tony who?" she blurted out, holding her napkin across her mouth as she stifled her laughter. "The Tony who told me about you last night?"

"That's the guy: Tony Mezzo Soprano. A cabby who owns a limo and cab company with some kind of contract with the archbishop. Also, he's the nephew of my tour guide Giovanni. The uncle saw the guys come and go."

"Why didn't he call the cops?"

"He thought they were electrical repairmen. He thought they were legitimate."

"You met him too?"

"I did. Instead of spending the night with you, I spent it in the room next to his."

"Wishful thinking. And his name?" She couldn't help saying it. "Was it Tony Soprano?"

"Giovanni Palmitessa is his name. And it was right in the middle of his tour that these two guys strolled in with their bag of tricks and somehow jimmied the whole electronic system of locks and security cameras. They strung a curtain across the chapel interior and were finished in seconds. Nobody saw the theft. Including me."

She gazed lazily around the room. "Excuse me. You mentioned sleeping arrangements."

"Hey, you have a better offer? An organic farmer?" he shot back. "Sorry, male pride."

He could see she was still peeved. A waiter greeted them warmly and stared with some interest at the olive oil samples. "Oops. *Scusi!"* She swooped them into her purse. "OK. I forgive you. I am so…serene — what else can I call it. Talk to me. Test my serenity."

They ordered coffee. Without a breath, he went on.

"I've got a hunch these guys were part of a, a — what would you call it — a syndicate. A secret society. *Cavalieri,* knights, of something or other. Giovanni says they turned and saluted him when they were carrying out the Shroud. Turned and saluted him." He raised his right arm to his brow in the military fashion. "He was so proud he was three feet off the ground.

"There is this organization called the Knights Templar, a secret society that was dissolved by the church in the fourteenth century. Some heirs of the society are still around, still plotting to save society from some scourge. So, eight hundred years later, exactly to the year when it was taken from your city when it was known as Constantinople, my very unprofessional hunch is that the society plucks the precious linen out of its case and takes it back to France. It was there until it came to Turin four hundred years ago. I think these guys weren't saluting Giovanni. I think they were saluting either the altar where the church keeps the blessed hosts or they were saluting the chapel of *la Sindone*."

He was still talking an hour later. "Traditional Catholics, still living in the Middle Ages. They feel threatened by some coming catastrophe and want the Shroud because it's got magic. Protection. Who knows from what catastrophe? Secular humanism? The growing power of Islam in France? Bioterrorism? Maybe something to do with the second coming of Christ, when the enemies of Christianity will be boiled in oil or some god-awful punishment and the faithful will be taken up into heaven; you know, the rapture, the *Left Behind* stuff. It's mind-boggling. So they hire somebody to steal the Shroud."

"You are reading a lot into a little Italian male bonding ritual, which is all that gesture means to me." She smiled, indulgently.

"Anyway, I'm fighting an aching back after forty-eight hours of standing on carpeting over concrete after a three-hour flight from Istanbul. Shall we talk about sleeping arrangements?"

"One more thing. I want you to meet the archbishop of Turin."

"Right. You met him too. OK — Tom. Are we — you and I — on hold?" It was a fair question asked in an unfair way — her specialty, he knew. "You talk like — are you going to miss my workshop Thursday on liquid gold, olive treasures of Turkey?"

Tom chewed on a biscotto and sipped his cold coffee. "I'm feeling guilty. Mea culpa. Listen: I had an appointment to see this archbishop so I could write off part of this junket. I am in the church when this Shroud is stolen. You and me, here together, this week — some underground current between the cathedral and the Lingotto convention center somewhere. More than..."

"…coincidence."

"More! Confluence. A magical stream. Go with the flow."

"And you can turn it off and turn it on, I mean, pursuit of me? Just like that?"

Tom read that question as a compliment — he did not cling. She had told him that was one of the things that attracted her to him.

"I came here thinking I might spend some free time writing a story about this Shroud, about the people who venerate it. Magazine piece; nothing deep. All of sudden, it's deep. You are at the *Salone del Gusto* up to your ears in friends and food. You are not at a loss for dinner companions, I've noticed. Me? — Think about it."

She took out several Euros and laid them on the table as he calculated the tip. "OK. Trattoria di Gianna. 'Gianna.' What a beautiful name."

"Tony Mezzo Soprano's dad Vittorio owns it. I think Tony owns Turin." He put a couple of Euros on the table.

"Tony is machismo on steroids."

"He's waiting for us outside. I want you to meet the archbishop. Can you take an hour from the *Salone?*"

Her eyes were misting. "Only for you." She stood and adjusted her skirt around her waist. "He may not appreciate this working woman's uniform. I'll change. You get one hour of my time, buddy."

CHAPTER 13

Tony Mezzo Soprano brought them to Rachel's hotel. After 15 minutes, she hustled outside, neatly dressed in white blouse, black jacket and skirt. She slid onto the backseat, watching the cabby warily in his rearview mirror.

"Nice outfit."

"Watch the road, Romeo." She sat in silence. Tom looked to be daydreaming. Tony dodged a motorbike, then stared at her in the mirror.

"I'm glad you dressed for the occasion. He's no prude, but you never know with the clergy."

She stared right back at him. Rachel had a lot on her plate that day. *Terra Madre* — the actual growers themselves — were holding sessions that afternoon, really important stuff — a big report on multinationals moving into organics, co-opting the movement in developed countries, their lower minions accused of beating up organizers in some developing countries.

"Excuse me, do you have the *Herald Tribune*?" Tony handed one back to her immediately. "Shroud of Turin sightings everywhere," read a headline. Nothing on the *Salone*. She read the Shroud piece to the end and looked up only when the cab stopped inside a courtyard tucked away under the watchful eyes of a statue of the Madonna and Child. Tony opened her door and she stepped out.

"This is his residence. The office is next door." He smiled icily at Rachel and leaned against the cab. "And get over your thing with machismo, because that dude in there is Eye-talian too." He caressed the "eye." He pushed his sunglasses up on his forehead and stared into the sky. His cool unnerved her.

She squared herself and, with a shrug honed on the streets of Seattle in the face of police and dogs and tear gas, walked toward the unpretentious building arm in arm with Tom. She caught a wedge heel between two of the stones and stumbled awkwardly before Tom caught her and she regained her balance. She straightened up, turned and glared at Tony, who looked away. She set her chin low and marched on. Cabbies were one thing; could she handle church patriarchs? "Resist authority" was all she could think of.

The press conference was just starting. A dozen journalists

scribbled and a half-dozen camera crews trained their lenses on the podium. A broad-shouldered monsignor strode in, talking as he walked. The monsignor had a military, barking, staccato delivery. He was a trained dominator.

The monsignor pointed to a screen behind him displaying the Shroud. "The linen is of herringbone weave, fourteen feet long, between three and four feet wide. The imprint of a man is visible, about five feet, seven inches tall. These appear to be blood stains, especially around the head, neck, wrist, feet and the right side of the chest. The man is dead. Who is it?"

"That is the question," Tom whispered to Rachel. Rachel sighed. "I want to meet the Reverend Tucci," she growled. "I hope this guy doesn't start at the beginning."

The monsignor started at the beginning. Thaddeus, the disciple who replaced Judas, was sent to evangelize Edessa, a city in Turkey. There he worked miracles, including one involving the use of an image of the face of Christ to heal the king of Edessa of his leprosy. In the second century the cloth went underground along with the local persecuted Christians and was lost until the sixth century, when it resurfaced in that city. Muslim forces overran the city in the 7th century. In the 9th century, a Christian delegation from Constantinople purchased the Shroud from Edessa. The church in Constantinople displayed it from time to time until the infamous 4th crusade. Crusaders looted Constantinople and brought the Shroud to France. It was displayed in different cities and towns, until the House of Savoy transferred it from Chambéry to Turin in the 16th century.

Looking at his watch, the monsignor leapfrogged to the 20th Century. In 1898, investigators used a camera to discover that the sketchy set of markings on the cloth was a photographic negative. Then ninety years later, a controversial radiocarbon dating in 1988 put the origins of the Shroud somewhere between 1260 and 1390 C.E.

"So there you have it. Many scientists declare that it's not Christ's Shroud; others disagree. And the church has not pronounced one way or the other, but reveres it as a singular reminder of the passion, death and resurrection of Jesus. Any questions?"

"Any clues yet?" asked Tom.

The square-jawed monsignor looked at Tom through his glasses with a kind of night-vision-goggle menace. *"Signòre, paziènza.* At this point, nothing." Then his face softened and he whined, "We are hoping the press will pass along information to us."

"We stand ready, Monsignor," shouted a man seated in the front row. Leaping to his feet, he introduced himself. "I'm Bruno Baumgartner of the Welt-Wanderer, a Catholic weekly in Germany." The Monsignor acknowledged him with a stiff wave, shut off the screen and marched out the door.

"You Christians," Rachel said, slyly. "It's a fake."

"Let's go right to the source." He dialed the private number of Michael Tucci.

CHAPTER 14

Next door, at the residence of the archbishop of Turin, a nine-foot-high wood-paneled door opened before them. Rachel was looking at a distinguished-looking elderly clergyman in black suit and Roman collar.

"Come in. I'm Father Michael Tucci. Thomas Ueland, I welcome you back."

"Pastor, this is my friend, Rachel Cohen."

"Rachel, *prego!*"

She felt self-conscious, not cosmopolitan at all; Jewish; the first bishop's hand she had ever shaken; the effect was tingling. What did she call him? "Father" was out of the question.

"Hi, Michael. Let's talk."

His forehead creased in surprise. But gradually his lips arched in a grateful smile. "Yes. Come in." The archbishop led the way into a sitting room. Not what she expected; it was not filled with overstuffed chairs and did not have plaster putti dripping from clouds painted on garish ceilings. If anything, it was austere; brocaded old chairs, modern abstract art pieces, some dramatic black and white photography. A particularly striking photo — three people in front of a cathedral. All in their twenties or thirties, from a time that looked like the nineteen fifties. Two men, one woman, she probably married to the more dapper of the gentlemen, and the other man more by himself, a dark-complexioned and good-looking fellow with long hair pushed straight back. She lingered, gazing at it and then the archbishop.

"You as a young man?"

"Yes. The swarthy one."

"I figured. Your friends are French, I am betting. Parisians."

"Right again. Old friends. Paul and Genevieve De Rosier. You live a long time, you have a lot of old friends. Dead or alive." He smiled at her, then turned to Tom. "They, thankfully, are alive. And they know a thing or two about magical thinking. So, please sit; the promised coffee is coming." Tom scribbled something in a notebook.

Rachel sensed that Tucci was waiting to see how sympathetic she was to his dilemma. "A terrible thing for your church. For you. I'm very sorry. As a Jew, I struggle with hostile, warped people all the time. They bombed my parents' old synagogue in Istanbul last year."

"A terrible thing. Religious zealots are terrifying. I had asked your friend Tom to consult with me on a theological matter weeks ago. Now zealots have made it a criminal matter. I am delighted he followed you to Torino for a..."

"Have you ever heard of the *Salone del Gusto?*" she asked, too sweetly by half.

"I was going to stop by the day the schoolchildren are there. They like seeing the bishop sampling the formaggio, holding my skullcap with one hand while I toss back a small glass of vino with the other." He acted out the charade. "The children love it and the press cover it. I call it the Episcopal flip and sip. The Catholic church has built its whole sacramental system around food, you know; *Cibus angelorum,* the food of angels. And I have many friends among the growers of Piedmont. I go every time. Perhaps not this year."

She laughed at his act, surprising herself, and felt her face redden. Never assume. He's got a graceful touch, this guy. Yet, underneath the gold cross on his vest, she was sure he was surmising, "Now, aren't you a charming little Christ-killer."

Michael asked Tom, "Well, that press conference — was it helpful to you?"

"About those words: 'The land of its provenance.' If the authenticators were right, its provenance could be any of the following: Palestine from thirty-three through fifty CE, Turkey from fifty through twelve oh four, France from twelve oh four through fifteen seventy-eight and Torino from fifteen seventy-eight to today. That's a lot of provenances. And why does someone need it today, eight hundred years to the year after crusaders sacked Constantinople? Revenge? Black magic?"

Michael Tucci sat back, fumbled in his pockets for something. He looked at Tom. "Why indeed? It is not the abduction of a Monet or a Picasso. They desperately want it to do something they can't do without it."

"Where do you think the Shroud is now?" Tom asked.

"In Israel, somewhere. And you — where do you think it is?"

Rachel watched Tom's expression change as he spoke. "I think it's somewhere in France." He looked at Rachel. "I'd like to make a short visit to Paris. To talk to your friends the De Rosiers."

The priest's eyes widened. "Of course. I'll give you their number."

CHAPTER 15

"You will miss my workshop." They were back outside her hotel an hour later, he with his backpack, she in slacks and sweater. "I am not happy about that."

"I'll try to be back. I will miss you." Tom drew her to him.

"Call me. And be careful, mighty crime scene investigator."

"To be continued."

"*Mazeltov*. I'm late for an appointment." She kissed him on the lips and was gone, swooped up by another Mezzo Soprano Company taxi.

***

He climbed back into Tony's waiting cab. Tony whistled. "Lovely lady. So. God be with you, Signor Ueland." Tony whisked a bishop's blessing back at Tom. "Stay in touch. *Zio* Giovanni has more to talk with you about. And listen to me. You are a soft touch, Signor Ueland. You need more hard edges. A man coming to Italy to be with a woman — nothing should stand in its way. I worry about you."

"Thanks for the analysis. I can handle myself."

The cab jerked to a quick stop in front of Stazione Porta Nuova. Tony jumped out, opened the back door and held out his hand palm up as Tom stood up on the sidewalk. Tom was about to slap the hand when he saw it contained the smallest cellular phone he had ever seen. "Stay in touch, *Signòre*. Your cheap phone may not work from Paris." Tony giggled. "Your fare is…"

"Run me a tab. And listen; Rachel. Look in on her at your father's restaurant. Don't be churlish with her. She'll stab you." He wagged his finger and walked into the station.

***

Alone, a cabby talks to himself. "What the hell is 'churlish?' '*Chiuso?*' It must mean, 'Don't hide anything.' OK. Time to ferry lunch to *Zio* Giovanni. What's today? Tuesday; Cannelloni, yes of course. Well. I have made a valuable contact with Tom Ueland, who might unlock the mystery of the stolen *Sindone*. And might put *Zio* Giovanni's name in newspapers all over the world. And maybe in a book. And…Martin Scorsese. It's going to be a good week." The cab headed back to Trattoria di Gianna.

CHAPTER 16

Staring absentmindedly out a window, Michael Tucci lingered long after his guests had left. His two priests hovered nearby. "Fathers, will you take all messages for an hour? Unless the highest authority calls." The priests' faces blanched as they measured his words. Michael smiled. To them "highest authority," of course, meant the pope.

What did the phrase mean to him? Alone in his study, he removed his coat, pectoral cross, vest and collar. He slumped down in a high-backed chair, reached for an unopened pack of cigarettes, threw it down and shut his eyes. He had shared the names and phone number of two old friends, as if Tom Ueland were just a college kid needing an introduction to old friends in a foreign country. What the priest had done was give Tom Ueland a key to his own past, just as someone yesterday had given a key to the Holy Shroud's very tabernacle to the thieves. He shook his head and ran his fingers through his hair. It was not just his own past — it was the church's future at play here. That was his highest authority: the church of the 21st century. And the fortunate fault of the Shroud's abduction might be the key to ensuring the future he had in mind. Politics was all.

He picked up a book lying on a nearby table. Its edges were worn, and bookmarks protruded from pages where he had underlined a sentence or word. It was a work by the Jesuit historian, Michel de Certeau. Certeau, born in 1925, had been a teenager helping the resistance in the Savoy region during the war. In the 1970s, Certeau became known for his use of the term "heterologies," studies of those on the outside — the "other," those not at the center of power. Only a dialogue between those on the inside and the outsiders could keep the search for truth on the straight and narrow path. Michael, a few years younger than Certeau, had sought him out.

Michael reflected on his own breathtaking role reversal after his friendship with Certeau, who died in 1986. He identified more with the "others," the outsiders, than with his own brother bishops. "I have more in common with Martin Luther King than with some of these comical figures," he remembered speaking into a live mike he assumed was turned off at a conference of the Italian hierarchy.

And today he identified with the young historian Tom Ueland, even now climbing aboard a train that would travel through Chambéry, where Certeau had been born.

"My prayers go with you," he whispered before he dozed off.

CHAPTER 17

"Paul De Rosier." Something about the name struck Tom's memory as he studied the card the archbishop had given him. The Rosicrucians, that was it. Another secret society, founded in the 19th century. It was easy to laugh off the holy-bloodline hounds and grail-seekers from a distance, but he was about to get up close. He looked up as the train chugged into Chambéry.

He stretched and yawned and grabbed his scribbled notes from the day before. Between 1502 and 1578 the Shroud had been kept in Sainte-Chapelle at Chambéry, France. Should he jump out and scramble around town? He reached for his backpack and swung into the aisle. A large woman was just coming aboard and blocked the aisle. The hell with it. On his return he would stop at Chambéry after he found out more from the archbishop's friends in Paris.

He pulled out a pamphlet that featured a map showing the Shroud's itinerary. From Turkey the Shroud had sailed west on the Mediterranean Sea to Marseilles after the plunder of Constantinople in 1204 in the 4th Crusade. Then north to Paris where it was kept until about 1307, just before the Templars were disbanded. It then moved to southeastern France for the next two centuries, in Chambéry for most of the 16th century, before Turin. He sat down, gazing out the windows at the mountainous terrain.

As the train pulled away from the station, he heard the lonely wail of an ambulance siren.

Hours later, he transferred at Lyon to the TGV, France's high-speed train. While it sped through the fields of Bourgogne, he scribbled a list of his plans for Paris. Get a room. Make a phone call to Paul De Rosier. OK, then what? That was up to Monsieur De Rosier — Tucci's old friend.

Gare de Lyon swallowed the TGV under its giant roof at precisely 9:30 p.m. Tom slid on the backpack and once outside joined the stream of travelers trailing their suitcases behind them. Was he being watched? Someone bumped into him. An older man, short, a scarf nattily tied around his neck, a black topcoat. The man was gone in the crowd. Keep an eye out for that man's face. Sure, his and seven million others'.

He stopped at a newsstand. The *Herald Tribune* headline, if not screamed, was distinctly murmured, "Mysterious Death in Chambéry, France." And underneath, "Linked to theft of Shroud?" Damn, why had he not just climbed over the seats on an end run around the big woman? "Police believe that the dead man, an elderly security guard, died of a stroke in the Sainte-Chapelle where the Shroud of Turin had been displayed before its removal by the royal family of Savoy to Turin. The Shroud was stolen by several unidentified men on Monday from the cathedral in Turin."

In the cab queue, he snapped open Tony's cell phone and turned it on. It played the "Chorus of the Hebrew Slaves" from Verdi's *Nabucco*. Over-the-edge Tony. Tom tapped out the Paris number of Paul De Rosier. He watched the screen, wondering whether the thing was roaming. Hardly. The phone was ringing. After three rings, a woman's voice on tape, an invitation to leave a message. He fished out the card with the number of his hotel from his pocket and said his name and who he was and where he was staying. At the head of the queue, he turned to see the man with the scarf far back in the line. Tom got into a cab and was whisked away.

The Marais district was no more than five minutes away from the station. Tom paid the fare, slung the backpack over his shoulder and entered into the small hotel's shoebox office. What looked like Christmas lights or red pepper bulbs were strung around a filmy mirror. In it, he saw the clerk, a thin, smiling woman in her 30s, merrily puffing away on a cigarette. She greeted him in English, gave him a key and a note. "The call came for you just when the cab pulled up. She said to have you call immediately."

"She?" Tom was puzzled, expecting the husband to be the main actor. The clerk smiled at him, a smile that said "Your lucky day."

"Thank you." He took the note and squeezed into the tiny elevator. On the fifth floor the door to his *petite chambre* opened on a downright petite room with a little pathway around one side of the bed. The price was right, about eight Euros a square foot.

He dialed the De Rosier number. When the woman answered, Tom spoke hesitantly. *"Parlez-vous Anglais,* Madame? This is Tom Ueland. I'm a...ah, an acquaintance of Archbishop Tucci. I'm trying to get in touch with a Paul and Genevieve De Rosier."

There was a pause, then breathing. A clear voice of an older woman came back. *"Bonjour,* Monsieur Ueland. My name is Genevieve De Rosier." Another pause. "My husband Paul lives in a home — for people with dementia." Tom sat down slowly on the bed.

"Archbishop Tucci thought...I'm sorry. I guess I shouldn't be bothering you. You see, I'm here in connection with the theft of the Shroud of Turin. I'm not police. I'm just following up...I mean."

"The Shroud. Of course. Come at 2 tomorrow."

CHAPTER 18

The white van was parked on a side street near Boulevard Port Royal. The bearded leader was gazing up toward an apartment window in a nearby building. His head shook. He was warding off unwanted thoughts. "We are at the northernmost point of the Holy Shroud's journey home, from Torino through the Alps to Chambéry to Paris. Here it lay five hundred years ago. Now we turn and head south in the Crusader King Louis' footsteps. How good it is when brothers dwell together, watching and waiting for the return of Christ the King! Do not falter, Sidonius and Trophimus. We have forsaken all for His sake: family, marriage, luxury, self-will. To live together as brothers."

He looked up again at the window. The curtains were open. Two figures were now moving about inside. Then the curtains were being drawn. He had not needed to tell his two companions why the van was parked here. They knew. The leader signaled for ignition, then held his arm out over the heads of his companions. "The sailing ship of the saints awaits us, we sail to Jerusalem — His own Shroud our guide under the constellations of the skies. Let us go to reverence the Shroud at Sainte Elizabeth."

***

Charles, the sacristan at the Church of Sainte Elizabeth on Paris' Rue du Temple, was as tightly wound as the church clock by which he timed his duties. But on this infernal day everything was chaos. A pack of Shroud vultures had left three hours earlier and he barely had time to reopen the doors for evening mass, attended by the usual congregation of pensioners, widows and young immigrant mothers cradling babies. What would tomorrow, Wednesday, be like, with the news from Chambéry?

The pastor was his usual buoyant ass of a self, oh yes, he thought. The priest did not have to deal with crazed fanatics trying to turn the church upside down looking for the Shroud. Oh no, the pastor, who had never done a day of manual labor, could give a little sermon on how the real clothing that comforts Christ's body is "the vestment of our souls, not the Holy Shroud." And the pastor could

47

feel smug about how he had transformed a mundane matter like the theft of the Shroud into a spiritual message for his flock who Charles knew would forget it as soon as they left the church.

So things he would have done before the service he now had to do at night. First he had dined on onion soup and a glass of wine at the bistro close by, where he could nurse his resentments. On his return, so as not to attract attention from Shroud seekers, he entered the church from the rear through a small gated area off Rue de Turbigo — and found the door unlatched. Had he forgotten to lock it when he left earlier after throwing out the fanatics? Yes, he remembered — he had been so utterly rattled by them that he stalked out without turning back. He sighed; no damage, no one inside. He cleaned the sanctuary with the vacuum cleaner, stored it away in the utility closet. Next he did the rounds of Sainte Elizabeth's nooks and crannies and doors and windows, picking up stray papers or bulletins, closing windows, locking doors. He thought he heard a noise elsewhere in the church but ignored it; the floors creaked all the time. He removed burnt-out candles from the side altar candle stand and put fresh ones in their place; Madame De Rosier would be here the next morning as usual to light one.

Charles' final duty was to lay out the vestments for the next morning's mass. He unlocked the sacristy door. The smell of extinguished candles from the altar had somehow drifted into the sacristy. Unmistakable, that smell; it was the scent of his work. He walked to the vestment case, opened it and began rummaging through the chasubles until he found the green one the pastor would wear the next morning. He could do his work in the dark; the only light was that from the altar in the sanctuary. He laid out all the vestments but the alb and cincture. He turned to the closet and something caught his eye. It was the wall vitrine opposite the vestment case. Instead of the old chasubles that hung inside the glass, something was covering the glass itself. An amber cloth, draped all the way across the vitrine wall.

It was dark in the sacristy; in the low light, he couldn't tell what the cloth was — *mon dieu*, maybe the Shroud that mob was looking for. He turned to flick on the light for a better look. And just then, out of the darkness at the far end of the vestment case, a figure rose from a kneeling position. A slight man, dressed in nondescript slacks and a jacket, his face bearded. The man started to approach Charles. *"Qui..."* Charles said no more. He felt his chest constricted by a rough rope that cut off the circulation in his arms. Then it was loosened, just enough for him to gasp for air. The bearded man spoke.

"Monsieur, you will say nothing of this to anyone. We have vowed to find the true Shroud. We have come here to reverence a replica of it in this chapel where it once was displayed. If you break the prayer chain — forged by the thousands of faithful who are united to us — if you disclose what you have seen, you will frustrate our purpose; you will stand against all the saints of God and on the side of the forces of Lucifer. And you will die a painful and accursed death and suffer eternal damnation in the deepest regions of hell. Do you swear to remain silent?" The rope tightened once again.

"Oui, je le jure," Charles managed to breathe out before he collapsed on the floor. He heard as if from far away a man speak in the Provençal tongue.

"The second station of the cross: The Savior's Shroud returns to Paris. Time is short. On to the Camargue!"

CHAPTER 19

"Rachel! Where are you all my life!" Did the wily Turk know that his English was not airtight? He apparently knew he could get the idea across. "Olives? Are you still stuck in olives? The future is in wheat, Rachel! Get on the program!"

When Yusuf Aktug sauntered down Rachel's aisle at the *Salone del Gusto*, she had been trading coffee stories with a small group of growers from Kenya. Yusuf waved to her; she waved back, the Kenyans turned to look and hellos were shouted in three languages. It was a *Terra Madre* moment — instant recognition, acceptance, a lovefest in an Eden of growers, mutual admiration sprouting like a seed among perfect strangers. She spoke in English.

"Meet my compatriot, Yusuf Aktug, the man who is organizing Turkey's growers against genetically modified organisms," she crowed as the circle broke to admit Yusuf. Yusuf bowed and shook hands with each of the Kenyans. When he came to the counter he took Rachel's hand and kissed it. She squeezed his hand in hers, flushing not only with pleasure but with the admiration she felt for courageous men and women in her native country.

Rachel Cohen had known Yusuf Aktug mostly by his reputation long before she had met him — the radical organizer of the small wheat growers of Turkey, the man who by himself had built them into a powerful force, a coalition of over 50,000 families and small corporations. Aktug had traveled the length and breadth of the country's interior and its coastal and mountainous areas for years, patiently roping together the frustrations and anger of small growers, keeping the pressure on government bureaucracy and big grain.

So here he was, ambling nonchalantly in the vast aisles the day before the *Salone del Gusto* officially opened, greeting old friends in the *Terra Madre* group of growers, shouting out ancient blessings, hugging and being hugged. A lean, mustachioed and bearded handsome man, with long hair and dark complexion, Yusuf Aktug looked every inch the model weather-whipped and defiant wheat farmer. Looking down his nose at olives.

"Not 'get on the program,' Get with the program, I think you mean to say. My dear man, one million eight hundred thousand metric tons of olive products produced this year. Turkey makes the best olive oils in the world! Homer's liquid gold! Look at this stuff! Smell it!" She pushed a jar of olives into his face. "It's great to see you again."

He inhaled and smiled. "All too many months between, my sister. Have you converted to Islam yet?" Yusuf's eyes darted back and forth from the Kenyans to Rachel. He had a reputation for begetting anarchy in the midst of amity. "I hear Islam is America's quickest growing religion. Join the club, yes?" The Kenyans smiled nervously.

"City girls don't convert, Yusuf. They are cosmopolitan." Not that he was really pushing conversion; his farmers' coalition embraced the swirling ethnic and religious mix that was Istanbul and the vast reaches of the country's interior. No wonder the European Union was cautious about Turkey.

The Kenyan contingent drifted off like swans in their graceful robes down the long aisle of booths, soon lost in the crowd.

"If you convert, wait until after Ramadan. You cannot believe how difficult to attend the *Salone del Gusto* during Ramadan! Here I am, surrounded by the most beautiful foods of the world, and I can eat nothing until after sundown! You are married? No? I see no ring." Fasting or not, he was impish with her — he had once admitted to her she was one of the few women with whom he could be relaxed.

"So, you know that we are working right now on the GMOs? I fear that we are losing, Rachel; time is getting smaller, shorter — how do you say. The big guys come together, preparing for takeover of Turkey. Feeding the multitudes, they are claiming. 'Insect- and bacterial-resistant wheat' able to be grown in shorter growing seasons. Grown more efficiently on bigger and bigger farms. The cities are filling up with farmers, Rachel, glad to be off the land and then suddenly on the dole. Life is beautiful here at the *Salone del Gusto*. But we are a — how do you say it — a dangerous species."

"An endangered species. Who are the big guys these days?"

"The biggest is Gregory Samaras. Made much money on the futures wheat market. Millions. Now he is making branches into real estate, investments, banking. He is ready to start up agribusiness on a big way — this is staggering us. And he honestly believes it will be for Turkey's goodness, not to mention his own pocketbook's fatness."

Rachel shut down the booth, came around the counter to the

aisle, took Yusuf's arm and kissed his cheek.

"No boyfriend?" Yusuf was probing again.

Rachel looked at him with a wry smile. "I have a friend who is in town." She was being evasive. "He's a professor at a college in Minnesota."

"The mightiful Mississippi?" Yusuf was showing off again. "Where it all begins, the chemicals, the bad stuff from all those farmers making the river a sewer to the Mexican sea? I hear..."

"I'm not here defending agriculture in Minnesota," she cut in. "I'm simply saying that a friend of mine from Minnesota is here, visiting Turin while I'm..."

"OK. I am just playing a game. I understand. You will meet him after this?" He was studying her.

"No. He had to go to Paris for...an article he is writing."

"Good." He showed little interest in either Tom or the article. "Then you can come with me and my friends for supper. You know many of them, I think. We are going to this restaurant recommended by some of our Torinese friends. Trattoria di Gianna. They say it is hot, hot, hot."

"Been there, done that," she laughed. "It is hot, hot, hot."

Trattoria di Gianna was jammed with conventioneers from every continent, motley in their kilts and skirts and dungarees and dharmas and loin cloths. She saw Tony Mezzo Soprano pushing his way among the tables; he was close to the table where she and Yusuf and some of the Kenyans and the Americans were comparing corporate outrages. He smiled knowingly, his tummy jiggling beneath a t-shirt that said "Duca d'URL: Wi-Fi and Internet Services." He whispered, "My cab will be outside if you need a ride home later."

He left before she could say anything. Yusuf leaned over. "The boyfriend?"

OK, how much should she tell him? Not much. "No. The boyfriend's cabby. His father owns this place, I think."

Yusuf smiled. "You Americans lead celebrity lives. Your own driver. I am very jealous."

"Don't be. It makes me feel a little creepy, like I'm being watched. I know the *Salone del Gusto* is like the Garden of Eden, full of caring sensitive people. But could there be...spies here? You know?" Rachel made a face. "I have made enemies wherever I go. I am so paranoid."

The teeth again — Yusuf smiled. "Hey, OK, why not? We sneak

into their board meetings, their stockholder meetings. Why not?"

"But we don't try to put them in jail. Or worse. You be careful, my friend."

"OK, big business is watching and waiting; they want to copy our — how do you say — our message. But this is not a dirt road in Anatolia. I don't fear a bullet here."

She stifled a yawn. "I should go. I'm still jet lagged."

He stood up with her. "I have an interview with a reporter in the morning. I will walk you to your hotel."

They stepped out into the cool Turin night. Tony's cab was across the street. He motioned to them. Yusuf walked over to him. "We are walking. Thank you. You are good to her boyfriend, OK?"

Tony grinned. "*Amico*, her boyfriend and I are *famiglia*. Welcome to Torino. My card." Yusuf shook Tony's outstretched hand, rejoined Rachel and walked arm in arm with her toward her hotel.

A college-age couple approached them. She was tall, athletic-looking, blonde. He was a chubby, bookish-looking fellow with glasses. They blocked Rachel and Yusuf's way. The young woman spoke first. "We are students in town for the *Salone*. We have friends at Istanbul University who know you. You have a problem with the businessman Gregory Samaras, we hear. We know him quite well; we interviewed him as part of a research report we did last year. We found him quite sweet." The preppy male squared his shoulders and kept blocking their path.

"He is who he is," Yusuf parried. Keep your mouth shut, Yusuf, she thought; these kids are trouble. The chubby one glowered at Yusuf and kept needling him.

"In addition to amassing a fortune in the grain business, he has become a power player alongside the Cargills and the Continentals and the other grain giants of the world. And he is in favor of allowing GMOs into Turkey. What's the problem with your movement?"

Could these two be serious? "Wait a minute," Rachel yelled. The tall woman bumped her with a muscular thigh.

Her partner poked Yusuf in the chest. "We know about you. Everybody in the field of agricultural economics knows about you, Mr. Aktug. You are the watchword for outdated libertarianism in food. The world market is going to GMOs but the road is littered with these little protests of yours that slow progress."

The young woman — an Amazon in jeans and a sweatshirt — stood eyeball to eyeball with Yusuf. "How does it feel going to bed at night knowing you have caused millions of children to go to bed hungry at that very moment? Yes, the children, their families' crop decimated by grasshoppers? This will be the way the world works into the future, Mr. Aktug. Engineered crops to sustain world population; you do know about sustainability, don't you?"

Yusuf put himself between Rachel and the students. "Go home to your rich friends and don't bother us, you little shits!" he shouted.

The chubby male started screaming. "We're registered participants in the *Salone del Gusto*, same as you! And we know the stakes in this game of food production. It's men like Gregory Samaras who will be the reason people in the Middle East and Africa and the Far East will not starve in years to come, because they will be able to grow grains without fear of pestilence. Isn't it about time you put your skills to work on the side of the people?"

***

Tony Mezzo Soprano's cab had been following Rachel. When he saw the students turn menacing, Tony leaped out of his cab and pushed the male aside. The young man thrust a fat elbow into Tony's ample stomach. Yusuf grabbed the student by the arm but was blindsided by the tall female who bloodied his nose with a whiplash back of her hand. A black Carmen Ghia sped up, the rear doors opened, the students — nimble as ballet dancers — disappeared into the backseat and were gone.

CHAPTER 20

Genevieve De Rosier's apartment building was nestled on the tiny street of Rue Flatters near the intersection of Rue Bertholet and Boulevard Port Royal. Tom unknowingly walked past her building three times. Finally he saw her name by the intercom. He punched the numbers.

"Entrez, Monsieur Ueland." Once inside, he rode a two-person elevator that took its time climbing to the third floor. When he got out he saw that the door of the apartment straight ahead was ajar. Number Seven, her apartment. He knocked lightly on the door.

"Une minute, s'il vous plait," she called from inside. *"Desirez-vous un cafe?"*

"Oui, Madame." Tom pushed the door open. She had not yet entered the hallway; he could see at the end of it a large room filled with the stuff of a long life: bookcases lining the wall, boxes of papers stacked in front of them, framed photographs hanging above the bookcases, a card table weighed down with magazines and legal pads, an ornate writing desk overflowing with stationery and envelopes. In the center, an oval oak dining room table. Despite the clutter, the place smelled fresh, new. Perhaps it was the flowers. They were everywhere.

"Bienvenue. Je suis Genevieve De Rosier." She appeared from another room, a tall, tanned, slender woman, apparently ageless but probably in her 70s, with an astonishing sweep of striking grey hair falling down her neck and back.

"Enchanté, Madame. *Je m'appelle* Tom Ueland. Bonjour. *Je parle un peu Français.* Ah, sorry." Tom stammered. She sighed, her breath seeming to exude some disappointment but not surprise.

"It is not a problem. *Entrez;* I have coffee; would you like milk?" She led him into a sun porch which did not see much sun, only the building across the tiny street, especially now in late October. There were two high-backed chairs and a love seat, all slip-covered with a rose-petal pattern, on either side of a glass coffee table. He stood behind one of the chairs. She disappeared into another room and returned carrying a tray and silver service. "Please sit down. Tell me what I need to know about you and how you came to have such...*amitie* with our old friend, Archbishop Tucci."

While she prepared his coffee, he examined her face. Green eyes, almond skin almost miraculously unwrinkled, high cheekbones, thin mouth. She wore a simple white blouse under a handsome pink cardigan sweater, with a grey, woolen ankle-length skirt. She set his cup down and her eyes met his. "Sorry, I'm staring," he blurted out. "You are a most wonderful-looking woman."

"Thank you. My husband Paul…"

"I'm sorry, I didn't know he was in a rest home when I called you."

"Of course. He loved it when someone complimented me as you did. I think he felt he needed someone like me beside him. His friends told me he referred to us as *"la belle et la bête."* His picture is over there; as you can see, he was not handsome but he was by no means unattractive. A dashing man."

Tom studied the picture of Paul De Rosier. He was dressed in the uniform of royalty; a coat completely buttoned neck to waist, thick collar Nehru-style around his neck, a sash around his waist, a sword hanging in its scabbard. He had a fine goatee. He was not handsome. But by god he was distinguished, an aristocrat. And the photographer had captured the man's commanding aura. "Is that his uniform as a Knight Templar?"

She laughed. "I'm afraid not. It's his Chevaliere du Malta plumage. He has long since shed the plumage — both the uniform and the goatee."

"Impressive. He's a good-looking man. I am very sorry he needs care in a rest home." Tom studied her. She looked down at her cup.

"He was a passionate man. He believed in the Catholic Church, its civilizing force, its power as the — how do you say — glue of society. We had a great many friends in the church. "

"Among them, Archbishop Tucci." He wished he had said something subtler, like "Yes. Of course." "Actually, I just met him Tuesday. It's all accidental."

"Nothing is accidental. I'm sure there is a reason that you are here."

"The coffee is delicious, thank you. Well, I came to Torino to be with a friend at the *Salone del Gusto*. I was also going to visit the archbishop to talk about — well, magic and religion. But first I made a visit to the cathedral — right when the Shroud was being removed by the thieves. So I met Pastor Tucci and, well, here I am. In the United States I teach American and European history at a college in

Minnesota." He paused; it was her turn to stare at him. "That's me."

"Ah, *oui, le* Mississippi," she sighed. From the coffee table she took a pack of cigarettes and drew one out. She rummaged for a matchbook, lit the cigarette, drew on it and exhaled a stream of smoke away from Tom. A performance by someone younger, a simple ritual for her. "I smoke only three a day. One in the morning, one in the afternoon and a third at night. A disgusting habit."

Her enjoyment of the disgusting habit was palpable. "So, Monsieur Ueland, the archbishop and you believe there is magical thinking involved in the theft, yes?"

"He thinks it's more politics — but he is open to another view: mine is the Shroud was taken — for its magical qualities, protecting one's friends, harming one's enemies, making a divinity act on one's behalf — does that make sense?"

"I speak to you as an anthropologist. Yes, a certain amount of sense. The sympathetic principle; you have read Malinowski?" She exhaled, the smoke crawling around the window.

"Some time ago, in post-grad study. I confess I have not been back to it."

"You should reread his entry entitled 'Culture' in the Encyclopedia of Social Sciences, nineteen thirty-one. When primitive people encounter an immovable obstacle and yet are driven by an irresistible force to continue, they resort to magic. If we can't understand or control something, if we feel impotent to affect an outcome — we resort to magic. We are compelled to fulfill a wish by other means. The sacrilegious thieves may have taken the Shroud to force heaven's hand — to bring about something."

Tom nodded. "If civilized people feel impotent to affect an outcome, what do they resort to?" Before she could answer, he added, "Religion?"

"Perhaps." She frowned, annoyed. "Violence, revolution, more likely. You might ask the archbishop. He knows many things — none very deeply, I recall."

"I wonder why Pastor Tucci did not know your husband was...not well? He had no idea, judging from the way he spoke about him." Tom waited for the mention of a falling out, a simmering dispute, or even the possibility that the aging archbishop had just forgotten, the way old friends can forget.

"We have not been in touch for years, except for an occasional Christmas card. And yesterday he left only a voice mail on our phone." She paused, a flicker of regret in the tone. "He became the archbishop of Turin, I think some fifteen years ago now. We began to diverge in our views about the church, Europe, the world, perhaps twenty-five years ago. We were great friends before. Now? Not so great. Paul was in the habit of sending him very angry letters when he read something that Michael" — she caught herself — "I mean, the archbishop, had said."

"Yeah, he is outspoken. Church disputes?"

"Mostly the Second Vatican Council and all that. Saner voices — Paul's — wanted the church to pull back from the council's theologically flimsy assertions. Paul and I saw Vatican II as a disaster for the church here in Europe, the beginning of this mélange of 'every man his own pope' we have today." She inhaled the cigarette and stamped it out. Tom noticed it was a Gauloise. Wow. Strong stuff, lady. She exhaled into the thin light from the street, her face hid in darkness.

He guessed that Genevieve De Rosier was not going to be any help. A grand but aged dame of Malta, all faded, delicate elegance. Yet, he stifled his instinct to cut her short. Her relationship to the Turin churchman was important — God knew why.

"Mrs. De Rosier, I'm trying to make some secret society connection with this theft of the Shroud. Can you help me?"

"Mais oui. You think a Frenchman stole the Holy Shroud, *n'est-ce-pas?"* There was the hint of a smile on her lips, Mona Lisa late in life, and then a tensing of her mouth. "Preposterous on the face of it. Yet I suppose these days anything is possible. Chambéry; the poor soul in that chapel. Who could have so frightened him? Were you there too?"

"I was on the train passing through Chambéry; they had just found the old man, but I couldn't get off. Maybe the thieves were on the train with me. With the Shroud..."

"A very unpleasant thought," she frowned. "Shall we go to the site where they burned Jacques de Molay, the last public leader of the Templars? The tip of the Ile d' Cité. Come, we'll talk as we go. I need the walk. In his saner moments, my husband says I should walk every day. And not smoke. He wants me to keep walking until some day they can't find me, I think."

Descending the steps, he was keenly aware of a vivacious sheen of good health glowing from her face, a subtle perfume from her body. "You walk a lot?"

"Actually, I go hiking in the hills of Burgundy regularly. You should walk five miles every day, young man." She had buttoned an ankle-length thick velour coat against the late afternoon October chill and drew from a pocket a smart cap that looked hand-sewn. She took Tom's arm. She walked with a vital stride that threatened to drag him along.

"Well, here is my response to your question — I suppose rather, to your theory. I believe rationalism is destroying Europe. My husband — in younger years — wrote about it, spoke publicly about it. The French revolution ushered in rationalism, and out went the aristocracy, the church, royalty, only to be replaced by the new aristocracy, those who pose as democratic politicians but are seeking the same absolute power as any king." She took a deep breath; Tom thought they might have to rest; no such luck.

"Bureaucrats run the country now. We need values. The magic of religion. Stability. That is what the old order bestowed on us. The church. Royalty. The nobility. For all its flaws, the old order kept things in their place." She paused, looking back over her shoulder. "My dear, it's a little further than I said to the Ile; here comes the Number Twenty-one; let's take it until we cross the Seine."

Minutes later, the bus had crossed the Pont Saint-Michel onto the Boulevard du Palais; They stepped out the back door and onto Place de Notre Dame. Genevieve crossed herself and then turned to go the other way from the church. She was a study in contrasts — sensuality, religiosity. "So as I was saying." Catching him staring at her, she smiled. "Oh *mon dieu*, what was I saying? *Quel dommage...*" There was challenge in her eyes. "Was I making sense?"

"We were digressing, I think." Tom noticed that passersby were staring at them, this striking dowager in her gorgeous frock and him, her young squire in a worn London Fog raincoat and corduroy cap. Mother and son. "So why did you burn your friend Jacques de Molay at the stake?"

They passed la Saint-Chapelle as they picked their way along the crowded Quai; she nudged him toward Place Dauphine, littered with golden leaves cascading alongside their footsteps on the stones. "The knights came into being in the early twelfth century to provide protection for the growing numbers of pilgrims traveling to the Holy Land. They were more than travel guides; they also became a fighting force. They built fortresses across Europe and the near East.

They were so loyal and so essential to the good order of society that they were given permission to name bishops and answered only to the pope. When the fourth crusade came together in the first decade of the thirteenth century, they had the funds to underwrite it." She stopped — for breath or effect?

They crossed Place Dauphine's triangular stretch of stones and stepped onto the Pont Neuf. Massive scaffolding had been erected to restore the statue of Henry IV. She led him past the statue, down the steps to the Square du Vert-Gallant, a small park on a spit of low-lying land. One of the tourist bubble-glass-top vedettes that roil the Seine had just moored at the dock, and a crowd was coming up the steps, gripping their guides and maps, getting their bearings. She spoke into the wind.

"I think of Auden's poem about the death of Icarus: 'How everything turns away, quite leisurely, from the disaster.' Here, look below the scaffolding — the plaque commemorating the death on that fateful scaffold; you can barely see it. None of these tourists ever see it. We are told that the Monarch, Philippe le Bel, watched the execution from the window of the palace." The wind was cold, biting. Tom wrapped the collar of his raincoat around him. He looked at Genevieve De Rosier. Her eyes were moist, whether from wind or emotion he couldn't tell. She crossed herself, looked for a bench, sat and continued.

"Jacques de Molay was burned alive at a stake built on this mound of earth not only because the order was rich and powerful and secret. He was burned alive because the order was no longer relevant. The church needs movements. It is an old institution that can only be reborn if movements come and go. It needs heresies and apostasies and fringe movements to continually subject it to cleansing — even if they are wrong, especially if they are wrong. It needs Archbishop Michael Tucci."

She looked at him, her eyes brilliant, intense. "In my life I have been part of many movements. To be old is to watch them all come to ruin on the rocks of greed, rigid ideology, self-will. Old age is being Lot's wife, turning to salt, yes, gazing back at what was once beautiful, now burning. Only the one rock remains, thank God. The Church of Rome. Of course it will endure, but it needs this continual cleansing to remain pure and worthy of survival. It is a divine institution run by all too human sinners!"

She shook her head. *"Mon dieu, pardonnez-moi!* I do go on."

"Do you have a guess which fringe movement is involved here?"

She stood, pulled her collar around her neck, and led him back up the steps. "My guess is that the thief wants to start a movement against rationalism. I sympathize with that. 'You, O Europe, are in danger of losing everything that makes you Europe. You are burning your values at the stake. In the name of diversity, you are allowing the religion of Islam to become as European as the Roman Catholic Church.' You see, my dear young man, the French needed Nazism to show them how much their culture had decayed, to revivify it. This theft is a misguided protest against heresy, against foreign religions. Perhaps against Michael Tucci's brand of Catholicism."

My god, here is Rumsfeld's "Old Europe," he thought. "With all due respect, what makes Europe Europe? It's not a single cultural worldview. Why can't people who have vastly different theologies live together and thrive? Why do some have to be heretics? I think the thieves are out to unleash a single grand vision that reduces all heresies to smithereens!"

After he said it, he studied her face for a clue. End of conversation? She was looking at the spires of Notre Dame. He continued. "I know from my tourist guidebook that at the other end of this island, behind the church, there is a memorial to the tens of thousands of French Jews deported to death camps. The leisurely turning away from disaster you spoke of, was that not the crime of thousands of faithful Catholics? Was that not full-scale retreat from rationalism?"

They crossed the street, dodging tourists promenading across the Pont Neuf. "I was sixteen years old in nineteen forty-one. I did not know Paul yet. I actually met Paul in America. And now I have lived long enough to see the real face of Islam, slipping into France less violently than Nazism, but no less deeply, no less insidiously."

The wind skimmed across the waves of the Seine and scooped up the water's frigid envelope of air, carrying it right through his London Fog. As they reached Place Dauphine, the city of lights was illuminating itself against the overcast dark sky. "Can I buy you a glass of wine and a sandwich?"

She nodded and pointed the way into one of the cafes ringing the square. It was warm, cozy, dark, with small windows opening onto Place Dauphine. They ordered a *croque-monsieur* and white wine. "I have a friend," he blurted out. "A woman who is working to create a new order, based on native seeds and untreated foods. The future will belong to those who can find commonality among very different cultures — even Islam. Her colleagues are uniting around sustainably grown and distributed foods. That is the future. It's not your vision of Christendom, is it? Kind of an earth religion. She's reclaiming our agricultural roots."

"Every movement has its dogmas." She wound her fingers around the stem of her glass. "Your friend and I would probably get along very well. Food is truly transnational. You must miss being with her." He grinned, slightly embarrassed.

She smiled. *"Pardonnez-moi, mon cher* Tom. Now you are looking for the Shroud of Turin. The thieves probably are the new version of Knights Templar, seeking to cure the church's sickness. That's why I took you to poor Monsieur Molay's pyre. Now I'm tired. Let me send you off to the Church of Sainte Elizabeth on the Rue du Temple near Rue Turbigo. It was a frequent center of activity for later Templar-claimants long after the order had been disbanded. Go to it; it's across the street from the Square du Temple, which is part of the original precincts of the temple headquarters of the order." She took out a piece of paper and drew a map of the landmarks.

"So. There is a sacristy in the church; you will have to sneak around to see it. It has a wall with a display case of medieval vestments. Perhaps the Shroud has been added to the collection." She smiled again, that guarded smile. She was baiting him. "I know the sacristan. Use my name."

She rose, ascended was more like it. "I hope I am able to help you. *Bonne chance, mon ami.* I'm sorry, I must go visit my poor husband. It's been a wonderful release for me, Monsieur Ueland. I mean it."

He realized he was going to miss her company — royalty, she was. He stifled his Minnesota democratic impulse, took her hand and kissed it. "I wish you all the best. Can I call you again if I come upon something?"

"You will hear from us — I mean — me, before you leave. And greet the good archbishop for me when you return to Turin. And ask him why the *Duomo* has that dreadful copy of Leonardo's Last Supper hanging on its wall. Does he believe Leonardo fabricated the Shroud? Maybe the archbishop is a Knight Templar in purple."

She winked and offered her face to be kissed; Tom held her hand as he kissed her cheeks. "And by the way, the sacristan's name at

Sainte Elizabeth is Charles. Be kind to him. He seemed very disturbed when I saw him at mass this morning. And if you have time, light a candle at the side altar."

"For your husband."

"Oui. D'accord. And for all who will make a wrong choice today. *Et pour moi."* And then she was gone, striding across the square, the valiant woman of the Old Testament, caring for the holy places while her senatorial-looking husband wandered the halls of a nursing home.

Tom started walking. Something about her unnerved him. She knew something about this Shroud, something that smelled of conspiracy. And she was sending him into the middle of it.

CHAPTER 21

The church of Sainte Elizabeth was a 20-minute walk down the Rue du Temple, which started out straight enough but then twisted and narrowed before widening again. It struck him how much that meandering path reflected his conversation with Madame De Rosier. Close to 80 years shrunk into one encounter.

Following the landmark signs, he first stopped at the Square of the Temple. From the outside, its tall trees masked the lovely playgrounds within. The trees' thick leaves formed a crepuscular canopy over the paths — almost a burial Shroud. He shivered. The lovely, delightful lady had sent him here with skimpy instructions, and he was projecting a dismal failure.

And then he saw the crowd nearby. About 200 people standing on the sidewalk and in the street, blocking traffic. They were outside a church. The Church of Sainte Elizabeth. What was going on? Had he missed the news? He realized he had not read the *Herald Tribune* that morning. It was a noisy crowd — maybe an "On Leonardo's Trail" tour sponsored by, oh, say, Occult Travel, Ltd.

He crossed the street and roamed the perimeter of the crowd until he heard English. "I don't believe it. Our good luck to be in Paris when the story broke!" "Damn right. Who'd have thought the damn Templars had any balls left?"

"What's happening?" he asked.

A beefy tourist eyed him suspiciously. "You haven't seen the papers?"

"Not a thing. What about the Templars and their balls?" The beefy one shoved a *Herald Tribune* into Tom's face, the story below the fold and down in the left-hand corner: "Templar link to theft of the Shroud?" The story quoted one rumor that the linen had been brought to Paris. The Church of Sainte Elizabeth.

"So they took it back?" His question was greeted with hoots.

"Hell yes, they did. It's always been a French relic. The Shroud didn't land in Rome. It landed in France. And you can bet your last worthless dollar that the Shroud's going to stay in France!"

At the church's entrance stood four gendarmes and a harried, terrified man in a black suit and tie. Charles? He was perspiring, caught in the fury of the mob. A small man, with protruding yellowish teeth, he snarled, hissing like a cornered cat whenever packs of aggressive and pushy Germans or Americans got too close to him. "Who's he?" Tom asked a woman, who shrugged and gave him a blank look.

An older man nearby, a note of weariness in his voice, shouted at Tom, "He's the sacristan and he's telling us to fuck off, go home; the church is closed. And the Shroud is not there."

Tom pushed his way toward the besieged sacristan. "Monsieur Charles! *Salut* from Madame De Rosier!"

A long look by Charles, a flicker of his tongue and then a quick snap of the hand to come closer. Not quick enough; five men and women — a group of Brits — piled on top of Tom, this new interloper in the London Fog, and the gendarmes had to pick them off one by one. Somebody was grabbing Charles in the confusion, pushing his glasses off, tearing at his hair, trying to push past into the church. Just as Tom reached him, one of the five Brits, a stout lady, raised a hardcover book over her head and brought it crashing down on Tom's skull. Charles grabbed him by the arm and led him past the cordon of police. The sacristan opened the door while the gendarmes heaved the Brits back. He pulled Tom inside and quickly slammed it shut.

Too quickly — the London Fog caught in the door. Charles swore in French and opened the door slightly — wham! — it battered him, spilling him on the floor of the church. On top of him fell the gendarmes followed by the five book-wielding Brits. Like marionettes the police nimbly bounced up and tossed the Brits out one by one. The stout lady landed a few useless blows on their headgear while they pushed the door almost shut; now the crowd was crushing against the unlucky Brits, and the lady started screaming and beating whoever was close by. Tom helped Charles up and the two of them lined up alongside the gendarmes, pushing until the gap between the door and the frame was about the thickness of the hardcover book which its owner had inserted in the crack. Tom lifted his foot and kicked the book. It popped free and the door closed and Charles sprang like a cat and double bolted it.

The sacristan showed the gendarmes another way out of the church so they could return to the frontline, wiped off his forehead and tried to catch his breath. This was a man who hadn't lifted anything heavier than a vestment in 30 years, Tom thought. Well, maybe a massive candle base or two. And his job was not crowd control. Where was the pastor?

Charles eyed Tom with chilling disdain. "Madame De Rosier? Monsieur De Rosier? *Leurs prénoms?"*

"Genevieve, Paul." He passed the test.

"Ecrivez votre nom, s'il vous plait." Charles opened a guest book and shoved a pen rudely at Tom. Tom complied. *"Bon. Je suis Charles. Que cherchez vous?"*

Keep it simple. *"Je m'appelle* Tom Ueland. *Ah, je suis un ami de* Archbishop Michel Tucci." Charles seemed to know the name but did not appear impressed as Tom fumbled for cognates. Was there a secret sign or password he should know? This Charles looked familiar: who? — Peter Lorre, yes — diminutive, fear in his eyes, cowering under Sydney Greenstreet's threatening gaze in *The Maltese Falcon.*

"Vous pouvez parler Anglais, s'il vous plait — merde!"

"Imperious asshole" didn't describe this guy — he was a lackey, a foul-smelling functionary. Suddenly, Charles grabbed Tom's arm and led him through the nave into the sacristy. And here he was, in the tiny room used for meetings by would-be Templars in past centuries. He had been prepared to sneak into it past the sacristan and now he was being conducted there by the nearly demented man. A wall on one side was filled with milky-glass-covered cases displaying faded vestments, chasubles and stoles from long ago. The room didn't look like a headquarters for a fugitive order.

"Rien." Charles flung open a drawer and then another, cabinet after cabinet until the place appeared ransacked. *"Rien, rien, rien, rien. Merde! Bonne chance!* OK?"

"Je comprends, Charles. *Il est...en* France?"

Charles' face boiled in tics, and he consented to speak in English. "How do I know? I am only a sacristan. I light candles; I extinguish candles. I am not Inspector Clouseau!" Tom backed up against the vestment case as Charles waved his arms wildly. "Of course it's not in this church. It could be anywhere. Anywhere. No! Tell your Tucci to look in Rome or Venice — those two dens of thieves have stolen half the world's great art treasures and precious relics! And the other half is in London. Rome, Venice, London!"

Tom was stumped. He was being berated at an incomprehensible rate, a peculiarly French indoor pleasure, to his mind. Charles was wiping his forehead with an already soaked handkerchief. He was too outraged by half; he was hiding something.

Charles sucked in his breath as if preparing to breathe fire on Tom. But he had no fire left. He exhaled, rolled his eyes and leaned against a cabinet. He hissed through his teeth in furious, accented English. "Madame De Rosier made a serious mistake to send you here."

Outside, the noisy crowd had been dispersed and it was quiet. Charles breathed more easily and said the next words as in a trance. *"L'Islam. Tout le monde. Terrorisme."* Charles studied Tom's face as if imploring a hint of understanding.

Tom nodded. "Ah." That was the dumbest thing he could have said. His audience with Monsieur Charles was over.

Charles grabbed Tom by the arm, propelled him toward the same door he had shown to the gendarmes and hissed, *"Bonsoir et bonne journée!"* Then Tom was outside, around the back of the church in a gated area off Rue de Turbigo. A buzzer sounded and the gate opened for him. He walked around the side of the church through a narrow alley.

Very slowly, he walked down Rue du Temple past the front of the church, fearing that the book-wielding Brits were hiding in the shadows ready to pounce on him.

What he did see was a tall figure — a man, standing near the church entrance. He was standing with his back to Tom, as if waiting for someone else. Tom would have to walk past him on his way back to the hotel. They were the only two people on the street. The dusk felt darker and colder. As he approached the figure, the man turned and blocked his way.

"OK, what's up with you, buddy?" Tom did not do bravado well. He blended well, he observed well, but he was not a naturally in your face kind of guy. So this was an effort.

"Pardon?" The shadowy figure actually took a step toward him. He was not a young man but still stood ramrod straight. His face had solid bone structure, and his wrinkled skin was stretched tight as a drum. His stolid expression pushed a panic button deep in Tom.

"I don't speak French well under pressure, so either you get this or you don't. What do you want?"

The figure just stood there looking at him. Maybe this is a source, a lead sent by Genevieve. *"Quel est votre nom?"*

The eyes of the man blinked; an owl's blink, unfeeling. Only the lips moved. *"Je m'appelle* Paul De Rosier."

CHAPTER 22

Bruno Baumgartner fancied himself the consummate private eye. His was the unblinking eye of the professional spook — no, of the Hubble telescope, peering into the deep space of human behavior.

This week, he was eyeing these food addicts who were slugging down organic cheese curds and locally brewed beer at the *Salone del Gusto*. He had been told to hand over to the client complete profiles of "problem people." Those so identified were getting in the way of his client making money. And money was being made in seed. Not seeds. Seed. He was told his client did not like the plural form.

He was told that by the Voice, his mysterious paymaster. The Voice had corrected Bruno more than once. "'Seed.' There is one seed. And it's our client's. 'Seeds' sounds like crossbows, a thing of the past. Now there is only the Seed. The one our client creates. Anybody who disputes that, find them, find out about them. I'll do the rest," said the Voice. Bruno never asked about the meaning of "the rest." He assumed it meant anything between "You need a rest" to "Rest in peace."

Bruno signed up for back-to-back sessions at the *Salone*. He was cruising from one crowd to another. The taste workshops had boring titles but so what — better than sitting around at a roofing convention stalking Mafiosi. "Meet the Maker: Merlot according to Cotarella." "Old Brown Ales from Flanders Weave Their Spell." "European Blue Cheeses." "Espresso Origins Compared."

What he really tried to crack — and was having difficulty doing — was the *Terra Madre* circle of growers. Bruno had a healthy respect for the business of food production. He had grown up and still had a home in Cortina d'Ampezzo in the Friuli Venezia Giulia region, son of a German father and an Italian mother who together ran a restaurant. He had put his provincial past behind when he entered the University of Bologna and graduated with honors in language and literature. He married, fathered children and took a job as a public affairs consultant doubling as a journalist.

The arson at the first McDonald's Restaurant in Rome in the 1990s was his initial encounter with these food freak types, but that episode quickly paled before the massive riots in Genoa at the 2001 G8 meeting. It was in Genoa where he honed his skills at learning the mindset and infiltrating the ranks of the protesters.

So here he was, fielding a press pass, based on actual credentials from a German newspaper. It was a publication allegedly serving Germany's Catholic religious right; "alleged" because it was little more than a Web site. A virtual newspaper was good enough, however, to gain him admission to the *Terra Madre* gatherings, where he had inveigled an interview with Yusuf Aktug. He was relieved to see Aktug stride through the hotel lobby into the bar. He rose from his chair, staring at Yusuf's swollen nose.

"Bruno Baumgartner, *Der Welt-Wanderer* out of Germany. My god, are you all right?"

"Never heard of you. Der Welt-who?"

Bruno figured Yusuf had an especially hostile relationship with reporters, especially European ones, who always had some racist axe to grind. "*Welt-Wanderer*. World Traveler, if you will. Traditional Catholic newspaper in Munich. Agrarian values, family farms. We're interested in what's coming out of this meeting."

"Who gave you my name?"

Bruno was ready. "My editor told me to find somebody from Turkey, because the issue of bringing you fellows into the European Union issue is hot right now. We want to know about the Turks because Europe is fading fast under USA pressures to admit genetically modified corn, soybeans. Frankenfoods, I think you folks call them. Will your people fight?"

Yusuf looked Bruno up and down and thrust an open palm at Bruno and felt along his shirt and jacket for bulges.

"Clean enough?" Bruno smiled. "Look, I got your name from somebody in the press office. You are a known quantity, sir. Are you and your movement going to stand up to the multinationals?"

"Tell your readers we are no, never going to surrender. Tell them about the big men who are ordering farmers to stop saving their seeds. The companies who are getting, how do you say, intellectual property law, that kind of thing, approved by their friends the politicians in countries around the world. They are making seed saving a crime. You hear me, Mr. Baumgartner? They are forcing farmers to pay penalties — just for saving their own seeds. And if they can't pay or refuse to pay the penalties, then jail. Jail!"

Bruno wrote furiously. "Slow down, please."

"Turkey and Europe are on different worlds when it comes to diversity. I tell you, many of the food species found in my country

69

are not found any place else in the world. We don't want GMOs coming in. We don't want the monoculture."

"Monoculture?" Bruno knew what it meant, but the rule was, Ask the subject what he thinks you might not know.

"Farmers growing one crop with modified seeds, destroying our indigenous seeds with this shit. Everything is cash crops. So farmers grow one cash crop. Diversity is gone, gone, gone. And then an insect discovers how to, how to crawl inside that modified crop and the farmer is ruined. We don't want our seeds filled with things put in them by people we don't know or trust."

Bruno asked, "So what are you going to do to stop GMOs from coming in?"

"We're going to resist. We are going to persuade the people of Turkey to defend the country against the loss of biological diversity. I think they get to it."

Bruno wanted to correct his English but held back. "OK. Good luck, Mr. Aktug. And take care of that nose."

Yusuf stood up. "Good day, Herr Baumgartner. Spread the word. We shall be overcome."

Bruno scratched some more notes while watching Yusuf get into a cab. Then he hailed another one and instructed the driver to follow the other cab at a respectful distance. This was a good hunting day. He did not look up from his notes until his cab stopped ten minutes later. Yusuf was paying his cabby and walking into a crowded bistro. Trattoria di Gianna. Bruno wrote the name down and waved the cabby on.

CHAPTER 23

Tom was panting alongside a purposefully striding and infuriatingly silent Paul De Rosier. This was a man in his late 70s who could keep up a four-mile-an-hour pace without breaking a sweat. The walk back Rue du Temple was slowed by couples sauntering arm in arm, mothers pushing strollers or old women scavenging with shopping bags on the narrow sidewalks, but every so often the field opened up. Did the old fart plan to walk all the way back in the darkness to his apartment at this clip?

"Are you a spook? CIA?" asked the old man.

"No."

"You are staying in the Marais?"

"I thought that made sense. If anything on this trip does."

De Rosier did not smile. "You made sense to Madame De Rosier. She is expecting us for dinner. I will tell you now, Monsieur Ueland, if you have not guessed. I have not reached a healthy eighth decade by opening my door to every Tom, Dick or Henri" — he stroked the French sounding of "Henry" — "who comes knocking, even if he uses the name of Michael Tucci as an entrée."

"Sir, I must tell you, that dementia line is one hell of a subterfuge."

"Works like a Swiss watch. I have thrown many people off their investigation."

Tom couldn't help sounding breathy. "I suppose it's easy to accumulate enemies in seventy years, but, sir — aren't many of them dead or really demented, unlike you?" Humor the old bird. "Or are you a tiny bit paranoid?"

"Not at all paranoid. Did you argue with the sacristan? He can be most disagreeable. There is a paranoid person for you."

"We did argue. He threw me out." Tom's response drew a grunt from his partner. "So, Monsieur De Rosier, are you now or have you ever been a member of the Templars?"

Paul grimaced. "Spoken like a prosecutor. I am a secretive man and I learned my lessons from the best. I was approached to join the knights over thirty years ago, but I declined. I knew plenty of knights in my day; in the field of law they were here and there, still stamping about, protecting their secrets. I think Michael thought of me because he knew I knew…how they think, what they would do next and because — well. Enough for now."

They were now over the Seine on the Pont Saint-Michel, retracing the route he and Genevieve had taken. Tom looked back and saw the Number 21 bus approaching a block or two away; De Rosier showed no sign of slowing down, despite the street's steady rise toward the Jardin de Luxembourg. De Rosier turned to him, saw Tom's sweaty face and also the bus coming down on them. *"Facilis descensus Averno."*

"Sorry?"

"'Getting there is easy. The return is difficult.' Vergil's *Aeneid,* Book Six, line one hundred twenty-six. Come, we'll take the bus." As Tom sat down next to him in the bus, he decided he did not like the old man. You, Monsieur De Rosier, are a pompous prick who's in excellent shape and delights in making younger men know it. They did not speak the rest of the way.

When Genevieve opened the apartment door on level three, she appeared to sense the old male competitive friction. *"Voila,* Paul has led you on the marathon." She took Tom's raincoat and hung it in a nearby closet. "He carries his dementia well, don't you think?"

Tom nodded an emphatic "yes" to Genevieve. "I should be so lucky to be that demented. Maybe your husband is preparing for the Olympics in Turin. Snowboarding, possibly?"

Paul led them into the sunroom carrying a tray of small glasses and a bottle. "The downhill was always my favorite. Here, Armagnac. From the southwest of France. *La France profonde.* Our Heartland." Paul poured three glasses and offered them to his wife and Tom. Her husband lit Genevieve's cigarette and then sat next to her on the love seat facing Tom.

"A votre sante, Monsieur Ueland." Paul raised his glass, Genevieve joined him and Tom held his nervously.

"And to yours, both of you." He sipped. The Armagnac had a most agreeably earthy, rich taste.

"To the matter of my secrecy — may I call you Tom?" Paul twisted his glass. His intensity matched his wife's but he was more aggressive. The lawyer. "Archbishop Tucci and my wife and I were good friends for many years. We became acquainted with one another after the war. Nineteen fifty-four to be exact. So it is fifty years that we have known each other. Is it possible, Genevieve?" Above the three of them, a small framed photograph of a young

Michael Tucci in Roman collar looked down on them. The paper was yellowing.

"Exactement. We met in Belgium," she said. "He was a very young parish priest in a small Italian village, and Paul and I had been married a year and living in a Paris suburb, Saint Cloud." She sighed. "Belgium was wonderful. Wonderful."

Paul continued. "The summer of nineteen fifty-four, we had gone to Antwerp to study the Young Christian Worker movement under Canon Cardijn. You are familiar with that movement? *Jeunesse Ouvrière Chrétienne."* Tom shook his head no. "Ah. Well, it became the center of our lives for a long, long time. Joseph Cardijn was a Belgian priest who was dismayed at the advances being made among the working classes by the Communists. You do know that the Communists were a powerful political party across the continent."

Paul's jaw tightened. "Unlike prosperous postwar America, Europe's economy was in a shambles and the Communists promised the cure — distribution of wealth to the working classes. Canon Cardijn was convinced that the future was bleak for the church in Europe. Young Catholic men and women in the working class were deserting the church and joining the party in droves."

Genevieve took a last draw from her cigarette and exhaled as she spoke. "So Paul and I went to Antwerp to be trained in the movement. Paul was a new advocate at the bar and I worked at a natural history museum. So there we were, very upper-class, starting a cell, leaving our pleasant suburban country house, side by side on picket lines with men and women who were coming right from a grimy factory or field work."

Paul sat tensed at the edge of his cushion, his glass held tight between his legs. "Another movement, the worker priest movement, was a spark from the same flame of activism. Priests all over Europe were taking off their Roman collars and buying work clothes and taking jobs in factories. Side by side with the workers, they began to draw young men and women to their apartments and residences. These were Christian cells, taking the good things of Communism and making them Christian."

Tom nodded. "And that is how you met Pastor Tucci. He was a worker priest."

"Oui." Paul reached for the Armagnac and refilled their glasses. "He had tired of the conventional life of a parish priest after only one

year at it. He came to Belgium the same summer as we did. Maybe ten years younger than we were."

"Only three," Genevieve corrected him.

"Plus ou moins. He spent a month of his summer vacation in Antwerp, living in a seminary where we spent twenty hours a day for four weeks being trained in the Cardijn method and learning the issues we needed to know. It was very exciting for us all."

"It sounds like the sixties in the USA. The anti-war movement, civil rights. Taking the battle to the streets, creating coalitions between academics and workers. What did you smoke in those days?"

"Gauloises. *Toujour* Gauloises." Genevieve modulated her voice in a deep growl. Effortlessly, she was sexy. Tom laughed with her. When was the leap from youthful urban missionaries to conservatives, Tom wondered. When and why did the break with Tucci really take place?

Genevieve picked up the narrative. "We did not want to let Michael go back to Italy. We were very close." She hesitated for the right word and then sighed. "Paul and I started a family. Paul did legal work for a cell and I taught them English. For perhaps ten years. And then? All three of us drifted from the Young Christian Workers. We were no longer so young. Paul's law practice was becoming successful; I had obtained a degree in Anthropology. We...changed."

Paul pointed a prophet's finger at a photograph of Notre Dame. "The church changed. It was no longer Communism that threatened the church. It was materialism, the Marshall plan. And theology was changing around us. No Aquinas, thank you, the excitement was with the new theologians, with Hans Kung and Michel de Certeau. The new 'openness to the world' thinking — the death of orthodoxy."

Paul's face was reddening, his voice choking on an old grievance. "So when my former friend the archbishop of Turin mentions our names, I am naturally perplexed. Especially when his voice mail message has to do with the Shroud of Turin and its disappearance — and now a death in Chambéry in some mysterious conjunction with its loss. Does Michael think I have something to do with these things?" Paul was still pacing. He looked directly at Tom. "Well, does he? Has he gone completely crazy? *Est-il devenu complètement fou?* If you think I am private, my young man, Michael Tucci is the master of privacy. I could tell you a good deal about the archbishop of Turin!"

Genevieve stood and excused herself. Tom was suddenly aware that there was the most wonderful scent coming from the kitchen and that he was very hungry. She spoke firmly, "We have said enough about the archbishop."

"It wouldn't surprise me if Michael Tucci had the Shroud stolen so he could cook up some liberal harebrained idea, like a homeless shelter in the cathedral of Turin. He's cut loose from his theological moorings. That is dangerous in a bishop. He's a shepherd who was bitten by the *aggiornamento,* the new and improved thinking of Vatican II. He never got over it."

"Paul!" The voice from the kitchen was a command.

"Pardonnez-moi. I am prone to ranting,"

Tom watched him go to the window, pull the drapes shut and disappear into the kitchen. Alone, he walked to the window and peeked through the thick tapestry-like fabric. Was the apartment being watched? No place to lurk in a parked car in this tiny street. How did Templars get around these days? If not horses, then — Harleys? Humvees?

He was seeing the world through old people's eyes, fanciful, bitter, their boat still floating but moored in another time. The ramble with Genevieve across seven centuries, the mad scene at Sainte Elizabeth's, the eerie graveyard feel that had enveloped him at the Square du Temple — everything felt unmoored. He was surrounded by the end-of-life senility of Paul and Genevieve De Rosier. He would be on the first train back to Turin and Rachel, first thing in the morning.

He could picture Paul challenging Michael to a duel. Tom looked up at Tucci's photograph; handsome devil. Could Genevieve and he have had something going? Was Paul more jealous of the priest's putative sexual prowess than angry at his church politics — now, at this age? Get over it already, you old fart. He walked toward the kitchen. She was ladling soup into bowls; Paul was slicing a baguette. "I have another opinion about Pastor Tucci," Tom murmured.

"Which is?" Paul flicked a crumb off the knife.

"He's worldly all right, but he reminds me of a pastor back in the states who resigned over your church's position against birth control. I met him when he spoke at my college about the nature of dissent. He called himself a reluctant dissenter. His face was both serene and sad at the same time. He had done the right thing and he was paying for it. I'll never forget his eyes — unbelieving, accepting. Unbelieving, yet accepting that he was an outcast from the bosom of his church. Tucci has that look — serene and very sad. *Très triste.*"

Some soup spilled from the ladle onto the floor. The bread knife sawed through the baguette and scraped on the counter.

A telephone rang. Genevieve wiped her hands on her apron and walked quickly to the phone. She spoke in rapid, agitated French to the caller. She hung up and turned to her husband and Tom. "That was Charles, the sacristan. He is hysterical. He has seen the Shroud."

CHAPTER 24

An agitated Paul De Rosier left the kitchen and returned minutes later to the dining room where Genevieve and Tom were sitting. "I've called our friend Inspector Toussaint to be here when Charles comes," he announced. Genevieve sat at the writing desk, rummaging through old yellowing papers. She looked up suddenly and stared at Tom.

"How would you describe my friend Charles?" she asked.

"Unfriendly, menacing, nervous. There was this huge crowd of Shroud seekers. He was anxious to get rid of me. Looking back, I thought at the time — this man is claiming to know nothing a little too strenuously — even with those wild people banging down the church door."

"Mon dieu, poor Charles. As faithful and good a man as one can find." Genevieve's voice was full of sympathy. How could she have such affection for this jerk? "He always makes sure there is a fresh votive candle." Tom remembered; he had not lit the candle he promised he would. For those who would make a bad choice that day.

He bit his lip. "He was furious with me for pushing my way into the church. I asked him if he was hiding the Shroud. I think he would have hit me with a candlestick if one had been handy."

The telephone rang. Paul lurched to his feet and pressed a number on the handset. Moments later, the sacristan appeared in the apartment doorway. As incoherent as he was in the church encounter with Tom, now he was ashen, drained of all color. He gripped Genevieve's hands tightly. "I am not to tell anyone — but I must tell you!" Then he saw Tom and froze.

"Please sit down, Charles. This man can be trusted," Paul said.

A rotund man followed the sacristan. He was perhaps 60, with a sharp-eyed countenance, a thick mustache and an immaculate suit and tie. Paul introduced him to Tom. "This is Bernard Toussaint, an old friend and an inspector in our arrondissement. Please, everyone, sit down." Toussaint nodded to Tom, appraising him with an investigative eye. Tom eyed him back; he looked like the man on the Gare de Lyon platform.

"My friend, Charles, tell us what happened," Genevieve said.

Charles wiped his forehead. He was shaking and spoke in French.

"I saw the cloth as I was laying out the vestments. It was draped across the sacristy wall, at least ten feet long, maybe longer. The sacristy was dark — I couldn't tell at first. I turned on the light. Two men held it tight. Then this bearded man came toward me. Someone tied a rope around me. I could not breathe. He looked at me with the gaze of an avenging angel. I can barely remember his words: 'Monsieur, you will say nothing of this to anyone. We have vowed to find the Holy Shroud. This cloth is only — only a replica. If you tell anyone, you will break the prayer chain — against all the saints of God; you work for Lucifer. And you will suffer eternal damnation in the deepest regions of hell. Do you swear to remain silent?'"

"And then, what?" Genevieve asked.

"'*Oui,*' I whispered, '*Oui!*' I fell down, afraid, half conscious, but heard him speak to the others in the Provençal of my childhood. He did not call the cloth a replica. He called it 'the Savior's Shroud.' And then they left me there. I may die a painful death, but I had to tell someone. To tell…you."

Genevieve gently explained Charles' story to Tom. Toussaint was watching him under a pair of bushy eyebrows that danced up and down to the rhythm of her words. Paul was rummaging through a bookshelf that ran the length of the room. He brought back a small hardback book with a cracked leather cover. He opened to a bookmarked page and recited a poem, in Provençal.

> *The pink flamingoes flock from the Rhône shore,*
> *The tamarisks in blossom all adore.*
> *"The dear saints beckon me to them," she said.*
> *"They tell me I need never be afraid;*
> *They know the constellations of the skies;*
> *Their bark will take us quick to Paradise!"*

He paused and looked at the quivering sacristan. "Did the dialect sound like that, Charles?"

"*Oui. Exactement.* The Camargue."

Genevieve walked over to Paul and took his arm. Stone-faced, side by side, they looked like guards at the entrance to a secret cave, alerted by the frightened Charles to intruders. Then she spoke to Tom.

"We must leave early in the morning. Inspector Toussaint is

convinced these men are linked to the Shroud. And we also are convinced."

Everything had changed, and nothing, to his mind. Her glassy demeanor startled him. "Where to? And how sure are you?"

"We go to the Camargue early in the morning. To confront the knights who took the Shroud."

"Can I come with you?" He was requesting entrance to the secret cave.

"Yes," Genevieve replied, before he could change his mind.

CHAPTER 25

At 10:55 p.m., alone in the De Rosier's tiny guest bedroom, Tom pressed the numbers for his contact at the *New York Times*, a special sections editor. She answered. Was she interested in his story?

"That would be…?"

"Sorry. The theft of the Shroud in Turin. I think I'm on to something."

A long pause. "OK. We'll look at it. Call me when you have it finished. Bye."

He punched in Rachel's phone number. "Rachel, pick up the phone. Rachel!" He hung up, dialed the hotel again. The night clerk said he did not awaken people in the middle of the night if it was not a serious matter. "I would not be calling if it was not serious!"

In muttered English, the clerk answered, "Oh yes, always. Always serious."

"Knock the damn door down, *subito!*" Tom vowed to hate all hotel clerks. Goddamned churlish lackeys, every one of them.

"Call back in ten minutes," the clerk spit out. Tom's return call was put through to a very disoriented sleeper.

"Rachel. It's Tom."

"Hi. Tom! Where are you? Oh yeah, Paris, right? What time is it?"

"I'm in Paris at the apartment of friends of the archbishop. I'm sorry, it's eleven o'clock. How are you?"

"I'm fine, I guess. Ask me in the morning. Are you OK? What's going on?"

"Have you been following the Shroud of Turin story?"

"What's to follow? They haven't found it? Have you? Have you found it?"

"Rachel. It's getting deeper. We are flying to the south of France early tomorrow morning. The police are involved. Tucci's two friends think they know who did it and where the Shroud is. Tomorrow, we may find the bad guys."

"My God, Tom. What kind of a wacky trip are you on? Are you smoking something? What the hell is happening?"

"I'll be back as soon as I can get there. I'll call you. I miss you, Rachel."

"I've got to tell you about these two kids..."
"Gotta go. I miss you." He hung up.

CHAPTER 26

Standing shoulder to shoulder shortly after dawn in the farmhouse chapel, the four brother monks were reunited in their monastery for the first time in a week. Maximim, who had been left behind at the farmhouse, had barely finished sewing a second replica of the Shroud — the first one went to Turin earlier in the week and was in the hands of the city's police.

Jean Baptiste looked at his three brother knights and thought of their intermingled lives. The farmhouse — the monastery. Home to the religious community for the last 30 years. The community had purchased a sheep farm that was crumbling. In the rectangular barn behind the house, the roof had collapsed. By their own labor, the brothers restored the house but left the barn roofless. They built an enclosed walkway from the farmhouse to the barn. The barn became the cemetery. The house, the walkway and the barn formed a continuous enclosure from the outside world.

The leader stood at the lectern and addressed his brothers. Against the wall, the Shroud of Turin hung supported by a long metal frame. The smell of incense lingered in the chill air. All four wore casual slacks and t-shirts; camouflage for the next step to Jerusalem.

"'At the trumpet of God, the voice of the archangel will call out the command, and the Lord himself will come down from heaven; those who have died in Christ will be the first to rise, and then those of us who are still alive will be taken up in the clouds, together with them, to meet the Lord in the air.'

"Maximim, Sidonius and Trophimus. I, your brother Jean Baptiste, proclaim these words of Paul to the Thessalonians to be meant for us; with these thoughts let us comfort one another. My brothers, we face the forces of evil in our quest to make straight the way of the Lord. These forces are the true evil empire, the domain of the Antichrist.

"All were put in our way by God, whether by chance or purpose, to test our resolve. And our resolve is great, as great as that of the forerunner himself, my patron, the Baptist. But our task is infinitely more difficult, and thus our resolve must be all the greater. The Baptist called upon people to repent. We know it is too late for repentance. The die is cast; the Lord will come to judge the living and the dead. And we are preparing the way of the Lord, making the rough ways smooth.

"We know there will be plague, famine, war, earthquakes — these are the signs portending the king's return. There will be pandemics like the Avian flu now spreading its wings, brought by birds to humanity. There will be murderers who, God forbid, may try to destroy this world before the Holy One returns, as they did on September eleventh, two thousand one — the day we firmly committed to begin this mission.

"Bonded together by our vows, we have accepted our mission: to bring this Holy Shroud back to Jerusalem, prepared to receive Him when He comes again. It is the *Vexillum Regis*, the standard of the king who conquers death. We will retrace the journey it made over the long centuries. Once in Jerusalem, we await His return.

"We trust He will be there. The heavens will open as they did over John the Baptist when he announced the presence of one whose shoes he was not worthy to tie. So be sober and watchful, my brothers.

"We will be on the waters of the sea shortly and begin the next chapter in our mission. Now we say goodbye to the monastery and to the Camargue. We have said our goodbyes to those who now lie buried here, awaiting the Lord." His mouth glistened; his eyes shone.

Outside, they gathered on the porch and stood arm in arm in a circle. An autumn dawn was breaking, red sky, frost-bearing air. A massive stone slab had served as their front door all these years. It had survived a fire at a bank in Arles years before, and the brothers had purchased it. To them, the slab was a reminder of the stone rolled over the entrance to the Lord's tomb, blown away in the thermonuclear blast of His resurrection. The great door rolled shut heavily behind them.

Jean Baptiste turned to the three. "Each step that we now take is infinitely more dangerous than the previous one. We once pledged ourselves to be nonviolent. But the world has become a violent place. We must be prepared to deal seriously with anyone who stands in our way of reaching Jerusalem. The Lord is with us. I, Jean Baptiste, and you my brothers, Maximim, Sidonius and Trophimus — the Knight-Precursors of Christ the King. We shall prevail. And the Lord will come again. Alleluia! Come Lord Jesus! Come!"

CHAPTER 27

Below the sleek Airbus corporate jetliner, Paris glowed at dawn, a misty urban mirage. The plane was a courtesy Paul's old law firm still extended to him. Bernard Toussaint was talking sotto voce to two lieutenants, big men in suits.

Genevieve looked fresh, eager; what a wonder she was to look at. Paul looked tense, alert. Tom leaned toward them.

"Our itinerary?" he asked. One of the lieutenants was passing around cups and filling them gingerly with coffee and milk. Inspector Toussaint sat gazing out the window.

Paul sipped his coffee. "Our destination is an airport near Arles and Nimes in the south of France. Flying time, less than an hour. There we drive by car into the Camargue."

Tom nodded, a forced gesture. He had not slept well in the De Rosiers' cramped spare bedroom and now he was stuffed between the Inspector and Paul. His world had become compressed. He felt as though he was being dropped into a hole in the earth, with less and less room to maneuver, defend himself, break free if he had to.

This ring of elders held too many secrets inside their already long and private lives. Now they had him involved — some kind of pawn or cover for their schemes. The archbishop himself had ordered the theft — he was no rebel, he was a Richelieu. These two French "old friends" were lieutenants in a grand design under the direction of the papacy. The church was to be seen as under siege from Muslim terrorists embarking on a step-by-step offensive to rid Europe of its Christian icons — the Islamization of Christendom. Tom was an innocent abroad who had stumbled into the plot. He was being flown as a hostage to a long detention in an underworld populated by the shades of Templars and their henchmen.

He shook his head. "Get a grip," he grunted.

"Are you all right?" Genevieve asked

"Yes, just jet lag. The Camargue. All right. Tell me about that." Tom had studied a little about this region. Cowboys. French cowboys. Horses.

Bernard Toussaint was nodding off. It was Paul who spoke first. "Let's start at the moment in time when we fell under the spell of the Camargue. Genevieve and I were instinctively distrustful of anything to do with the nineteen sixties. May nineteen sixty-eight, the worker and student protests. Revolution was utterly repellent to us. There was one revolution we did join, however. It was in the world of museums."

"Paul was the lawyer; I was the anthropologist," Genevieve went on. "I became a museum educator right about the time something called the *eco-musée* movement became popular. We who were trained in a museum discipline had to learn how to become more involved with real people in their lives and traditions. You see? It fit right in with our Young Christian Worker experience in the nineteen fifties."

By now, Monsieur Toussaint's snoring was almost sonorous, a base violin, while the big guys made like tubas. Tom was struggling himself. Only the two elders looked to have a normal pulse. Genevieve seemed to draw energy from her memories. "Museums can be such unreal and possessive places. What we wanted to do was to restore the museum to the real world where people live and work. And that is how we became involved with the Camargue." She stiffened against a small tremor.

Paul glanced at his watch. "That is the Rhône delta, west of Marseilles. It comprises over two hundred square miles of marshland lying between the two arms of the Rhône River emptying into the Mediterranean. This is plains country, home to the famous Camargue horses and the *Gardians,* the cowboys who tend them. Here black bulls are raised on bull farms for bullfights in Arles."

"...where the bull is *not* killed," added Genevieve.

"A widespread system of nineteenth century canals and drainage ditches greatly expanded agriculture in the Camargue. Like other fragile parts of the world, tourism and agriculture together threaten its primitive character. So in the nineteen seventies, the government designated it as a botanical and zoological nature reserve. The museum of the Camargue lies about halfway between Arles and the seaside town of Saintes Maries de la Mer. It is located in an old sheep barn that once belonged to a farm. Genevieve helped design some of the exhibits in the nineteen seventies."

Paul stopped and put his hand on Tom's arm. The lecturers had finally run out of steam and so had their audience. All three dozed off. After what seemed like only minutes, Tom heard Paul speak. "We are beginning our descent into the Nimes-Camargue airport. Wake up, my friend."

Tom rubbed his eyes and peered out the window at the ribbon of the Rhône below, snaking its way through the landscape. Camargue. What did all the arcane stories Tom had read over the years — snippets about Knights Templar and the Holy Grail, the small boat bearing Mary Magdalene and Joseph of Arimathea as they fled Jerusalem and landed in France, the Priory of Sion and Rennes Le Chateau — what did they have to do with this journey? He wished he knew half as much as the mob of camp followers of the Holy Grail and the Shroud of Turin whom he had met outside that Paris church. A world of myths and legends — even these two senescent recluses next to him were delusional. Dangerous. He was alone in an underworld of dotty strangers. How had he gotten snared in their gnarled old hands?

"As I was saying, a large part of the *musée* is dedicated to life on the farm in the nineteenth century and the repercussions of the industrial revolution," Paul continued as if there had been no interruption. "Farmers produced great quantities of salt and rice and they raised bulls on land drained by an enormous dike, a seawall and an elaborate drainage system."

The seat belt sign was on, the swooping motion of the jet had leveled out and Tom could see the flat terrain only a few hundred yards below. Genevieve was pointing her finger accusingly at an imaginary museum visitor. "We challenged visitors to think globally — yes? — as they looked at life on a Camargue farm. Wake up! Go home, we said: look at your wetlands that have been drained to increase the agricultural acreage; your park preserves, hastily built to protect the small bits of undeveloped land. Someday your homeland will look like this barren land if you don't stop it. Technology, progress — rationalism — is killing the land." The bump of wheels on the runway jostled Bernard Toussaint and the big guys into consciousness.

"Mon dieu, ce n'est pas possible!" shouted a disoriented-looking Toussaint.

"Mais si, Monsieur Toussaint." Genevieve smiled. *"Bonjour."* The big men stretched and yawned in tandem. Minutes later the crew had opened the door and the entourage hustled down the stairs to the tarmac. An unmarked Renault minivan awaited them.

Tom followed Paul and Genevieve into the rear row of the van; one big guy in the front passenger seat, the other in the middle seat with Toussaint. The driver was a small wiry man introduced as

Inspector Michel Poirier. He did not look as though he wanted to be on this escapade — a lacquered sneer layered over a grouchy attitude. Poirier had pressed a large package of sandwiches and fruit and a jug of coffee into the hands of the big guy in front. After the inspector had selected a sizeable sandwich, the aide took the second largest one and passed the package back. All ate silently, gratefully. When the coffee made it to the rear and he had taken several good sips, Tom sat forward. Poirier was moving at a fast clip down a highway bristling with "Camargue" road signs. A bridge carried them over a river — "La Petit Rhône," Genevieve said. She and her husband were getting excited. Back to earth.

Genevieve smiled dreamily. "The people drawn here are romantics, cowboys, those who see life in cosmic terms, living on land's end, below the sea, a sense of rugged individualism, yes, of magic." To Tom, the terrain itself seemed to waver, misty, moving, as they sped past.

Paul craned his neck to see down the highway. "We are going to observe a farmhouse near the *musée*. How do you say 'observe' in such a context?"

"'Stake out,' 'case.' We are going to stake out a farmhouse. Whose farmhouse, Paul?" Tom felt his own muscles growing taut. Monsieur Poirier slowed down, as if to catch a flamingo unaware. Everyone was staring out the windows.

"When we were assisting with the *musée* — I should say Genevieve was assisting and I was taking holidays — we noticed an old stone farmhouse not far away, oh a mile or two miles distant. We drove by each day from where we were staying in Saintes Maries de la Mer."

Genevieve pointed ahead. "It's not far now. The *musée* is coming up on the left; here, see the sign. There is a small hill between here and the farmhouse, just a few kilometers ahead. We'll pull off the highway there and drive up a road that leads to the top of the hill. From there we can observe — stake out — the farmhouse — home to a religious community of men."

"One day, we had a flat tire near the farmhouse," Paul said, his breathing more shallow. "One of the members of the commune came and offered to help us change the tire. We accepted. In the course of the conversation, the member told us more than he should have. I think he was disaffected, and I'm sure he did not survive the hard life. And this is what he told us." The Renault had now pushed off the highway and was grinding up a gravel road to the top of the hill, not more than 20 feet above the highway. "He said, 'We are a French Christian community of men awaiting the return of Christ, who shall judge the living and the dead. We are unlike other Christian communities awaiting the return of Jesus Christ.' I am sure I looked totally ignorant of his meaning. I asked him, 'How are you unlike?' There was something very ominous about his bearing. The poor boy went on, 'We aim to create the conditions which will make the return of the Judge of the world possible. He who has redeemed us without our help will not save us without our help. We are turning back our time to His time.'"

The minivan rolled to a stop and Genevieve turned to face Tom. "I asked them, 'Do you have a name? And how do you create the conditions necessary for the Christ to return?' And this is what he said, 'Our name is *Equites Praecursores Regis Christi.*' The Knight-Precursors of Christ the King. And I repeated, 'How do you bring about the conditions?' And he paused and then answered, 'In due time we will turn back history to the time of the crucified Christ. Saint Louis is our hero, seeking the return of the holy lands to Christendom. He set off on the crusade from this region. So will we. The nations, the cities, all civilization will be destroyed. Crushed down to salt, like much of Camargue. All accretions, all dogma, all churches formed since his holy blood — that pristine source of power poured forth from his side — will be carried away. Christ the Ruler of all will return to earth, borne on a cloud, and reclaim His burial garment, His robe of glory. And then shall begin the tribulations of the earth — the earth will end and the righteous will be saved!'

"The poor boy was no more than twenty-five. A young zealot." Genevieve shuddered as she stepped out of the van.

Poirier had turned off the motor. The hilltop was just a small rise, some 15 feet in diameter. Desolate, thought Tom. A good place to die. A panorama of marshland dotted by sparse vegetation lay around them. A chilling breeze from the north whipped across their faces. Paul and Genevieve motioned for Tom to follow. They were still holding hands. The path led to the edge of the hilltop. One by one they lined up behind scrubby trees and a thick growth of bushes. Bernard Toussaint passed a set of binoculars to Paul. Tom saw him aiming down into the flatland, a spot just off the highway not more than the length of two football fields from where they had pulled off the road.

"The farmhouse," Paul spoke slowly in mixed French and English, "looks little different now than it did some ten years ago. Perhaps in worse condition. There is every sign it is still being lived in. No one is outside. Here." He was shaking. He passed the glasses to Genevieve. She looked, shuddered again and turned her eyes away. Their old encounter with the Knight-Precursors had left an imprint.

Tom took the binoculars from her and adjusted the lenses. What he saw was a hardscrabble rural Minnesota scene, lots of junk piled up outside the house, some old machinery, appliances, furniture. A stunning stone front door. He passed the binoculars to Toussaint. How could this Tobacco Road setting be the mainspring of the high-tech break-in and theft of Christianity's most revered material relic? This was a bunch of Christian hippies, roadies, a fringe community on the edge of a fringe community, that couldn't jimmy an unlocked door much less an electronically fortified chamber.

This whole junket smelled of mossy, hallucinatory fantasies derived from the couple's hardened dogmas. These two had lived a long life of privilege and religiosity after hanging up their Young Christian Worker overalls. Hell, if only a rifle shot would ring out from the farmhouse, to shatter the creeping sense of wasted effort, to give some credence to an old couple's wild goose chase into flamingo country. He gave the glasses back to Paul and looked at the notes he had been scribbling.

"You said you were here ten years ago. But the museum work was in the nineteen seventies. Why'd you come back?"

"The twentieth anniversary of the Musée de la Camargue." It was Genevieve who answered.

The sound of an engine starting somewhere crackled through the air. Paul quickly raised the glasses and spoke in French. Perhaps they had been seen by a farmhouse lookout. "I can't see well enough to know if the sound came from the farmhouse. Monsieur Toussaint, what next?"

Poirier was giving instructions to someone over a cell phone. He spoke tersely, then repeated instructions to Paul. The two officers took up positions where the gravel road met the hilltop. They peered down the approach to the hilltop and listened for the sound of a car racing up the gravel toward them. Moments passed; it became clear nothing was going to happen.

Poirier was a leonine contrast to the laconic Toussaint, punctuating his barked directions with "no, no, no," and repeating himself crisply in French. "What we heard was only a passing car. Only a passing car." The harsh static of the inspector's phone was the wind's only competition.

"I think," Paul spoke with a bitter edge, "perhaps, they have escaped to heaven."

Genevieve turned to Tom. "He is talking about Monsieur Mistral. Explain yourself." Her face was taut. She took a Gauloise from her purse and lit it. Tom knew she had had more than her three cigarettes that day.

Paul, chastened, said, "The book I read to Charles last evening. Mistral's heroine Miréio, while crossing the barren land of La Crau, suffers a sunstroke. As she lies dying, she has a vision in the chapel of the pilgrimage site. A boat from heaven bearing the local saints, Magdalene, Maximim, Sidonius, Trophimus, comes to carry her back to heaven. Poof. Gone. *Envolée.*"

Tom watched the two inspectors, heads bobbing together, arguing back and forth about the next step. "Where are the cops?" asked Tom. "Who has this guy been on the phone to?"

"Poirier is not calling them to come help us; I suspect he is requesting that we be arrested. To him this is only an old man and woman's demented scenario. Only his respect for Toussaint is keeping him in this 'charade.'" He spit the last word out. "That's what he calls it."

Tom wanted to say, "I am with Poirier. You are crazy." He didn't.

"Merde," Poirier snarled. Toussaint winced, his mustache shriveling. Tom suddenly realized this might be a fatal fiasco. They were staking out a farmhouse where a holed-up band of religious fanatics might be planning a Waco-style last stand. And he, the wannabe *New York Times* stringer, was embedded with an assault force of embittered old folks hell-bent on stoking the flames.

CHAPTER 28

All had gone well until the marina. The four knights had left the farmhouse and driven directly to the deep Etang de Vaccares lagoon. Jean Baptiste had encouraged them to take moderate pleasure being outfitted as just another jeepload of rowdy male tourists making the most of a gorgeous dawn in the preserve, digital cameras at the ready. What glorious sights! Rose flamingos smudged the grassland with their pink feathers. Here and there black bulls foraged. The lagoon teemed with gray herons, purple herons, great egrets, little egrets, cattle egrets, squacco herons, great bitterns. "Pleasure" was not a word in the brothers' vocabulary, except as part of the world they denounced. Their pleasure lay solely in anticipation of the second coming. But this Camargue, this Eden, yielded a foretaste of the heaven to follow.

The "tourists" waved to the *gardians,* the cowboys of Provence, whose wild horses owned the trails. As they rounded the Etang's east end, they headed south on D 36, the jeep jostling back and forth over the ruts and then down a series of empty back roads — empty but for the oncoming Peugeot on one of them. Leaning forward into the wind like astronauts in combat with G-forces, their jeep bouncing around on the rough gravel on a curve in the road, they sent the Peugeot driver into the ditch as the careening jeep skidded from one side of the road to the other. Jean Baptiste looked back only for a moment; no damage done. Fools to bring a Peugeot here. He exulted in his brethren in their long-sleeved shirts and full-length pants, their floppy wide-brimmed hats, their dark glasses, their resolutely erect torsos, the sun-blocking salve glistening on their taut faces against the dawn glare.

"Are they hurt?" Maximim had asked, looking back at the Peugeot, wheel-deep in swamp. "Should we not help them?" Jean Baptiste had shaken his head no. Soft-hearted Maximim would always be the one left behind to guard things. Sympathy is a dangerous trait in a comrade in battle.

Finally, Aigues-Mortes, the medieval seaport built by Saint Louis, lay before them. They skirted the town and drove to the marina. "The sea, the sea, the great Mediterranean Sea," cried Trophimus. The four men joined hands tightly, transmitting the molten energy that flowed like a deep river among them. Then, each leapt from the jeep, carrying their cargo, on a dead run. Among the backpacks and suitcases and boxes of equipment were two smooth, slender, molded plastic containers, carefully cradled in their arms. Jean Baptiste was ecstatic; in minutes they would board the *Colombe*, named for the dove hovering over John the Baptist as he acknowledged the Christ.

They approached the sleek *Colombe* as she lay tethered in the slip. They recognized one last fool who might obstruct their crusade. Lounging on the deck was the assistant manager of the marina. They would have to deal with him — quickly.

"Saint Louis, *priez pour nous!"* intoned Jean Baptiste. This encounter had not been in anybody's forecast of what could go wrong. The fool had admired their boat for a long time, ever since they had rented a slip the previous year. He had reminded them during their frequent rehearsal jaunts that the license plate on the boat was about to expire, and they had taken care of the matter. What was this bureaucrat doing on their boat now, at this early hour?

"Should we return to the farm, Jean Baptiste?" Maximim whispered. "He may report us before we leave port! We can return later; he will be gone, perhaps." The leader looked back at the jeep. He hesitated. The official shifted his weight and spoke.

"I'm glad you showed up, my friends. Would you mind letting me inspect below? New port regulations just put into effect this very week." The man slurred his words; he had been drinking. He would not scare easily, thought Jean Baptiste. Rolling with the lapping current, his body idled lazily on a deck that sparkled in the bright sun.

Jean Baptiste's cell phone rang. He listened to the caller. Totally out of character, he kept listening. For a full 10 minutes, he said nothing; the knights looked uneasily at one another. The manager remained smiling, insolent.

Jean Baptiste closed the phone. He had never seemed so unsure of what was to happen next, and his brothers sensed it. He motioned them to return to the jeep.

The bureaucrat stood unsteadily. "Forget something?"

"Yes. The keys," Jean Baptiste grunted.

"I've done that enough times. Well, I'll be here."

Dejection settled like a pall over the jeep. The reversal hollowed out Jean Baptiste's anticipation of traversing the passage down the long Canal de la Roubine to the sea, past the ramparts and the Constance Tower built by Saint Louis. Jean Baptiste had often lectured his brothers on the symbolism of their embarking from Aigues-Mortes, which had once been a vibrant port but had silted up, and the town had lost its seaside prominence to Marseilles. On earth, all things tended toward corruption. Pride, like drifting sand, choked all life underneath.

They returned by another road to avoid the Peugeot. Past the rose flamingos, the black bulls, the herons, egrets and bitterns — the jeep sped back toward the farmhouse, a molten dust-devil sending clouds of dirt heavenward. No one asked him about the cell phone message.

Jean Baptiste finally spoke above the wind. "The situation at our next station is unstable. The Shroud — it's needed, now. An agent of the benefactor will meet us at the farmhouse in fifteen minutes."

CHAPTER 29

Keeping the others back on the small rise, Poirier and his two lieutenants decided to use a bullhorn to talk to the farmhouse's enclosed brothers. There had been no response. The farmhouse lay silent.

"We will storm the monastery," Toussaint announced. Everyone tumbled into the van. Poirier eased the vehicle down to the road, turned toward the farmhouse and then parked it 50 yards away on the side of the road.

Poirier and his two lieutenants circled the entire enclosure and returned minutes later to the front door. Tom and the others were waiting behind a thicket of bushes near the Renault. Poirier's bullhorn startled some nearby egrets that whooshed into the sky. No other answer. He approached the great stone door slowly, knocked and waited. He called out again. Nothing. He pulled the brass handle. The door creaked. Poirier opened it just enough to set a tear gas canister on the floor and pull the plug. He darted back quickly to the surrounding bushes. They heard the hissing gas fill the house and then stop. After a half hour, the two inspectors and the big guys filed in. Shortly after, windows were thrown open. Poirier motioned to the others; it was a solemn procession that entered past the stone door.

"Smell them," Poirier ordered. "Still warm." "Them" was a bank of computers against a wall — incinerated. Their hard drives had melted down; the heat had sculpted the cases into twisted plastic hulls, a jarring sight in this monastic setting. The only picture on the wall was a large copy of Titian's *Entombment* showing the burial of Christ's body, wrapped in a long winding sheet.

The other rooms in the house held no surprises. There were a large kitchen, a dining room with a long wooden table with stools set around it and bowls of half-finished soup on it. Upstairs there were bedrooms with single cots lined up hospital-style, their mattresses thin as blankets, the sheets still in disarray. On a wall in the hallway, a copy of Andrea Mantegna's *Dead Christ*. Poirier ordered the two lieutenants to secure the barn — the brothers could have retreated there to make a stand.

When they were coming down the steps, they saw a door opening to a long narrow room on the back side of the house. It must have been an addition to the original structure. The chapel. A series of *prie-dieu* were lined up in rows before an altar. Behind it, on the wall, overpowering the entire chapel, an enormous copy of Michelangelo's *Last Judgment*.

The air was pungent with the odor of incense. A thurible rested on the altar platform; the ashes inside the cup were fresh. Paul and Genevieve both had brought white cotton gloves, which they fitted on their hands. On the lectern, a Bible was opened to Saint Paul's *First Letter to the Thessalonians,* Chapter 4. Genevieve came alongside him. "Open to the inside front cover," she whispered. Paul marked the page, closed the book and then opened the cover page. Adjusting her glasses, Genevieve read the inscription. "'To J.B. LaRocque, from the community of the EPCR.'" She was trembling. "'J.B.' Jean Baptiste, the precursor. And here is the passage, 'And the Lord said to Moses, "Stretch forth your hand over the sea that the waters may come again upon the Egyptians, upon their chariots and horsemen. And when Moses stretched forth his hand toward the sea, it returned at the first break of day to the former place; and as the Egyptians were fleeing away, the waters came upon them." *Exodus,* chapter fourteen, verse twenty-five.'"

She caressed the book softly and handed it to Bernard Toussaint, who was busy taking fingerprints on surfaces in the chapel. Toussaint paged through it carefully. Poirier was snarling about what a waste of time this was. Tom leaned on a *pre-dieu.* Who was this Jean Baptiste? Why were these two old coots being so goddamned secretive and protective? They were both demented.

"You mean as in John the Baptist, cousin of Jesus?" Tom asked.

Genevieve sighed. "Yes. That John the Baptist. The leader of the Knight-Precursors of Christ the King sees himself as his reincarnation." Near the altar was a silver pail, with a sprinkler in it. Tom picked up the sprinkler. "Go ahead, Tom. Sprinkle it. Holy water." Tom shook the sprinkler and tiny jets of water splatted against the wall. Genevieve watched the drops descend. "The Red Sea parted and the Israelites passed through. I think our precursors look forward to a second cosmic flood. They and the elect alone shall pass through, dry-shod. The rest of us — Oh, these holy fools, these madmen!"

Poirier's aides returned and spoke in quiet French with him. He motioned to the others to follow them. Toussaint remained in the chapel, occupied with paging through the Bible. Paul took

Genevieve's arm and nodded to Tom. They processed through the enclosed walkway and stood at the entry to the barn. The ground was dotted with small crosses. The community cemetery: 1978. 1981. 1996. 2003 — the dirt under that last cross still fresh, mounded. Tom walked alone until he found himself at the far end of the barn. He saw a vegetable garden behind the enclosure; the brothers had been subsistence farmers: potatoes, carrots, eggplant, squash. A purple patch of lavender bloomed nearby, the only soft and pleasant feature of this harsh homestead. He thought of Rachel.

He was standing with his back to the others, looking at a white van that had been left under a nearby canopy of trees. Near it was a silhouette of a human figure traced on a piece of thin plywood that was bound to a stack of straw. Target practice. Behind him, he heard rustling noises, then a gun being cocked. This was it. He had been lured out here because he was a threat to the conspirators — Michael Tucci, *éminence grisé;* Paul and Genevieve De Rosier, priest and priestess of some ancient cult. Tom Ueland had always doubted his courage under fire, but whose fire was it? The Knight-Precursors in the surrounding brush? The old couple and their fake inspector? He took a shallow breath, turned and waited for another Waco to erupt.

Poirier was lowering his pistol. *"Rien."* An enormous heron took off into the sky. Tom was sweating heavily. Toussaint came out and spoke in French with Paul and Genevieve. He handed them a folded sheet of paper, which they opened and studied. They turned to Tom.

"The inspector has found one last clue." His hands shaking, Paul handed Tom the yellowed paper. "He found it in the Bible." Etched on the paper was a crude map, a clumsy hand drawing; it illustrated the contour and focal points of a journey from Europe, through the Mediterranean Sea and the Sea of Marmara, to the Middle East. A pencil line, accompanied by arrows showing the direction, ran through a series of small circles; the circles had names next to them. Turin; Chambéry; Paris; the Rhône delta; Istanbul; Edessa; Jerusalem. Around Istanbul, the circle was jagged, not smooth. Above the last circle around Jerusalem, the Greek characters chi and rho, the first two letters of the name of Christ. The map was dated: September 12, 2001.

The Rhône delta today. Next — Istanbul.

"Believe us; the knights are sailing to Byzantium," Genevieve said. She took his hands in hers and squeezed them. "They drew this the day after Nine-Eleven. Their answer to terrorism: the return of

Christ. Believe us."

A hump-hump-hump whirring of helicopter rotors interrupted the quiet. The fleeing heron had heard it first. A jeep with four hunched figures in it braked sharply off the highway and crunched the gravel of the farmhouse driveway. Poirier, Toussaint and their lieutenants pushed the elderly couple and Tom down behind a burial mound of dirt. From the open-air cemetery, Tom could see everything happen in bewildering cinematic speed.

The four Knight-Precursors of Christ the King formed a line from the jeep a short distance to where the helicopter was descending. One of the men held what looked like an AK-47. When the chopper landed, the men handed baggage into the cockpit — last were two molded plastic cases. In fewer than 30 seconds, all four scrambled inside.

As the helicopter rose, Tom saw a bearded man leaning out of the cockpit, his binoculars trained on the intruders hiding in the cemetery. Even at a distance an unearthly aura of ferocity emanated from the figure. Was that the AK-47 alongside him? Was somebody aiming it at them? They were all exposed. The bearded man held up his arm in front of the weapon. Tom started crawling toward Paul and Genevieve. The blast of the rotors sent dirt and gravel flying all the way to the cemetery, blinding everyone. Tom saw Paul stand and begin to shout, but his voice failed and he slumped back to the ground. Had he suffered a heart attack? The old man lay silent until Tom leaned close to take his pulse.

"The benefactor. God damn him," Paul whispered.

CHAPTER 30

Toussaint suggested the group spend the night in Saintes Maries de la Mer; his men would stay at the farmhouse. They checked into a small hotel near the historic old church of Notre Dame de la Mer. The seaside town was preparing for the saint's day — Mary Salome; men cleaned streets and women decorated sidewalks for the procession to the beach for the blessing of the sea.

Genevieve's mood was in stark contrast to the holiday spirit outside. She could be an irritable old woman — the flip side of her elegance. Tom had diagnosed the change as her old age rubbing against his arrogant youth. At supper, she ignored him and spoke in French to Paul. The couple had suffered some kind of psychological collapse and were withdrawing. He leaned forward, elbows on the table, and interrupted the couple's *tête-a-tête*.

"So the theory is that this Jean Baptiste and his band of brothers are turning time on its head by retracing the steps of the Shroud, from the tomb in Jerusalem right to where it lay three days ago in Turin. Christ is waiting offstage, ready to start his descent to earth when his burial cloth is returned to his tomb. He flies back into the tomb and begins the last judgment. It's like an old movie reel run backwards. And then it's over — really over. And you've known about them for years." He paused. Nail the old coots, his inner brat whispered.

"Tell me, why did you keep these people to yourself? Why didn't you tell Bernard Toussaint about such a fringe group before — when you were hiding in your private museum world? Didn't your experience after World War II…" He hesitated.

Genevieve glanced at Toussaint and Poirier, who were at a different table, deep in muffled conversation. Her words pounced on Tom. "How dare you lecture us? Paul and I are not comfortable with any fringe group. But these people were not lawless; they hurt no one — until now. They were innocents. Not much different from you. And no less certain they are in the right." She was shaking again. Too much stress this day for anyone. But it was their idea to come here, right?

Genevieve shook a wrinkled, waxen finger at Tom's face. "You are the kind of academic rationalist who would have reported the early monastic communities to the authorities. Wild men, living in the wilderness, keeping watch for the return of Christ. You would have turned them in! But they had something to say to their times, 'The Lord will come again. Be sober and watchful!'" Genevieve was resolute; she glared at Tom. "Don't accuse us of irrelevance! *S'il vous plait!*" Her face was creased, her cheeks flaming, her breathing raspy.

"*Je suis très désolé*...shouldn't have said that..." He leaned back in his chair. The rest of the meal passed in silence. Genevieve and Paul excused themselves.

Tom left the hotel, walked to the beach and dodged the waves rolling in over the sand. Tony's cell phone was blinking low battery; he had never turned it off. He pressed Rachel's number.

"*Pronto,* I mean, hello? Tom?"

"Hello. Rachel, yeah, it's me."

"Where the hell are you?"

"A seaside resort on the Mediterranean. And I've got a low battery. I just made my two old guides crazy mad. But I want to say, I'm OK, I'm tired and I miss you."

"Will you tell me what this is all about?"

"It is all about magical thinking. I'm surrounded by it."

"That's what you wanted. And you missed my workshop."

"I know. 'Liquid Gold: the Treasures of Turkey's Olive Groves.' How did it go?"

"If you have to know, it was dazzling."

"What?"

"Dazzling! Oh, your damn phone is fading! What are you doing at a resort?"

"We've met the suspects. My French connection believes they are heading for your hometown, Istanbul. And something about a benefactor. One minute I believe them, the next I want to check their luggage for hallucinogens."

"Get your ass out of there."

"As soon as I can. Tomorrow."

"Shall I call Michael?"

"Leave him out of it for now."

"Tom, I'm scared. My friend Yusuf Aktug and I were walking back to the hotel when these two students started harassing us. I'm spooked."

"Did you report it?"

"Of course; no suspects yet. Tony's working on it."

"Rachel, I didn't bargain for this. I really want to get back. But what if the *Salone* and the Shroud and the bishop and his two French friends are all one piece? God, the answers are so elusive."

"It is you who are elusive, friend. The dude that eludes me. You are the mystery, Tommy boy."

The phone went dead.

CHAPTER 31

He sat down to a quiet, tense breakfast with the De Rosiers the next morning. Tom apologized again. The two inspectors were still in muffled conversation at their table. Then they joined Tom and the couple. Toussaint shrugged and addressed his words to the two of them, and they translated. The helicopter had been tracked to a gated estate near Marseilles. It had landed at a private heliport and its occupants had been whisked away before police arrived. The estate's renters leased from a holding company and knew nothing.

On the ride back to the Nimes-Camargue Airport, Poirier harangued Toussaint about the futility of their escapade. Toussaint dozed throughout. Paul and Genevieve huddled together, leaving Tom to his thoughts. They said a hurried goodbye at the airport, Genevieve held his hands tightly and Paul promised to telephone the archbishop on their return to Paris. "Remember, Istanbul!" he said.

Tom boarded a plane to Marseilles and transferred there for a flight to Turin. Airborne, he looked over the Mediterranean below. Somewhere down there, either by sea or by air, the Shroud of Turin was going home to the land of its provenance. These were the same people who had bamboozled the Turin church, these manic believers who lived in brotherhood in their dingy farmhouse, the ones who sprinkled holy water around them, the ring of radicals who had commandeered a mysterious helicopter apparently sent by some enigmatic benefactor.

How was anyone going to find them in the megalopolis of Istanbul — if that was truly their next stop?

"Next steps," he scribbled in his notebook. "The parting of the Red Sea? The theory that a volcanic eruption under the Mediterranean Sea near the Greek island of Santorini in 16th century BCE sucked the Red Sea dry and then hurled a tidal wave across the dry land. Does the theft of the Shroud have anything to do with the threat of earthquakes or volcanoes? The crude drawing in the knights' Bible — Istanbul surrounded by a jagged ring, not a circle. 'Coming catastrophe.'"

He had succumbed to the magic. With Genevieve's touch still vibrant on his hands and Paul's prophecy ringing in his ears, he plotted the course he would follow on the trail of the knights to the edge of Europe, to the mysterious catastrophe that only the Shroud could avert.

***

On the jetliner heading toward Paris, Genevieve looked out the window at the great rocky central massif below. "LaRoque. The Rock. Peter. The disciple who lied to save himself — We should have told him the rest," she whispered to her husband.

"We made a promise." He spoke as if in a trance.

***

And below them all, a privately chartered aircraft lifted into the sky from the Marseilles-Provence Airport and headed east to the Aegean island of Santorini.

CHAPTER 32

Bruno checked his notes from the Yusuf Aktug interview and walked toward the *Salone del Gusto*. He avoided the registration line and the Lingotto convention center and picked his way among the arriving crowds that flowed into the piazza. Entering the adjacent shopping mall building he rode up the escalator and walked to the left, past knots of teenagers hanging out, took a right down a corridor and stopped before a door that was locked. He took a key from his pocket and opened it. Another hallway, with an elevator. He called for it; once inside, he pushed the button for the top. When the door opened, he stood amazed at the sight.

The test track for Fiat spread out before him, a one-kilometer rectangular autodrome around the edge of the flat rooftop, banked at both ends. How ironic — for Bruno still treasured irony — that the *Salone,* the pinnacle of local, clean, natural agricultural and viticultural biodiversity, was occupying a part of the old Fiat factory, an epicenter of industrialization, mechanization and automation. Not to mention the source of a big chunk of the greenhouse gases frying the planet.

From his perch along the rooftop edge, he could see the crowds lining up for the *Salone,* another world 50 feet below. Bruno loved being at the fault line, the grinding edge between two tectonically opposed mindsets. But he didn't like the half-man, half-cloud of smoke he was about to report to. He whistled under his breath as he retraced his steps to the elevator. He got in and ascended one floor to the architect Renzo Piano's glass bubble that crested the rooftop like an alien spaceship.

This was the moment he always dreaded. Reporting to the alien within. He pushed through the door like a man in a dream dragging two-ton legs. He felt his pecker dribbling a bit of pee. Before him, in the very center of the bubble, surrounded by a ring of empty chairs placed around the perimeter, sat a thin human figure. It was propped up atop a motorized wheelchair — a bishop's throne in a glass sanctuary. Wires led to and from his body, whether for electronic devices or intravenous feeding, Bruno was never sure.

"Hello, Bruno. How goes the battle?" The man's voice coiled and unwound in a disembodied fashion, like a cobra or a wisp of smoke. The echo in the huge empty chamber amplified the ghostly effect. And his every utterance, no matter how common, sounded absolutely sibylline to Bruno.

He also chain-smoked. The bubble's glass interior was milky from the smoke. Ashtrays stuck to the wheelchair arms like leeches.

Bruno coughed and steeled himself. "Our catch of the day is Yusuf Aktug. Turkish. Probably the most radical eco-fanatic of the crowd. A thorn in the side of Gregory Samaras. Our two young students gave Mr. Aktug a piece of their mind. They got a little carried away but maybe he will think twice before taking on Mr. Samaras."

"No one is to point a finger at Gregory. He knows nothing of our project. But he has the Greek Orthodox Church — whatever that is — on his side, which is our side; he's very religious, but with every fault there is a redeeming circumstance." The Voice claimed the absolute last word, planting periods on any and all topics. "So. Our next step? What do you think, Bruno?" The air seemed thinner in the room when the Voice inhaled his cigarette. He sucked up energy.

"I have a list of possible…"

The Voice cut him short. "Eschew lists. I would suggest we pay a visit to Archbishop Michael Tucci, head of the Turin archdiocese. A gift from the foundation to the church in its time of grieving that the Shroud of Turin has been ripped so untimely from its resting place." Bruno took a sheaf of notes from his briefcase and began taking dictation. "The entire Roman Catholic church is shaken at the temerity of this theft. They need a friendly voice from the business sector, 'Your holiness, we feel your pain.' Have you been following the story, Bruno?"

Bruno hated to feel the ground shift under his feet. Of course, he had been following the story. But why doesn't the son of a bitch thank me for a job well done?

The Voice could read minds, damn his extrasensory perception. At least Bruno's mind. Bruno began, "Of course, I interviewed Monsignor…"

"No resting on laurels, Bruno. We must make friendship between mother church and multinationals. What the world needs now is love sweet love." He hummed a tune which Bruno recognized, some pop one-world pap, then tapped it out with his yellowed fingers on the wheelchair arm, then croaked it scratchily, "We…We…We are fami*leee*." Bruno wanted to kick him in the balls, but he knew he himself did not have, metaphorically, the matching set. So he just agreed as he sweltered before his boss.

"Done. I'll see to it. When, how much, in whose name and for what purpose?"

"Gutt Mann, Bruno. Deliver it tomorrow and release the story simultaneously. One hundred thousand dollars. Half from the Consolidated Food Companies Philanthropic Foundation. Make the press release datelined from New York. Headline: "A reward for information leading to the arrest of those responsible for the crime against the Holy Shroud." I'd love to bring Samaras here to present the check, but we've got a Finn for this year's consortium chair, so get him down here. Aho Enterprises; he'll provide the other half. The two of you go the archbishop; when you give him the check, plant a little device on him. Have a nice day, Bruno. *Auf wiedersehen."*

He left the Voice's presence, stumbling like a cringing dog. This windswept autodrome was a perfect place for this...this thing, this shrouded sound box, this piece of multinational machinery in a humanoid body propped up in a state-of-the-art wheelchair throne. Reflexively, he looked behind him, fearing the Voice's mind penetration might reach out 30 yards to where he waited for the elevator.

Emerging from the locked corridor downstairs, he was soon back among real people; shoppers. Sometimes, and this was one of them, he wished he had a real job and a home to go to every night and kids waiting for him and a frau who would kiss him and make him feel good and send him to the grocery store for milk and bread. His frau and their three kids did not see a lot of him for months on end.

It was hell, this working for a multinational. Oh his kingdom for a boss. So damned many shell corporations, corporate spin-offs and charitable foundations. His livelihood resided in a Swiss bank, which wrote out his remuneration on checks registered to a Panamanian bank.

Once outside, he felt lighter, liberated, loosened from the Voice's grip. He jumped into a cab that had pushed its way to the front of the taxi queue outside the shopping mall building. The cabby swung the car out into traffic and had not even asked Bruno where he wanted to go. "Banca di Roma, *schnell,"* he ordered, before looking at the face in the rearview mirror. Tony Mezzo Soprano's face, wearing a predatory smile. Bruno felt weak.

"Banca di Roma; *Jawohl, mein commandant.* I had the Carmen

Ghia checked out."

"Which Carmen Ghia?"

"The one that scooped up your rowdy students. Registered to a Bruno Baumgartner, it seems, in town for the *Salone*. For *Der Welt-Wanderer*." The predatory smile turned into a horrible sneer.

"Better not to lease cars in this town under your own name, Bruno, for I am the prince of the fucking ferrets. I catch rats. And now, I take you on a ride; carpe diem, *amico*."

CHAPTER 33

CNN reported that French officials were combing the countryside, as well as Paris, but had no serious leads in the theft of the Holy Shroud. Officials were quoted as saying the Shroud's probable destination was "somewhere in France." Rachel watched the news between showering, drying and dressing. Friday night. Where the hell was Tom?

The coverage had turned to the ghoulish, the fringy. The anchorwoman ticked off one crazy episode after another: bloggers announcing that the Shroud had turned up in Hoboken or Madagascar; Web sites selling Shroud knockoffs at a discount for as long as it was missing; radio talk show hosts larding their commentary with talk of satanic rituals or Islamic terrorism; bishops of a hysterical persuasion hinting the faithful should prepare for martyrdom at the hands of anti-Christian armies; rich Romanian widows sending money to the Vatican to fund detective work.

The anchorwoman cut to the reporter in Turin, speaking against a background of churches where services were being held day and night, offering prayers for the return of the relic. The crowds grew bigger as each day passed without news. Women in long black dresses paraded outside the cathedral, eyes filled with tears, mourning the loss of their holy cloth.

Inside the cathedral, the cameras showed Archbishop Tucci presiding at a special liturgy to pray for the return of *la Sindone*. Rachel thought he looked more confused than sad. He wore a heavy stole over his alb, making him look as though he bore the weight of the crucified one. "You make good press and photograph like Mother Teresa," she growled at the TV.

The anchorwoman appeared to overhear the remark. "The archbishop has the affection of the local pious people more intensely than ever in his fourteen years as archbishop of Turin. He has always kept an emotional distance in public. A good but private man, a holy cold fish. But crisis had made him a public idol. The local newspaper has dubbed him 'Rudolpho Guiliani da Torino.'"

***

Rachel had spent the last 24 hours shuttling back and forth between the *Salone* and Yusuf's hotel room; she had moved her luggage to another room in his hotel. When she had dressed and gone to his room, she held an ice-filled towel to his nose.

"So where is Romeo?" Yusuf sputtered. Rachel had been mum about Tom since their brief conversation. She knew Yusuf knew her well enough from encounters over numerous crises that she had a hard inner core, unflappable. But here she was, biting her nails, acting distracted, switching CNN on and off, pacing the floor.

"If he doesn't call in the next hour, I'm calling Michael Tucci."

"Who's that — another boyfriend? No wonder you are looking a little pale."

"Tucci is the archbishop of Turin, not a boyfriend. I'll bet he's terrified that Tom's in serious danger. Yusuf, I'm scared." Yusuf said nothing.

She watched him and waited. "What are you thinking?" She tried to interpret his eyes, which always narrowed to slits when he was analyzing.

"I'm trying to make connections. I come here since nineteen ninety-six and it's always so...so..."

"Mellow."

"That's it. Like honey. This year, bang, bang! Kids telling me to shut up and quit fighting innocent Gregory Samaras, the most powerful grain merchant in the Middle East — and then this holy thing stolen and now your boyfriend Tom AWOK."

"AWOL." She smiled. "What's the K for?"

"Without OK, AWOK. Absent without OK. So paint for me a big picture."

"*The* big picture, actually. I can't believe that Mr. Samaras is involved with the students — is he dumb enough to think the biodiversity movement is going to be derailed by creepy kids?"

"The answer is 'no.' I know the man."

"We've been at this business of biodiversity a long time, Yusuf. What the hell do we expect? We are being taken seriously. I guess we ought to be grateful."

"I think you ought to be grateful that some guy is giving attention to you."

"Sure, some guy steps into my life and then he steps out. Thanks, I am overflowing with gratitude."

"I think you are worried he is not the right guy for you, Rachel.

Am I right?"

"He is so damned abstracted. He's like all teachers. If you can't get involved, then teach. I don't know what gets him passionate, makes him want to go to the barricades, whether he even knows there are barricades. Rootless, clueless American gentile Joe."

Yusuf felt his nose and again winced. She scowled at him. "Keep your fingers away from that beak." The phone rang and she jumped at it. Yusuf grinned.

"Rootless clueless Americano gentile Joe, I bet on it. Mellowwww." He shut up when she shot him a volley of scowls, mouthing the syllables of "gentile."

"Where are you, Tom?"

She set the receiver down and turned to Yusuf. "Gentile Joe's back in Turin."

Yusuf closed his eyes. When he opened them, Rachel was holding the phone close to his face. "Call her." Yusuf smiled and took the phone. "I'll go downstairs to meet him. Be right back."

Rachel walked through the lobby and saw the cab pull up. How should she greet him — happy, angry? He got out of the cab and was almost running to the hotel entrance. Oh, that's good, she thought! She felt a glow inside. She pushed her way through the lobby and embraced him before he saw her. He held her tightly for a long time. Tony tapped her on the arm. "Say, *amica*, Italians don't find public displays of affection to be, ah, in good taste, *per favore.*"

Tom stepped back, looked at her and whispered, "Hi. Missed you."

Whatever he'd been through showed on every facial muscle, she thought. She squeezed his hands. "Mutual. Very mutual."

They both turned to Tony, who gave them a Groucho-like roll of the eyes. "See you guys soon." He waved goodbye and sauntered out the door. *"Dormite bene!"*

So this is how the first night shakes out, she thought as she felt his embrace around her waist in the elevator. In his sleep-deprived, jet-lagged, cops-and-robbers state of mind, will he just fall asleep? When they reached the door to her room, she asked, "Did you bring one?"

"One what? Oh my god. I was going to buy a package at the..."

She rummaged through her purse. "Here. I never leave home without one. What do they teach Lutheran bachelors in Minnesota?"

"I'm sorry, I'm kind of spacey. No way to start off, is it? Look, I can sleep on the couch."

She opened the door. "*Voilà!* No couch."

She faced him; he gripped her shoulders. "I was hoping that was the case. Got a shower?"

"There's room for two."

So they undressed, showered together, and jumped into bed. She taught him what she knew, and he was a willing learner and generous lover. An hour later, when she turned off the bedside lamp, she giggled. "You can *shtup*, my friend."

***

In his room, Yusuf had finished the conversation with the children, with his wife. He went to the window and looked at the setting sun. Turning his back to it, he knelt on the floor and then prostrated himself. He said a few words and then, dizzy from his posture, pushed himself back up with the help of a nearby chair, wobbled back to the bedroom and turned out the light.

CHAPTER 34

Giovanni Palmitessa celebrated his release from protective custody with a Saturday midday feast at Trattoria di Gianna with a hundred of his closest friends and relatives. A heaping dish of Sarass del fen — ricotta matured in hay — made from goat, cow and sheep milk. A serving of mortardella, a sausage from the Val Pellice region. A sea-salty risotto negro. He was wiping his mouth with a napkin, under the watchful eye of his brother, Vittorio, and his nephew, Tony. It was midday in Torino's Old City area, where 60 years earlier Giovanni's father and thousands of other Napolitani like him had found cheap lodging in beautiful old residences vacated by their owners who had moved out to the new Torino rising after the war. Vittorio and Giovanni's father tired quickly of working for Fiat and found a shuttered storefront that became Trattoria di Gianna. Vittorio inherited it.

Today, a steady stream of Giovanni's male contemporaries kept approaching the table, hallooing and shouting his name; his brother kept sending them on their way. "He's eating. He'll talk later."

"No he won't, Papa." Tony stood. "No interviews. His story has been sold to the movies. He is not talking." Tony was playing the fixer.

Vittorio groaned. "Hey, you young one. Who are you to tell these old friends that they can't hear the story from Giovanni's own lips? What is this movie bullshit? Which studio? Here you are, a cabby, telling your elder what's what."

"È cosi, Papá. These are your brother's own wishes, and if you give him time to wipe his chin on the napkin, he'll tell you so." Giovanni was just then folding his napkin, which bore colorful stains. He belched quietly, sipped his Chianti and nodded to his nephew. Tony raised his hand. The room quieted. "Five minutes."

"Ah, you bastards know me too well. I would keep you here day and night with what I've seen. But Tony's right. We have received phone and fax messages from across the world. Magazines, moviemakers, newspapers, TV, radio. Even somebody named Al Jazerra. I think it is an American black music station. But we are holding out — Martin Scorsese. When the call comes, we are talking to him alone. And Tony says it won't be long. So, paziènza, *bastardi!"*

Men rose off their chairs, shaking their fists, shouting out their opinions, pointing fingers at Giovanni, gesticulating toward their hearts. One mean-looking featherweight, 80 years plus, proclaimed above the din that this whole business was being orchestrated by Berlusconi and he didn't believe anyone. It was momentarily quiet as he stomped out the door, adjusting his helmet on his bald head. His Vespa engine ignited and his tires squealed for 20 seconds. The room erupted in laughter.

"Silenzio!" shouted Giovanni. "You all think I do nothing but shake collection plates at tourists. Shoo away women in shorts." Raucous cheers rose from his audience, some of them impersonating women in shorts swiveling their hips. *"Silenzio!"* he thundered and glared at them. "I'll tell you." He fingered the firefighter lapel pin.

"So these signoras from Naples were all around me. I had just finished explaining history to them, when I saw this man at the back of the group, an American from the looks of his jeans and shirt collar — you know, self-conscious around strangers. He was taking notes, unlike most Americans. I felt good about that.

"I led the group toward the next side chapel — like the priest during the stations of the cross." He stood and took a few solemn strides. "I saw two men entering the church. They were ignoring my performance, heading directly for the Shroud chapel. They did not have that easy way we all have when we come into church, blessing ourselves with the holy water and figuring out how many of our enemies have arrived ahead of us." His audience pounded the tables in appreciation. "And they looked suspicious — not Americans. Germans? Just like their damned Autobahns. In a hurry to get to wherever they were going. No — these two were too skinny. Protestants, ill at ease in the house of the true church. No, wait; both of them were in uniform. ENEL — *si, La Nostra Societa Nazionale di Elettricità.* They carried large, sleek, plastic suitcases marked with the orange flame logo. They saluted me, nodded and then clutched their hearts. Italians after all." He smiled broadly. The audience murmured while he drew a breath.

"No one else was in the church — except La Prostrata, the crazy woman from the home for the feeble-minded. Today she was clutching her rosary, behaving."

He spread his arms wide. "Then they disappeared. But Chiara saw the electricians string a large ENEL curtain across the glass wall

of the chapel. It blocked the view. She motioned to me to wait —
stall the group.

"I said to the ladies and the young American, 'The Holy Shroud
was saved by the brave firemen of Torino seven years ago. A fire
had broken out in the church. A brave fellow swung a huge hammer
against the bullet-proof glass reliquary. He smashed it and removed
the Shroud. He and I could hardly breathe. Everywhere the walls
were falling, so I cleared a path through the flaming debris. And I
would do it all again and give my life to defend it against danger or
threat from an enemy.'"

He was perspiring right through his polyester shirt. He rocked on
his feet, crouching, grappling, fighting the inferno again, rotating his
arms in a dramatic axe-swinging arc.

Silenzio. Then the restaurant rumbled with shouted "bravos."
Giovanni held up his hand. He started softly but steadily rose to a
crescendo. "But on Monday no one saw the two workmen remove *la
Sindone* and place it in one of the suitcases. They took down the
curtain. They did their work. Then the two came out of the hallway
near the chapel, carrying their sleek plastic suitcases. I studied them.
Why was I not told they were coming? Then they stopped, turned
and saluted me goodbye. I saluted back. I looked at my Napolitani —
still kneeling before the Shroud — which wasn't there. The Yank
was still taking notes, distracting me. I clapped my hands together.
'Basta.' I pointed to the donation stand. 'Thank you in advance for
your donation to the *Chiesa Cattedrale.* Have a safe journey to your
homes.' Chiara rattled a donation plate. I took a phone from my coat
pocket and called the chief of security. *'Mi amico,* ENEL — *che
cosa fanno?'* There was no answer. I ran toward the door.

"La Prostrata jumped out of her pew, fell on her hands and knees
and started crawling toward me and the pilgrim ladies, their eyes as
big as pizzas. Now Chiara and I had to shove her into a wheelchair.
She shrieked at us. We rolled her out the door. The American was
still writing.

"Outside, there was no ENEL van. And no cabs; Chiara and I
pushed La Prostrata home, wailing like a demented queen. And then
it was over."

Giovanni signified the end of the session with another sip of
Chianti. "Where did you get this stuff, Vittorio? *È terribile.'*

The café owner threw up his hands. "Big head, Giovanni. *Capo
magno!"* That outburst loosened up the house, the laughter sprouted

alongside the curses, more coffee and Ampari were drunk, more arguments erupted, more fists raised. Men threatened violence against one another, swearing vendettas, insulting old friends, walking out on relationships that had been nurtured for half a century. All an act, the stuff that made old age bearable and kept them alive for another decade. The malcontent on the Vespa soon roared back, strode into the bar, took off his helmet and placed it on the table in front of him, finished a half-drunk glass of wine and promptly fell asleep in the midst of the racket.

Tony flashed his watch at his uncle, pointed to the digits and approached his chair to help Giovanni up. "Where are you going?" Vittorio demanded.

"Martin wants to see us." Tony said with a straight face, steering Giovanni out the door.

The chorus of elders and seers screamed epithets and shouted observations about who Martin was and what he would say if Giovanni and Tony got within earshot of his bodyguards and how he would throw these liars out on their backsides before they could say "Scorsese."

Alone in the cab with his uncle, Tony maneuvered the streets of Torino. "I've been at the Internet café, *Zio* Giovanni."

"OK."

"And I gave Tom Ueland a ride from the airport to his girlfriend's hotel. And you forgot to mention, he's innocent."

"Si."

"You know, *la Sacra Sindone* belongs to the little people — you and me, even La Prostrata. Torinesi who make their living off it."

"Si."

"Well, Tom Ueland says *la Sindone* is on its way to Istanbul. But the Internet says Istanbul is in trouble: earthquakes. Us little people need to organize an expedition."

"OK."

"We are going to need a seaplane to get us there and a fire truck to get around in. And plenty of water. I'll get the plane; you call your firefighter friend in Istanbul."

"Quando?"

"Domani."

"OK. *Si.* OK!"

CHAPTER 35

"This band of brothers is like a Christian cargo cult." Tom lay beside Rachel on the hotel bed. They had spent the morning relearning the lessons of the night. And then Tom told her about Paris, about Paul and Genevieve De Rosier, about the Camargue and the mission of the otherworldly Knight-Precursors of Christ the King, about the monastery, about the helicopter and its airborne, bearded, magical figure in the sky.

"What kind of cult is that?" she asked, running a finger down his arm.

"After World War II, cargo cults sprang up in places like New Guinea where the islanders had seen the marvelous material goods dropped to the troops from the skies — food, medicine, clothing, weapons. The natives built airstrips and control towers and wore wooden headsets, thinking they could persuade their deities to send their people the good things they had showered down on the Americans."

"Your fanatical friends are covering themselves in this Shroud to force God to send Jesus back and finish off the Jews for good."

"You got it. They aren't looking to the skies for food and clothing, they want the Son of God himself, whose teachings have been disregarded and distorted by a faithless world. He alone can give them their reward: life forever in heaven."

Rachel propped herself up on her elbow. "Amazing. And you — you're different. My Minnesota lover is no longer an outsider. I miss the old ambiguous outsider, the professor."

"Anything for the story. I'm just your garden variety paparazzo."

"Oh, I think it's more than that. You fell in love with the lovely Genevieve, I think."

Tom blinked. "I did. She's amazing. I went through every stage."

"Except consummation."

"At that point, a different kind of passion took over. Her passion. Paradise lost. Love and death. I can't explain it."

Rachel closed his eyelids with a soft finger. "I want to meet her. And her man. I imagine I could snuggle up to him easily enough."

Before he could answer, the phone rang. "That's Yusuf. I'll get it. Hello? Yes. Are we up? Of course we're up. It's afternoon." She hung up. "You are about to meet a Turkish alpha male. Yusuf Aktug is all hard shell and soft heart."

"Istanbul?" Tom stood, his eyes narrowing.

"Istanbul."

"Could he...help us there?" Tom asked.

"Us?" she shot back. "There?"

When the firm knock on the door came 15 minutes later, it was Tom who went to open it.

Yusuf was grinning under his bruised nose. "Gentle Joe?"

"Gentile Joe!" Rachel screamed.

"Come on in, Yusuf. I'm Tom Ueland." Tom put out his hand, Yusuf clasped it and then put both hands on Tom's shoulders. Tom liked him immediately.

"If she say Yusuf is an alpha male, I am not. I don't know what it means, but I am regular guy. I am happy to meet you, Tom Ueland."

Before Tom could close the door, Tony marched in, arm in arm with Giovanni. "Hey, everybody, this is my Uncle Giovanni Palmitessa. *Zio* Giovanni, you've met Tom; this is Rachel Cohen." Giovanni bowed to Rachel. "And this is Yusuf Aktug, a friend of Rachel's. I told you about him and me and the smart-ass students."

The horn-honks and Vespa-buzzes from the street below were deafening. "Tom, what are we doing in this sound chamber?" Tony asked.

"Unbuggable. Even by you, Tony. Try imagining what it was like sleeping here." The bed sat there, half-made, pillows askance.

Tony screwed up his face. Yusuf broke into a big grin.

"I'm trying!" Yusuf and Tony said at the same time. Rachel and Tom turned the red of new wine. "Yeah, I bet you're exhausted," Tony jabbed again. "Too tired to even get up and shut the windows."

"Buon giorno," Tom greeted Giovanni. It was their first meeting since the hotel detention episode.

In Italian, Giovanni responded. "You're the one who I thought was with them. Maybe I am still right." Giovanni waited for the reaction as Tony translated. Tom saluted him and offered Giovanni the one padded chair in the room. Staying close to his uncle, Tony turned a desk chair around and straddled it as Tom started to explain, pausing for Tony to translate.

"On Monday, two people posing as electricians steal the Shroud right under my nose. I spend Monday night in detention after

116

meeting Tony and Giovanni. On Tuesday, I meet the archbishop and I take the train to Paris. On Wednesday, I meet with an old man and woman whom I will never forget. I am with them for two days — the Shroud is sighted in Paris. On Thursday, we go to the south of France to hunt down the crazies who took it — and we actually encounter them — and lose them. Today is Saturday. Can we go back to Monday in the church?"

CNN flickered silently in the corner. Yusuf kept looking at the TV, distracted. Tom walked over to Giovanni and tried to get a smile out of him. "Tony, I want *Zio* Giovanni to tell me something those two guys did that we haven't heard a million times already. Something's missing that might make sure we're on the right track."

Giovanni mumbled a question to Tony, which Tony rendered in English as, "He wants to know if Tom works for Scorsese." Laughter. Tom shrugged.

"I work for me. Tell your uncle I'm going to do a story that will get picked up by a famous newspaper, and if he wants his fifteen minutes of fame he will talk to me."

Tony jerked a thumbs-up in Tom's direction that said "He's the man," and translated for Giovanni and then rendered Giovanni's long answer. "Tell the American I have already told everything to the police. These two guys looked Italian, maybe Spanish, scrawny. They didn't talk to anybody. And they were dressed like electricians. Electricians all look alike. They got in; they got out. They stopped and saluted me. Your friend thinks maybe they were saluting somebody else or paying their respects to the holy place. That's all boolshit. They were honoring me, the guide, the fireman, the savior of the Shroud. That's what they were doing."

"I caught 'boolshit.'" Tom leaned forward toward Giovanni's chair. "When they got to the door of the church, after they saluted you, they stopped at the holy water font, right? And you said they made the sign of the cross. Did they do anything strange there, anything else before they left? Please, Giovanni."

Giovanni looked at Tony as he translated, then back at Tom. Blank stares. Giovanni shrugged. Tom came closer. "Did either one take water from the fountain and sprinkle it on the suitcases they were carrying?" He had practiced the question since the Camargue, when he had sprinkled holy water in the farmhouse. "Did either of them act like they were blessing something or spreading holy water, like priests do at funerals? Were they treating whatever was in the cases like it was something holy or important?"

Tony pantomimed Tom's funeral liturgy. Everything seemed to get quieter. Even the street noise. Giovanni looked at Tom. His face brightened suddenly. Then he went on for five minutes, talking to Tony, gesturing, mimicking, mugging, breathing hard, pouring out words. Tony turned to Tom and translated. "Yes."

After the others stopped laughing, Tony said, "Can't take anything for granted with Americans. OK, the bastards made the sign of the cross over the cases and they shook the leftover water onto them. Like they were blessing the casket, the way the priests do at funerals. And then they were gone. That's it. Nothing else."

Tom scratched his head. He looked at Yusuf, then at Rachel. They were not watching him, but the television. "Hey, you two, next stop, after we see the archbishop — Istanbul."

"I don't think so." Yusuf's gaze stayed on the TV.

"What's going on?" Tom turned to the set. Giovanni crossed himself. Tony moved closer to the set. Images of ramshackle huts broken up like brittle pieces of overcooked pita bread.

"Earth tremors near Istanbul. Foreshocks: warnings of more to come. Maybe big. *Ai Ai!*" Yusuf slid off the bed and thumbed the buttons on his cell phone. He went out into the hallway, while the others watched the screen.

Tom blurted out, "Istanbul. Earthquake. The Red Sea parting. The 'coming catastrophe' of the note left in the church."

Moments later, Yusuf returned. "Thank Allah. She and our kids left the city today and went to her parents. Her brother is watching the house. They're OK. So what is it you were saying? I don't have time."

"Come with us to Istanbul," Tom replied.

CHAPTER 36

"I'm going home. Everything I have is in my house. Then to my family."

Tom was losing the one prop that could stabilize his flimsy scheme to intercept the knights. "Yusuf, we need your help. These are very deranged people — the men who stole the holy linen from the church this week. Something dangerous is happening in your city under cover of the earthquake. You know the territory. Come with us to see Pastor Tucci."

"Look, you want me to make time to chase some crazies who steal a piece of old linen? During an earthquake? Who is your boyfriend, Rachel? Superman? You know what earthquakes in Turkey do? I like you alive, taking care of Rachel here."

Yusuf went to the door. He looked at Rachel. Her expression was pleading. His body relaxed slightly. "If you find anything that tells me that your enemies are my enemies, that may make us friends, Mr. Ueland. Rachel has my cell phone number." And then he was gone.

Yusuf's exit took the air out of the room, or was it just Tom's own confidence deflating? Rachel's expression turned cool, distant, her back to him — what did that mean? What a contrast with the utter desperate need of the night before.

"There is nothing more important to a Turk than his home, his family. If all hell doesn't break loose, we'll see him again."

"I think he'd like a shot at Bruno," Tony blurted out.

"Bruno? Who's Bruno?" asked Tom.

"A journalist covering the *Salone*. There is a connection between him and some Greek guy."

"Gregory Samaras," she said.

"Who's Gregory Samaras?"

"He is the proto-Alpha Male. Turkish grain tycoon. I'll tell you all about it on the way to Michael's. Maybe we can make a connection between Yusuf's goals and yours. I mean, ours. But we have to work fast, before he leaves."

Tom's eyes widened. "You'll come with me to see Pastor Tucci? And then...whatever?"

"Blow off the *Salone,* you mean?" She took a breath. "OK. Whatever."

CHAPTER 37

Michael Tucci hung up the telephone. It was the first time he had heard Paul's and Genevieve's voices in 30 years. And the past came rushing back as he listened to their words — shakier, but still gently, censoriously, French.

He remembered the Young Christian Worker movement of the 1950s. The cell meetings with alienated young Catholics who were tired of ecclesiastics preaching about accepting one's lot in life and the evils of Communism — the young who knew the clergy didn't have to put food on the table every night. Michael gravitated to young men and women — not that much younger than he was himself. And they liked him. He preached the end-of-the-century encyclical of Pope Leo XIII, *"Rerum Novarum,"* that workers had a right to a living wage that would feed them and their families. He worked in the assembly-line with them, he invited them to his apartment for food and wine and he celebrated mass around the dining room table. They were heady days for a young priest brought up in rigid Italian seminaries.

Paul and Genevieve. Another story. She was a teacher and a cultural anthropologist; he was a lawyer. Every bit Michael's equals in spirituality, and then some. Genevieve taught young factory workers how to read faster, write more cogently. Paul taught them the law and how to speak before a crowd. Michael grew to appreciate the sacrifices they were making. He didn't buy their Christendom kind of thinking, their "Holy Roman Empire" way of seeing the world. The arguments that they had, nightly, made him lament the gap between the couple and him even more. But oh, how he loved the arguments with real people, rather than classmates busy making church careers for themselves.

Michael had grown very close to both of them. And he struggled with the feelings he had for Genevieve. She was the most beautiful woman he had ever seen, a dazzling, worldly Parisienne.

Whenever they touched in conversation or hugged at the greeting of peace during the mass, he felt the most wondrous thrill. And prayed over it. And threw himself into his factory work and his apartment housecleaning, whatever distraction came his way. But mostly he prayed. And as he prayed, he forced himself to become emotionally attached to Paul, for he knew that was the one way he could conquer his sexual awakening. If he grew to love Paul, surely he would not betray him with his wife.

But Genevieve knew, she had to know; he was sure she knew. Sometimes she would look at him and he would grow flustered and stammer. One day, with the gracefulness of an angel, she took his hands when they were waiting for Paul and spoke to him. *"Mon ami,* we are friends, you and I. It is very difficult to be a friend to you and I think it is the same for you. So be at peace, accept it as a gift from God, honor yourself, honor me, honor Paul. All will be well, Michael." That was her goodbye on the telephone today. *"Tout ira bien,* Michael." The voice was now less robust; it was drier, reedy with the fine thin texture of wind through stalks that had cracked here and there. He was stirred again.

Not all had been well back then, however. Genevieve became pregnant in 1965, after almost a dozen years of marriage. They had tried for years to have a child and only now in the heady days of the Young Christian Worker and the worker priest movements, in the nights of late suppers with Michael — and others, but mostly Michael — had she gotten pregnant. Paul knew the pregnancy was his doing, but somehow the fact that Genevieve had conceived during a time when Michael was an intimate in their lives lodged in Paul's brain, and a coolness between the men developed. Michael baptized the child and then returned to Italy and threw himself into the *"aggiornamento"* movement, making the church relevant to the modern world. A movement that this time the De Rosiers wanted no part of.

Michael had often thought over the years if his life had taken a different turn, if he had been a young priest not in the 1950s, but in the 1960s and 1970s, when so many young ones had left the priesthood. But he was a child of the Second World War; he had been involved with partisans as a teenager in the last year of the war, fighting the retreating Nazis near his hometown of Montepulciano. Priesthood for him was a way to continue the work of seeking a more just society; so was being a worker priest, so was his espousal of liberation theology. But would he have stayed a priest had he been ordained in the more liberal and unstructured church of the 1970s, where friendships with women were encouraged by the new theologians?

Elevation to the episcopacy in 1976 under the ailing Paul VI had snuffed out these doubts, and he threw his vigor into being a bishop. First assigned as an auxiliary to the cardinal of Venice, he acquired the reputation as a liberal. Not too liberal, just outspoken enough to make him a poster bishop for movements of social justice. He became a diplomat for the Vatican and spent a considerable number of years both in America and in the Middle East, with postings in Beirut and Istanbul and innumerable ad hoc itineraries in between.

At what price, he often reflected, had he exchanged a wife and family and children for this clerical world. She, Genevieve, had asked him that very question that day on the littoral of the Mediterranean in the seaside town of Saintes Maries de la Mer. She and Paul had invited him to visit them in 1974 when she was working at the Museum of the Camargue. They had a summer villa on the sea. Paul had been called back by his law firm to Paris on the last day of Michael's visit. Michael and Genevieve went for a long walk that day. For three hours they hiked the inland pathways and then along the shore. She slipped — was that how it happened? — on a damp clump of leaves; he reached out and held her so she wouldn't fall. It happened so fast; she was in his arms and taking his face in her hands she kissed him. Flustered, he gripped her tightly and held her close for an agonizing moment of indecision. They had never held each other before like this; always the chaste embrace, the ritual kiss of peace, always in Paul's presence. She drew back and looked at him — then broke away and walked ahead for some distance.

"I'm sorry," she finally spoke. They were five feet apart. "It just...I have great feelings for you, Michael. You know that. Paul knows that. We just must...forget, now. And forgive."

"I will not forget, Genevieve. I care for you very much. At this moment, I can only forget I am a priest. My God, how I hate to remember, here, with you!" He started to walk toward her. "I...we should go back now."

"Yes, of course." As they walked back to the villa, she asked, "Are you sorry now you never married, never had children?"

"At midlife, yes, I can say I am sorry. I miss those things I set aside — home, family. Yet, I chose rightly, I think. Many good things have come to me. But sometimes it seems so puny compared to this."

"This." She hesitated. They were now facing the sea, the wind catching their breath. She took his arm and quickened their pace as they joined the tourists strolling on the beach. "This is the nature of our beastliness. We are beautiful and we are beasts, yes? It does not change what we have chosen. Yes?" She smiled at him, begging him to say yes. He thought her the most radiant creature he had ever met and was burning to kiss her.

"Veramente." He took her hand as they reached the villa. *"Au revoir.* Tell Paul I hope to see you both soon." He watched her out of the rearview mirror as he drove away and then the overgrowth of the Camargue came between them.

He looked up at the fading photograph of her and Paul and himself. Oh God, to be young again. He saw himself in Tom Ueland, the outsider who might help him create a surprise ending to the theft of the Holy Shroud of Turin. And he was bringing his friend Rachel. Good, Michael enjoyed her spirit — like Genevieve's. And Tony. And *Zio* Giovanni. And maybe this Turkish community organizer Tom had mentioned.

And they were coming here because he asked them. Cast in the role of the Shroud's official protector, he was the shepherd whose sheep had been scattered in turmoil over the loss of a piece of linen whose dubious pedigree laid claim to the most intimate mystery of the faith, the death and resurrection of Jesus Christ.

Why had he allowed these people to get involved in this? Michael shuddered over the gnawing regret that he had ever mentioned the names of Paul and Genevieve to Tom, that he had not just taken Alitalia to Rome and held the media's hand. This was a time to show some gravitas, for God's sake. He remembered some American theologian's apt summary of a particularly imperious cardinal; "He has spilled gravitas all over his shirt."

He should be spending his days accepting the world's sympathy — like the press conference that morning at which he accepted $100,000 from a Finnish pasta company and some foundation from New York. Somebody named Bruno Baumgartner, as oily a fellow as any churchman. "We feel your pain, Archbishop." Ugh! *"Suavitas"* was the right Latin word for that oiliness.

Michael knew his aura was not gravitas; much closer to the *suavitas* of Bruno Baumgartner. Sweetly pulling people into his web, attracting rather than compelling anyone. So transparent was his own web — the lonely dissenter, exposing the church's failings and faults. His motives? Anything but transparent.

He turned to the east, bowed low and said out loud what he had been thinking for years. "Istanbul is the fulcrum on which I will right the wrongs. The Shroud belongs to Istanbul! And the Church of Rome must become the Church of Rome and Istanbul! Power to the Other!"

CHAPTER 38

Tony's cab raced toward the archbishop's residence. Tom and Rachel held hands while Giovanni gazed out the window. Tom spoke quietly to her.

"This morning you said I was different, not the old outsider. You know, I've felt like an embedded journalist with the troops as they chased the bad guys. Not anymore. I feel like one of the troops. All four of us."

"I know you're some kind of expert on magical thinking. I didn't know you were obsessed with it." She shot him a pained expression.

"The knights are out to end history. I'm here to write it. They're on my turf. I'm a knight-historian. I think this piece of history in the making needs an intervention — stop these freaks before they hurt somebody."

He saw Tony's face in the rearview mirror. He was smiling at Giovanni. The cab pulled into the courtyard and the archbishop was walking fast toward them.

"Buon giorno! Hello, my friends." Tom tried to read that face for signs of uneasiness, regret. This encounter, of distinguished churchman and ragtag motley characters, was surreal.

Giovanni knelt down on the stones to kiss Michael's ring, grabbing his hand and nearly pulling him down. *"Lei, sta in piedi,* Giovanni."* Giovanni remained kneeling until Tony half-lifted him back up.

"Pastor Tucci, ask Giovanni what else he saw that day," Tom said. Michael looked at Tom and then at Giovanni. Tony translated.

Giovanni was on his feet, like a fireman answering a two-alarm blaze. He pantomimed the entire routine, from the electricians' authoritative entry into the church and through the locked door leading to the chapel interior, to the crisp salutes the two offered him as they came out of that hallway and into the nave of the church, to their fumbling with the holy water at the entrance to the church. And when he came to reenacting the scene at the holy water font, he paused and looked at Tom. Very carefully he made the sign of the cross — not on his forehead and chest — but over the case. Then, raising his hands in quick motion, he brought them down in a dramatic sprinkling of holy water on one of the cases.

"Solo uno?" The archbishop stopped him.

"Uno. Solo," insisted Giovanni. The blessing was just over one of the cases.

"Who are these crazies?" asked Tony. Michael looked at Tom — a signal to jump in.

"When you and I first met this week, Pastor, I was talking medieval history. My belief is that these knights came to their messianic outlook gradually — like medieval Christians. First they fled the madness and corruption of the world brought on by materialism, capitalism, secularism, Islam, Zionism — the list goes on. They retreated to the Camargue and set up housekeeping. As time went by and nothing changed, they began to plot how to make history, not just suffer it. Then Nine-Eleven happened and they went ballistic over Islam. There's enough ammunition in the Book of Revelation to convince them God wills it and they are his agents. The returning Christ against the marauding infidels.

"Giovanni's sprinkling connects the dots. This particular group is on the fringe of the fringe, dedicated to the idea that Christ needs them to return his burial garment to Jerusalem so He can return to earth. Anyone who stands in their way has been terrorized into silence, in order that the divine command can be carried out."

"Reverendissime, troviamo questi stronzi!" Giovanni was on his feet after Tony told him what Tom had said. *"Sì, sì."* Giovanni mimed a fireman carrying a wriggling hose toward a fire, planting one foot in front of the other as he edged once more into some burning *Duomo*. Tom sensed that of all of those in the parlor, Giovanni was the one he wanted by his side in a confrontation.

Giovanni raised his hand for silence, then spoke just above a whisper. When he finished, a somber Tony translated. "The Shroud. It is my life now. *È la mia vita*. Without Catarina, it is my life." The room grew quiet.

After a pause, Michael turned to Tom. "And now?"

"If Paul and Genevieve are right, then the Knight-Precursors are speeding toward Istanbul by sea or they have already arrived by air. The Shroud's presence there is connected to an earthquake, the 'coming catastrophe' of the prayer note. Once there, who knows? They will plant the Shroud somewhere in the city until it's fulfilled their religious agenda. They will deal harshly with whoever gets in the way of their expedition to Jerusalem."

Michael passed his hand over his furrowed forehead. "There are one or two places in Istanbul the police should watch." He felt in his shirt pocket under his suit coat, as if he was fishing for a cigarette. Tony reached into his own pocket and pulled out a rumpled pack of Marlboros. "No, *grazie*, Antonio. Just an old reflex." He clapped his fists together.

"This used to be my town, Michael. Where would you look?" Rachel asked.

"Of course, you know the first place: Hagia Sophia, once the great mosque of Istanbul, now a museum. In ancient times, the seat of eastern Christianity. Then again in the Golden Horn area, the church of My Lady Saint Mary of Blachernae, still standing. Third, the Pharos chapel in the Bucaleon palace of the emperor, by the lighthouse facing the Mamarean Sea — today, ruins. It once stood atop the great seawall that made Constantinople impregnable."

"So in a metropolis of thirteen million people, you are going to find the Shroud in an interval that could be less than an hour during an earthquake?" Rachel asked. "I know I sound cynical like my friend Yusuf, but all you have is a Jewish girl from the US and her friend from Minnesota and a guy named Tony Mezzo Soprano and his uncle Giovanni. We're looking for four kooky knights and an unknown benefactor."

Michael blinked and again went to his breast pocket. Tony offered another cigarette. Michael took it, smelled it, crushed it.

Tom pointed at Rachel. "The benefactor — somebody with a lot of money who needs the Shroud for protection and will return it when the danger is past. That's got to be the mysterious benefactor Paul mentioned. Magical thinking again, Pastor. I am thinking he discreetly advertised for assistance in getting the Shroud and he made a deal with the Knight-Precursors and did not know their true agenda. They had the passion, he had the funds to buy them what they needed to have. They promised to make good. And they have. So far. When the time comes, if it has not already come and gone, they will treat him as an impediment, another sign confirming the right path they have taken on the road to salvation. And it will not be pretty."

Michael threw his hands up in desperation. "Is there a wealthy, devout Christian in Istanbul who might have financed this entire incredible theft of the Shroud?"

Rachel turned to Tom. "I have a hunch that the person you are looking for — the benefactor — is Gregory Samaras."

"I know that name!" Michael shouted. "He has been to Turin many times, I am told, to pray before the chapel of *la Sindone*. He has been pointed out to me. He leaves a generous amount of cash in the poor box. Perhaps it was he who left the note."

Tom turned to Tony. "If we get a picture of Gregory Samaras here, do you think your uncle can identify him?"

The cunning nephew of Giovanni Palmitessa made a time-out sign with his fingers and then translated the request. His uncle shrugged, *"No problema."*

"Yusuf?" Rachel's cell phone was at her ear. "Thank god you're still there. Can you come right away? Hello — It's me, Rachel. Of course I don't sound like myself; I'm not myself. We need you. Don't ask. Please come to the residence of the archbishop of Turin. The cabbies all know it. I know you're leaving. Yes, I know you're worried. So are we. No, you can't go back there yet! Are they OK? All right, so there's no danger where they are. Let that relative watch your house. We need you here. Now. Please."

Bounding into the room like Sumo wrestlers, Father Fiddle Dee Dee set down a laptop and Fiddle Dee Dum plugged in a power cord. Soon Tom was surfing "Gregory Samaras." There were 47,432 references to the guy, and a few with pictures. Tony led Giovanni over to the table. Tom zoomed in on the picture so the old man could get a good look at Signor Samaras. Giovanni put the flat of his palm to his forehead when he saw the industrialist's picture.

"I know that guy. He comes to the chapel once every couple of months. He prays for a long time in front of *la Sindone*. Yes, Tony, I recognize him. But I never met him. I never wanted to interrupt his praying."

Tony nodded to Tom and translated; Tom signaled he wanted more details. Tony went on. "Does he leave things around, like little sheets of paper, asking for a cure or help or a good crop or God knows what. You know what I mean, *zio.*"

"I don't know, Antonio. The regulars all do. Wait; yes; he does. Very quietly. He always is dressed nice, suit and tie, and crosses himself backwards after he leaves a prayer note."

"You mean he ended up on the left side, over his heart?" Tony made the sign of the cross "backwards."

"That is what he did. He ended up over his heart."

"OK. When was the last time you saw him?"

"A month or so ago — I'm not sure. He's always there in the

afternoon, right when we open at two. I figured he was a businessman who traveled to Turin every month or so."

"Did he leave a prayer note?"

"He always does!"

Tony looked at the archbishop and translated for the others. "He knows him. He's there a lot. He prays. And he's Orthodox, not Roman. And he left a prayer note a few weeks ago."

"Hurry up, Yusuf," Rachel whispered.

CHAPTER 39

"Thank God, you came." Rachel threw her arms around Yusuf and he winced when she touched his arm. "Sorry!"

She led him to Michael. "Archbishop this is Yusuf Aktug, a friend of mine and a fervent foe of genetically modified organisms threatening his beloved Turkey."

"Why would Gregory Samaras be so desperate to have the Shroud?" asked Tom. "That's the question, Yusuf." Tom gave him the note left in the church.

Yusuf read it over and scratched his head. "Five years ago, on August seventeenth, nineteen ninety-nine, at three o'clock in the morning, there was a big earthquake. It destroyed Izmit, fifty miles east of Istanbul. Twenty million people live in that area, one-third of Turkey's population. Below is the North Anatolian Fault, where most of our earthquakes rise up. Some scientist had predicted that Izmit was going to be hit. And he is predicting that sooner or later the stress along the fault will move up the line to Istanbul, with our thirteen million people. Samaras paid for the University of Istanbul to get some, how do you say, GPS receivers. I think he bought a couple for himself and put them in his basement. They measure movement of the earth's crust — as small as my small finger shaking. Mr. Samaras is very much afraid of an earthquake. That's the one good thing he's done for Turkey."

"He would do anything to stop a quake," Tom said. "Samaras contracted with the Knight-Precursors, a religious fringe group of Frenchmen, to steal the Shroud. He underwrote all their expenses. Now he thinks they're heading his way with the Shroud of Turin, as they promised him they would do. Only what he doesn't know is that their plan is not to leave it. They will keep right on moving toward Jerusalem after dealing with him — harshly."

Giovanni whistled with each successive revelation. He stopped Tony in mid-sentence and spoke in rapid Italian. "Now I remember the first time I met this man. It was right after the fire, April nineteen ninety-seven. It was a big news story, 'Firemen of Turin save *la Sindone*.' After the cathedral was reopened, he was there the first day. We had a huge thanksgiving service. The choir was singing the *Te Deum* and he was in the church. He was very moved by what had happened. The firemen walked down the aisle dressed in our uniforms, and he came to the aisle and shook everybody's hands. Of course, so did everybody else, but I remember him."

When Tony finished translating, Yusuf looked at his watch. "OK. So Samaras took the Shroud and now he's in trouble. Is that it? I'm going back first thing in the morning."

"Wait a minute, you bullheaded dope!" Rachel shouted. Yusuf was picking up his pack.

"What is 'bullhead'?" asked Yusuf.

"Pastor, it looks to me as though we are trapped in our own private detective world," Tom said, scribbling notes and then reading from them. "If we tell the police we think Samaras is a suspect, we face some big slander charges. We have nothing to go on. There are no clues he is even an accomplice, much less a mastermind. And if we don't get in touch with him, he's in danger. Jean Baptiste and the Knight-Precursors may do anything in the name of the Lord. And with an earthquake ready to blow there, they will slip in, give him a fake Shroud, get their money and slip out as fast as they can. If we tell the Turkish police that we think his life is in danger because of this gang — at best the cops will do triage and tell us to come back at the all-clear and then they will want a motive. And I don't think we have one. We have to find a way to do this ourselves and we need a guide."

Yusuf held his head up a little higher, as if daring anyone to touch him. "I am not a guide. And if I am a guide, who do I guide?"

Rachel shouted, "You would be guiding Tom Ueland and Rachel Cohen."

"And who protects them from these bad boys?" Chuckling, Yusuf was moving toward the door.

"You do." Rachel blocked his steps, growling. "In exchange for our wringing concessions out of Samaras. We change his heart."

"It will take more than you two to make this man have a change of heart. It will take…"

Rachel cut him off. "…An earthquake. And the sparing of the city through the intervention of the Shroud. We can handle the argument stuff. You get us there."

Yusuf was encircled, except for Tony and Giovanni who were murmuring back and forth in Italian, so that not even the bishop could hear what they were saying. Yusuf looked at Rachel. "The city — saved?" Then he challenged the archbishop. "Sir, you will allow your friends to go into danger? You will be responsible for their safety? If your Shroud does not protect the city, they will die, just like thousands of others there. And then there will be many terrible things happening later: cholera, starvation, plagues, thieves, murders. This is what your conscience tells you is OK?"

"They go because they choose to go. I can only suggest. They choose to be…players. And besides, Mr. Aktug, you are going there. I trust you will keep them safe."

Yusuf looked from face to face. "My friend's plane is too small for five people. And where do we land the plane?"

Michael gently laid his hand on Yusuf's shoulder. "Your city is very big. My guess is that the thieves will make landfall tomorrow and rendezvous with Gregory Samaras at the Bucaleon Palace."

"I know it well. *Inshallah,* we can join them there, but we will need…a seaplane."

Tony stood. "We have already arranged for that. My *Zio* Giovanni and me."

"OK," Yusuf said. "When do we meet at our seaplane?"

"We need until tomorrow. Noon. Time's wasting," replied Tony coolly.

"Seriously?" Tom asked.

"Would I kid about this, yank?"

"Do not doubt the word of Antonio Palmitessa and his uncle, Giovanni Palmitessa," said Michael. "I don't know how big their network is, but it reaches far. Now, I will call the patriarch of Istanbul, who is my friend. He will not betray us. I think he can be helpful."

Rachel poked her head between Tony and Giovanni. *"Scusi, signori.* Does this seaplane really exist? Does it have wings?"

"It has all the extras, wings included." Tony took his uncle's arm. "Let's go."

"It's late in the day. We are fiddling while Istanbul burns," Michael said. He pushed the group out the back door and into the street, shaking hands, returning Tony's high five. Rachel kissed him on the cheek and he blushed. Giovanni turned back to the priest, straightened his shoulders and saluted. Yusuf and Rachel joked about the odds facing them as they got into the backseat.

Tom gripped the priest's arm. Michael looked at him with that laser gaze. Tom expected a blessing or a lofty thought. What the priest said was, "This is serious. No more pissing around!"

CHAPTER 40

"Deo gratias," Jean Baptiste whispered. A sunny and gloriously calm passage through the Aegean Sea was almost finished. The benefactor's yacht, the *Thaumaturgos*, knifed through the glistening water. Its ancient Greek name meant "Wonder-Worker," ascribed to Gregory's patron saint, Saint Gregory the Wonder-Worker. It was a wondrous boat — 44 feet long, sporting a colorful main sail, white polymer keel and polished wooden deck. After Istanbul's Ataturk Airport had been closed, the benefactor had granted the knights' wish that they complete the last leg of the journey by sea.

To passing yachts, its owner looked to be a sultan or viscount, his boat registered to the port of the island of Santorini. He was out for a month of leisurely cruising and island-hopping. And sex. The bronzed, sun-kissed females lying on the deck engendered more lust than suspicion; three gorgeous and languorous-limbed creatures, attired in no more than necessary to cover their crotches. They lay motionless under the Aegean sun, as the craft slapped the waves relentlessly, slipping past the last of the Greek isles, northward. Near their perfectly shaped bodies lay bottles of wine, bowls of fruit, books, plastic water bottles, suntan lotion, makeup kits.

"Hey, have any passengers you want to share?" Shaking his head no, Jean Baptiste earnestly played the reluctant pimp, waving off lascivious inquiries from passing yachts. Shouts of "Hot babes!" wafted over from passing boats as the *Thaumaturgos* sailed by. A Greek fisherman whistled and called out to them. "Nymphs! Goddesses! Come aboard, let me board you!" But they just lay there, supinely disdainful of everyone who passed. And who would ask for anything more from three store-window mannequins?

Jean Baptiste knew these were not the usual camouflage ruses the Knight-Precursors would be expected to use — sport fishermen's rotating chairs on a chartered speedboat, or nets and tubs on an aging fishing trawler, or discreet telescopes mounted on a Greek Isles touring craft. Wrong, wrong, wrong. Who would have guessed the pure and pleasureless Knight-Precursors, custodians of eye and imagination equally, would come up with nubile mannequins, stretched out in sensual poses, hard as metal, alluring as sirens. No matter how many passes a search plane might have made in a sea-hunt, no one would have taken this boat seriously. The sirens, yes; the boat, no.

So the ladies were the benefactor's idea. Jean Baptiste was grateful for the testosterone-fueled counterfeit if not for the ersatz female company. Even from the fast-moving maritime security boats plowing past the *Thaumaturgos*, the craft occasioned nothing more than second and third glances. And when a passing boat seemed too curious, one of the knights would be called up by the captain, to saunter on deck in shorts and a t-shirt, lie down near one of the mannequins and stroke its arms and legs carelessly.

A complement of two knights was always on deck as navigator and helmsman. Below, the other two knelt in vigil before the Shroud. The linen had been draped with care on a long table, where it could be unfolded to perhaps two-thirds of its total length of four and one-half meters. Alongside the cloth lay one of the oversized suitcases. In the event of the *Thaumaturgos* being boarded, the two knights could fold and hide the Shroud in the suitcase under a dummy jib sail in 10 seconds. Jean Baptiste was at the helm. A shipboard sound system enabled him to hear the chants and prayers from below. "Deliver us from evil," he recited with those below. The last of the Shroud's stations on the European continent awaited them — Constantinople.

In the narrow strait of the Dardanelles, when the *Thaumaturgos* had slowed to a safe speed, he saw the roads approaching ancient Troy off the starboard side. Jean Baptiste remembered studying Heinrich Schliemann and his digs through the rubble of Troy. The treasures that rot. But down below him was the treasure that never crumbled, linked by some mystical ladder to the treasures that awaited them above. In his mind, the sky was never just the sky. There was more life up there than the poor earth could sustain: angels, saints, the heavenly city, where rust did not destroy nor thieves steal nor age enfeeble. "Lay up for yourselves treasures in heaven," he entreated the men below.

Passage through the Dardenelles was excruciatingly slow and called on all the seafaring skills Jean Baptiste had learned over the past year. The sea lanes were crowded. "Take the mannequins below, change them," he ordered. The brothers hustled the shapely forms below, re-dressed them and brought them topside, transformed into elderly tourists. Lounge chairs were set up on the deck, umbrellas swayed overhead and thick blankets flapped around the old ladies' ankles. The boat was transformed into a floating Elderhostel. Now and then, two capped and sweatered brothers from below would limp topside and engage each other in chess, while the ladies watched impassively.

Only a few more hours and they would be in Istanbul. They prepared for landfall at the edge of Europe. Jean Baptiste could hear the others' chatter after they folded the Shroud and returned it to the suitcase. He spoke into the intercom. "Remember, our destination is the landing near the ruins of the ancient Pharos Lighthouse on the Kennedy *Caddessi* ringing the old city's seaward edge. Nearby lies a park where the successful transfer of the false Shroud will take place." His voice trembled; this endeavor was momentous.

The benefactor had demanded delivery of the Shroud to the site of the old church of Saint Mary Blachernae, but that destination they immediately rejected as too risky, given the traffic on the Golden Horn. They needed an easy escape route across the sea to Asia Minor where a souped-up Land Rover, traditional Muslim garb stashed in its trunk, awaited them on the Asian side of Istanbul. Besides, the Saint Mary site was near the Cathedral of Saint George, the center of the Orthodox Catholic faith in the Fener district of the city; if believers knew their Shroud was nearby, they would kill to get it back. Finally, the knights were in no mood to test providence by sailing into the jaws of the earthquake that might flatten Istanbul at any moment. No. They would touch the southern tip of the city lightly and dash across the Bosphorus to another continent.

"We must be careful. Any injury to this man will unleash a worldwide manhunt for us. So he must not recognize the counterfeit. Maximim, you are as skilled in the art of historical restoration as any museum curator; we depend on you. The benefactor will know he cannot examine the delicate *Sindone* at the transfer without exposing it to the putrid air of Istanbul. Let him believe he can command the earthquake to cease with the Shroud in his hands. By the time he realizes the monumental deception, we will be on our way to Edessa." Cheers erupted from below.

Jean Baptiste heard Maximim say, "I swear that no devout believer will question the cloth."

Jean Baptiste reached for his cell phone.

CHAPTER 41

Gregory Samaras had two objects of veneration in his palatial residence on the Bosphorus. A global positioning system receiver, which recorded the slightest movement of the earth — anywhere, and a replica of *la Sindone*, which was draped over a massive wooden cross in his private chapel. A relic of the true cross was wedged into a tiny chamber at the foot of the cross.

When he was not monitoring the one, he was praying before the other. And this day, as the rumbles from below the earth's surface continued, he shuttled anxiously back and forth between the two adjacent rooms where the objects were kept.

He was a heavy man with a thick chest and salt and pepper hair. On the coolest of days he still perspired and on warm days the wetness of his body flowed freely. He changed shirts five times a day. Each time, he would remove the gold cross and chain he wore around his neck, wash, dress and then kiss the object before replacing it on his chest.

He was tall enough to not have to look up to most of his fellow citizens and business associates, whether Turk or Greek. He felt most challenged when face to face with western Europeans. He did not like dealing with people who towered over him, but these days there was little choice. His stature lay in his empire, not his height.

Gregory, reputed to be a billionaire many times over, had long ago moved his household to a compound in a gilded suburb north of the city, leaving behind the Fener district where a tiny remnant of the ethnic Greek population still lived. He had been just a toddler when his Greek parents had bundled him and his brothers and sisters into a truck outside their small house in Fener to escape the nightmare of looting and burning of Greek homes and shops in the 1950s uproar over Cyprus. But he was no stranger to Fener and gave generously to the church. He and his wife Sophia had seven grown children; yesterday, she and all their children's families had been airlifted to country homes in the interior.

Cosmas, the patriarch of Constantinople, known in the secular world as the patriarch of Fener, had a tight and confidential relationship with him, not only because of Gregory's largesse and standing in the wider community, but also because he was a devout

Christian layman. They would discuss at length the latest research on topics like the motifs and designs in an 11th century fresco of the Mandylion, a cloth believed by some to be the Shroud folded to show only Jesus' face. The fresco was in a church in the Cappadocian valleys midway between Constantinople and Edessa. The fresco, according to the paper Samaras had read, showed the Mandylion wrapped in a soft, woven fabric. It was kept folded this way between public displays of the entire length of the cloth, the first of which was apparently in the year 1025. The patriarch and Samaras would pore over the research far into the night. And when they had finished a final coffee or brandy, Samaras would look squarely at the patriarch and muse. "If only we could look upon its splendor again. Here. In the land of its provenance."

He would bristle when the patriarch, in response, would only sigh, chuckle and give him his blessing, admonishing him, "Its ultimate provenance is Jerusalem. And you live in Istanbul — not Constantinople, Gregory Samaras."

Gregory Samaras. This celebrated figure among the 100,000 or so Orthodox Christians in Istanbul, this respected — even if Greek — leader in the secular world of politics and commerce and philanthropy, was the alpha bull in Turkey's business community. His regular columns in Turkey's largely bullish-on-business newspapers extolled free enterprise without government restrictions. His mantra, Let Turkey feed Europe so the EU will embrace Turkey. He infuriated Yusuf Aktug and the anti-GMO movement by labeling them woolly-headed elitists and latter-day Communists who didn't want to feed the starving world with grain that could withstand all manner of pests and growing conditions.

He had watched with amusement as the skillful Aktug sought international pressure to force Turkish merchants to sign an anti-GMO statement — with no success. Despite Aktug's appeals, the United Nations Food and Agricultural Organization was unwilling to take on Samaras and Turkey's powerful grain merchants.

Today, Gregory Samaras was not thinking about grain futures. He was contemplating the future of Istanbul. He was waiting for a phone call, preparing for a rendezvous near the Bucaleon with a group of men he had met only once.

Eight years it was already, since he had found a Web site devoted to the Holy Shroud that stood out from all others. It was not research. It was prophecy. He was startled by it. He made contact with the site. They wrote back. And when Jean Baptiste LaRoque met him in Turin in 2001, the idea for a partnership was agreed upon. Jean Baptiste's mission was to return the Shroud to Jerusalem. He needed money. He was willing to bring the holy cloth from Turin, agreeing that it would remain in Istanbul for a period of no more than 100 years, to be watched over by a select group of next-generation Knight-Precursors. Samaras agreed to the proposal, inwardly knowing that he could engineer another solution after he had paid off these wild men with more money than they had ever dreamed of. The Shroud must go back to Italy — but only after it saved Istanbul from what he knew was coming, a violent earthquake. Pray God, the sacred cloth would arrive before the main shock broke the city apart.

And so he secretly financed the entire operation of this ragged but determined band, computers, advanced software, pirated instructions on probing and breaking into electronic security systems, vans, jeeps, boats, sailing classes, and a host of other instructions and paraphernalia. And they had actually pulled it off.

The tiny, troubling, foreshocks recorded on his receiver had begun as the knights made their way by car from Paris to the Camargue. Gregory had demanded that they fly rather than sail. And then the tremors multiplied in number. Ataturk Airport was shut down. He outfitted the *Thaumaturgos* for the knights after his private plane landed at Santorini near his marina. And now they were just hours away, when the Holy Shroud would be transferred to his care. He would go to the meeting place by helicopter; only his trusted pilot would accompany him. Not even Patriarch Cosmas knew of the plot. He had given the brothers detailed maps showing the landing's proximity to the foundations of the old Bucaleon palace; they could venerate the Shroud near the palace where it had been kept 800 years ago. And then he would take possession of it. Through Gregory's holy act of public service today, the glory of ancient Constantinople would be restored and the city saved from nature's rage, 800 years after being razed by crusaders' lusts.

These new crusaders — they had no lusts. They had rage. Had their mad quest driven them mad? He had not dealt with insanity since the Cyprus riots — only the routine give-and-take of commerce. Should he take his handgun? No, this was a holy act.

His cell phone rang. The moment had arrived. "I'm coming," he answered curtly and disconnected. He pressed another number. "Bring the helicopter now."

CHAPTER 42

It was a cool, blustery late afternoon in Turin. Not a good day for Bruno and Signor Aho to be out on the autodrome of the Lingotto Fiere. The Finnish captain of industry had demanded they stop there on their way up to the Voice so he could walk around on Fiat's oval test course. "Watch your step, Aho, or this gale will blow your ass right off the roof. Hurry up. *Schnell!*" Bruno dragged Aho back on the elevator and pressed the bubble button. Immediately he sensed his confidence wavering. Why did the Voice overpower him this way? The Voice had a chip *in* his shoulder, a circuit implanted and controlled by some other voice in some other galaxy.

It had not been a good 24 hours for Bruno. The bastard cabby had driven him to the worst slum in Turin yesterday and pushed him out of the cab. No other cab answered his repeated calls; *tutti occupati.* Fending off menacing street people, he hiked the four miles to the bank and his hotel. Then the check presentation to the archbishop had not gone well this morning; poor Aho, the clueless Finnish pasta maker, had become tongue-tied in front of the media, announcing he had a plane to "crash" when he meant "catch." And the priest — ah, a sly, cagey slippery devil; planting a tiny microphone on the back of his collar demanded all Bruno's tactile skills.

"Well?" Even the obtuse Aho shuddered at the croaking sound. It arose from the center of the darkened sphere, where the Voice sat, smoking cigarettes — three in one hand. Bruno had warned Aho that the consortium's director had been stricken with throat cancer and held court in a wheelchair. He watched Aho's eyes enlarge at the sight of this wraith wreathed in the smoke pouring out of his mouth, his voice clotted with coughing spells.

"How did it go? Did you get a plenary indulgence out of the bishop? Are we in the good graces of the church? The story had better be above the fold in the *Herald Tribune*. Keep your edge, Baumgartner. You did a good job planting the mike." A compliment?

A very long drag on the shortest of the three cigarettes buried that compliment deep in the creature's lungs. "Don't fuck it up now," he croaked.

Bruno blinked at the warning's intensity. He felt the need to reassure Aho, who was gasping for breath. "I think the coverage will be excellent. I saw much press." Aho nodded nervously in agreement. "But there is a mystery unfolding here."

"Yes?" A huge puff of smoke escaped from the center of the globe.

"Signor Aho and I stopped for coffee near the priest's residence to write our report. Yusuf Aktug arrived at the bishop's doorstep just as we were leaving to come here. I think the archbishop may be friendly with the foodies — even the Muslims — and that can mean all our positioning as friends of the church means nothing in the face of some pastoral statement on biodiversity and all that bullshit — maybe Yusuf will get him to name names of companies that are threats to biodiversity, and with the *Salone del Gusto* getting some more attention because of this Shroud business, that will do none of us any good, and — " Bruno could never find a period when talking to the Voice " — with the trouble Samaras has had with the protesters in Turkey, Yusuf in particular, this could be bad — also I think there is some woman involved here, I saw her with Yusuf. We could spread some gossip, but…"

The Voice said nothing. All that seemed to come from its mouth were yellow smoke rings floating toward Aho and Bruno, the smoke crawling inside Bruno's eyes. Aho, a nervous twit if Baumgartner had ever seen one, lit up a cigarette too, so the air was thick with acrid fumes. Then the Voice spoke. "I have been listening to our priest's plans for an expedition to Istanbul. Yes, this is a mystery. Perhaps we should contact Mr. Samaras. I don't like to do that. The consortium does not like to involve its members in its business unless absolutely necessary. On second thought, perhaps we need a presence in Istanbul now. Someone to advise him at this juncture. Just a friendly bit of assistance from the consortium at a difficult time for him."

Bruno did not want to go to Istanbul. "There was an earthquake in Istanbul. Did you know that?"

"You mean, those puny shocks they are experiencing? Nothing over three point oh on the scale, I am told. Terrestrial farts, nothing more. Nothing to worry about. We will send Mr. Aho back to the airport and I will have the consortium jet ready for you in the morning." He crumpled up in a wracking cough. Bruno felt a twinge of hope; oh, that the Voice would aspirate and die right then and there! The Voice recovered quickly. "Bruno, we have discovered that Gregory is a frequent visitor to Turin, to pray before this holy cloth. I would not be a bit surprised if he had some connection to its disappearance. If that is the case, be careful. We don't want to get involved in that kind of thing. I wish Gregory were just a womanizer or profligate. That we can deal with. But this religious obsession, this *idée fixe*. We should call on the American Vice President to see how he co-opts the religious right — right? Ha ha ha!"

Bruno sagged. The man is delusionary, manic; the smoke has coalesced into parasitic tendrils nesting against his brain synapses. Bruno turned to Aho and tried to play happy. "Ahoy, Aho. Let's set sail."

A crackle issued from the smoke. More coughing. "Yes, yes. Ahoy, Aho. Very good. Land ahead! Ahoy, mates! This land is our land. This land ain't your land. From California to the...the New Hebrides Islands. This land was made for the almighty Seed — and me!" The Voice crumpled on "me" and fell silent. Aho was about to reach his hand into the smoke to shake hands, but Bruno caught his elbow and backed him out of the glass bubble, hoping to avoid further insults.

"Auf wiedersehen, ahoy, Aho, *gute reise,* Bruno! Ha ha ha!"

The grinding of the elevator gears was accompanied by a steady cough tattoo from the bubble until the wind blew the hacking sounds off the edge of the roof. Out of the Voice's hearing, Aho asked Bruno why he had not let him shake the man's hand. "He has no hands, Aho! Claws! You know that German doctor who plasticizes bodies of dead people and puts them on exhibit? Well, I think he drained this man's fluids and replaced them with a polymer solution and kept him alive when he should be dead." Aho laughed nervously. "I mean it. He is a mid-level android who fancies himself master of the universe."

"I would not want to be his enemy," Aho gasped.

"Come with me, Aho, and you'll meet some. Istanbul."

CHAPTER 43

Late the following morning, out at the Lingotto cabstand, Bruno checked out the cabby's identity before getting in; no more rides with Mezzo Soprano. "Airport. *Schnell.*" Within the hour, the consortium jet was streaking over Turin, bound for Istanbul. Bruno loosened his seat belt as a comely cabin attendant served him coffee and Danish. One of the few perquisites of this dead-end job — flying in style. He was glad to be rid of Aho; one last "ahoy" had sent that simpleton back to Finland last night. Bruno smoldered with murderous urges toward the glass bubble visible atop the Fiat test track rooftop below. If Bruno survived Istanbul, he had better get a Mercedes for this one.

***

On Lake Maggiore, another Istanbul-bound plane was just then lumbering into the sky. Tom knew about this aircraft from its role in fighting forest fires in Minnesota's Boundary Waters Canoe Area. A Canadian-built, propeller-driven air tanker, the Bombardier CL-215, built for low swoops over the water during which its tanks could scoop up 1400 gallons of water.

The pilot announced in broken English that the flight plan was registered for a round trip to Istanbul to assist in putting out fires or whatever needed doing and was authorized by a special mayoral edict that named Tony Mezzo Soprano and Giovanni Palmitessa as special envoys. Dressed in military fatigues and shiny boots, Tony and Giovanni sat ramrod straight on a bench bolted into the wall across from him and Rachel. Tony turned to Giovanni and gave him a thumbs-up.

Rachel and Tom were huddled together. Tom watched a third stowaway up in the cockpit; Yusuf was with the pilot and copilot, the latter giving Yusuf a blow-by-blow radio report of the successive foreshocks. Yusuf would occasionally come back to the group and relay the data. "Some of the poor housing on the western ring of the city has been destroyed, but most people were outside on the streets. Two people dead. We have stayed lucky." And then the bushy smile. "The Shroud we are looking for, maybe it works!"

Rachel squeezed Tom's arm. "I can't believe this is happening. Oh, Tom."

"Sorry about the *Salone*. Did you get someone to cover the booth?"

"No. I left a sign. 'Back soon. Maybe.'" She pushed her head against his. "Tell me, Professor Ueland. Do you think Michael Tucci believes all this stuff about the Shroud of Turin?"

Tom shook his head. "When we talked about magic and religion, all I could do is read between the lines. Publicly, he calls it holy. Privately, he thinks it's a hoax. His old friend Genevieve agrees with him."

"He is one of the most political animals I have ever met, religious or atheist. Or maybe it's something really personal, like — he's got a secret." She joined her hands in a gesture of prayer. "Michael Tucci, you better have really, really good connections with fate, because I don't want to die yet. Really good, Reverend. *Ciao* Torino, *buon giorno* Istanbul!"

The engine noise forced the passengers to shout. After two tense hours, during the passage over the Thracian Sea, Tom jumped up and belted out a tune over the earsplitting drone of the aircraft. "Istanbul was Constantinople. Now it's Istanbul, not Constantinople." Even the peripatetic Yusuf paid attention.

Everyone clapped when he finished. Tom high-fived the others. "I like it," yelled Yusuf. "'Nobody's business but the Turks!' You are cool bananas, Yankee!"

"Don't quit your day job to be a singer," shouted Tony from across the fuselage.

CHAPTER 44

In the archbishop's residence back in Turin, Michael Tucci was listening to Paul and Genevieve De Rosier on the telephone. He felt warm. Absent-mindedly, he took out his handkerchief and dabbed at the back of his neck. He felt a tiny bulge under his collar but ignored it.

Paul was speaking softly. "We don't know where they are. Inspector Toussaint traced the flight plan of a private plane that left the Marseilles airport at about the same time we returned to Paris. Its destination, The island of Santorini in the Aegean. They may now be on a boat to Istanbul. Genevieve and I guess that they will make contact with Samaras at night. Given their situation, I am confident it will be the Bucaleon Palace, near the site of the old Pharos lighthouse, on the outer drive facing the sea. There, the symbolism of reversing the Shroud's path to the west is perfect. It offers a better escape situation to Asia than the Golden Horn. And an easier way to dump Samaras' body in the sea. We are trying to track Samaras' cell phone; apparently he has several. These knights" — he paused, swallowing — "are truly demented, dangerous men."

Genevieve spoke even more softly. "Michael. *Tout va bien?*"

"Hello, Genevieve. *Oui, merci. Et toi?*" He could still feel the awkwardness in his demeanor with her, after all these years. And now they had conversed twice in a week. The even keel of his old-age life was being tossed in middle-age waves. He was sweating. "And you — are you all right, my dear?"

"I'm fine. I trust we will live to see this crisis resolved. But I think about you often these days and pray for you. All my love. And be careful, Michael."

"I will. Pray for all of us here."

"Oh yes. Lovely young Tom; tell him the same. Make sure they understand the plan — the lighthouse." Her voice was spindly but still had the full-throatedness that always amazed him with the sensations it aroused in him.

"Of course. I'm in touch with them. Thank you, Genevieve. We will pray for the safe return of our friends."

"And the Shroud," she added. There she was, forever the feminine censor, wasn't she? He could never have lived with her.

But he had often mused in his last 40 years how difficult it was to live without her — or someone like her.

"And the Shroud," Michael sighed. "I am glad you both were unhurt in the Camargue. I trust we will see each other soon. The Shroud has brought us together again. Happy fault. Crooked ways the Lord has." The words sounded formulaic to him and he regretted saying them.

Paul and Genevieve signed off and Michael set down the receiver. He felt he should kneel and pray, but he went into the study and turned on CNN instead. He rubbed the back of his neck and felt the bulge again; this time he pulled at it and a tiny device tumbled out. He knew right away its provenance — yesterday morning, Bruno Baumgartner, the suave philanthropist, had given him an *abbraccio*. "We feel your pain, your Grace." *Suavitas* indeed.

For the first time since the theft on Monday, Michael Tucci realized there were other spider webs besides his own, perhaps drawing him in unknowingly. He was just one tactician among thousands, all vying to alter the grand strategy of some institution or other. From Eliot's *Murder in the Cathedral* he remembered a fragment, "Only the fool fixed in his folly may think he can turn the wheel on which he turns."

***

Across the mountains, in Paris, Genevieve went to her husband. He smiled and they walked together into the bedroom, sat on the edge of the bed and removed their shoes and lay down close to each other. "Oh, Paul, I know you are very afraid of what is to come. I feel we had no choice but to tell this much of our story. Are you angry we went to Camargue?" Paul kissed her and caressed her hair and then pressed his head against the slight outline of her breasts.

"No. I consider the case closed." She knew it was very much open. They held each other against the darkening sky outside.

***

Across the city of Turin from Michael Tucci's residence, atop the Lingotto Fiere, the Voice had been listening to the archbishop's conversation. He set down the earphones on the wheelchair arm and lit another cigarette. He was smiling. "So, the archbishop is not just another chanting holy old man. I should have known. A mysterious French connection. Some kind of lighthouse rendezvous with Mr. Samaras." He started punching the numbers on his cell phone furiously. "Where the hell are you, Baumgartner? Turn on your cell phone! Dickhead!" He knew Bruno loved to shut him off this way. Passive aggressive shitbrain. "Why the hell can't I hire good help?" he screamed, the echo carrying around the glass globe.

CHAPTER 45

Gregory Samaras checked his GPS receiver one last time as his pilot lowered the helicopter onto the helipad outside his residence. The LED tracer jumped intermittently, monitoring the earth's pressure points. On the wall were a series of maps full of arrows and flash points detailing past earthquakes. One map depicted stress points along the 1,500-kilometer North Anatolian Fault and in cartoon fashion showed it snaking between the Anatolian and Eurasian tectonic plates. Far down at the southern edge of the map, arrows captured the Arabian and African plates pushing northward against the Anatolian plate, which then, domino-fashion, rammed against the Eurasian plate, after which it ground west toward Greece along the fault. The 1999 Izmit earthquake map recorded the grim statistics of its last thrust; 20,000 lives lost, some in Istanbul, 100,000 people homeless. A graphic illustration of how the progression model worked clearly pointed to the next epicenter — within a few decades, The Sea of Marmara, near Istanbul.

He had hung nearby, as if to quiet anxiety, a gorgeous photograph of Hagia Sophia, still standing, still defying the unsteady earth, 1,500 years after being built by the Byzantine emperor Justinian. Hagia Sophia was not the symbol of endurance that Gregory Samaras wanted, however. It must be the Shroud itself, which had survived the thermonuclear blast of the resurrection and recorded the outline of the Lord's body upon it for all to see. Against the Shroud, no power could prevail.

Within minutes, aloft, looking down from the helicopter, he observed the city at sunset, a smoking welter of contrasting chaos and order. The ancient solidity of the domes and the mosques beneath them, the steady graceful needle-like thrust of the minarets into the faintly sulphurous air, the powerful rolling hills all suddenly fragile. Small fires burned here and there in the darkening landscape, where the earth had snapped electric and gas lines and cracked storm pipes; sirens whined, the gears of fire trucks meshing frantically. He gazed at the streets, which had been converted to vast pedestrian zones as residents camped out near all their earthly possessions. Observant Muslims were breaking their fast after a day of enduring hunger pangs and foreshocks; he wished he could inhale the scent of freshly baked *pide* bread below, but knew it was mixed with the smell of burning wood-frame homes.

He saw other Istanbullus leaving the city in a slow stream of cars, trucks, motorcycles and bicycles. He felt a twinge of kinship, knowing that they all had their radios tuned to the same government bulletins he was listening to, prescribing evacuation routes and proclaiming shoot-to-kill orders against rioters and looters. Boats clogged the Golden Horn and the Bosphorus, streaming out in whatever direction they believed safety lay.

Above him, other helicopters circled the crowded skies over Istanbul, jockeying for the perfect angle and position to see the big "shake and bake moment," a witticism favored by the young glitterati who had been living there before deserting the city in their Lear Jets. The media and film company helicopters were shooting live footage of the scene so the whole world could have the real-time experience of an earthquake; those below could watch themselves on TV, ants riding the rolling folds of the earth.

***

On the sea to the south, the *Thaumaturgos*, a solitary craft heading against the exodus, was now encountering these scattered flotillas. Sailors waved this wrong-way vessel, with its cargo of the elderly and the infirm, to turn around. Jean Baptiste kept the wheel steady as the great city came into view. In the distance he saw the stream of cars heading west on the Kennedy *Cadessi,* the main drive facing the sea. He checked his maps. The three other knights stood awestruck at the sight of the ancient city rumbling atop the unstable earth.

CHAPTER 46

Flying low above the sea, the tanker craft thrummed along, the faces of its passengers glued to the small windows. Yusuf reported that the pilot had radioed Ataturk International Airport for instructions on landing on the sea. Dusk rose out of the earth and settled over the smoke-filled city.

Tom heard Yusuf tell the pilot to request permission to land near the *cadde* and to taxi to a landing tucked alongside the road not far from the Bosphorus. Controllers told him it was too dangerous, then relented — the plane's water cannons were desperately needed; fragile houses were burning in narrow, abandoned streets where big fire rigs could not go.

Tom held Rachel's hands tightly as he watched the pilot bring the plane into a steep dive over the Sea of Marmara. "My god, the boats," he said. "Where is he going to put this thing? They better get the hell out of our way." The tanker threaded a path among fleeing boats to land on a clear strip of choppy water. The copilot taxied the plane as close to the landing as he could.

The pilot opened the aircraft's hatch, blew up a rubber raft and tossed it into the churning waters. "Sure you want to go out there?" he asked Tom as they all crowded toward the door — Giovanni right behind Tony.

"We're going to hook up with my old comrade, Adnan," Giovanni announced. The pilot scratched his head and nodded. "Adnan and I attended a firefighting training school back in nineteen seventy-two. He's meeting us with a rig that can go anywhere. Pretty soon, those big fire trucks will be tied up in knots." The pilot was staring at the firefighter's pin on Giovanni's chest. The old man thanked him with a fierce handshake and scrambled out the door and into the raft with Tony's help.

"Don't wait up for us. We've made arrangements to stay with friends," Giovanni boasted to the pilot. He and Tony yanked Tom, Rachel and Yusuf one by one onto the bobbing raft. Tony took the tiller.

Tom watched the plane pull away from the rocky shoreline and back out into the sea. It splashed along, slowly gaining speed, churning up spume, barely lifting out of the sea before the mast of a lone sailboat came into sight sailing straight for it. The tanker's fuselage cleared the boat's mast by inches.

The raft bounced corklike toward the landing and swept past a concrete breakwall, almost crashing into the rocks. Tony yanked the tiller and spun the raft to port, safe behind the breakwall. For one instant, the world felt calm. Giovanni crossed himself and grinned. Tom twisted around and saw a vintage fire truck swerving into the entrance from the Kennedy *Cadessi*. It rolled to stop in front of them, the driver waving. Giovanni yelled, "Adnan, is it you?"

And Adnan answered in broken Italian, "Giovanni, you old sinner! God keep you. *Andiamo, amico!* Who's the kid? Your son?"

"No, I would not acknowledge this schemer as my son. He's my brother Vittorio's. Meet Antonio Palmitessa, although he calls himself Tony Mezzo Soprano, after some anti-Italian TV show in America." Tony started pushing rope and axes into the back of the mini-rig while Giovanni was slapping Adnan on the shoulders and positioning himself as hose-master.

"Any friend of my uncle Giovanni is a friend of mine, no matter how unsavory his past," shot back Tony as he jumped on the running board. "And these are my friends Tom, Rachel and Yusuf."

Adnan bowed to Rachel, shook Tom's hands and immediately addressed Yusuf in Turkish. Yusuf was shaking his head. "Watch!" Adnan bellowed. He stepped on a gas pedal that was as big as a clown's shoe. The rig coughed, bounced forward and coughed again.

"Shit!" Adnan braked and let the engine idle. "It needs to warm up. We should make a plan. Most lanes on the *cadde* go west. We are going to need this gadget here." Adnan turned on a switch, and the old rotating light on the cab roof squeaked and started turning fitfully. In the intermittent beam of soft light, Tom saw Giovanni's face glow, the flickering image of a happy old firefighter, glad to be back.

"Tell me about this thing!" Giovanni slapped the rig's metal surface. He was standing on the running board next to Adnan; Tony was hanging off the other side.

"Vintage steam pumper from the nineteen thirties," roared Adnan. "I've nursed it along for forty years." The sound of steam hissing in the chamber echoed his claim; this old engine worked.

"Where we going, old friend?" asked Adnan as he shielded his eyes against the car lights on the drive. "Every way — the wrong way. You and I, Giovanni, it's OK if we die in this, but your friends, all young."

Tom watched in disbelief. This ancient rig and these two old men were going to thwart a dangerous plot in the middle of an earthquake? He felt sickeningly puny, unprepared. He turned to Rachel and Yusuf. "You believe in God?"

Rachel held her breath. "I believe in miracles."

"*Inshallah,* we will have one god perform one miracle. It just takes one," said Yusuf.

"What comes first, the Pharos lighthouse or Hagia Sofia?" Tom asked, crumpling his map of the city. Yusuf stepped in front of the shaking, spitting old rig and pointed.

"The old lighthouse has nothing left but a stone base. It's a hundred meters west. See it? Near the stones of the old Bucaleon Palace on the *cadde*. Up the hill is Hagia Sofia. You can almost see it from here." Yusuf pointed across the *cadde*.

Tom saw nothing but puffs and streamers of acrid smoke. He retrieved a pair of binoculars out of one of the packs and looked back along the shore to the west, then out to sea. "The knights will put in at the first place they can land." Then he froze; coming into view was a sleek 40-foot sailing vessel — he remembered the plane almost clipping off the top of a mast minutes before. He couldn't read the ship's name, but he could see a single figure standing on the deck. And he could see the gleaming barrel of what looked like an AK-47 slung over the figure's shoulder. Tom watched the man make the sign of the cross with his right hand, the left hand holding the rifle. Now a little more than 200 meters away, the boat was slowly approaching the very landing on which they stood.

"We're in luck. Cut the light, Adnan! Quick!" Tom yelled. Adnan hit the switch. "Tony, get Adnan to move this rig over there to the park — we've got to get out of sight fast." Adnan put the engine in gear, let out the clutch and the truck jerked until it settled into a slow roll across a scrubby park to a parking lot shrouded in the fading light. A tall light standard near the landing had been darkened by a power loss.

Tom watched the boat maneuver its way around the breakwall to the slips; one of the sailors tossed a rope around a mooring post. He could make out three figures scrambling up the concrete apron to the outer drive; one of the men was carrying a large suitcase. The fourth person with the assault rifle must have stayed on board. The three were dressed in long robes.

"They're here." He handed the binoculars to Yusuf.

"Why putting ashore in this place?" Yusuf asked. "They've got to have a slip at a real marina nearby; why here — why those Imam robes?" Tom and Rachel looked at each other. The Knight-Precursors had landed.

The three knights charged boldly across the *cadde*. "I think someone should go watch that boat," Yusuf said. "Those three — why go across the highway; why? There are only ruins there." He handed the binoculars back to Tom.

"I think they're looking for what's left of the Bucaleon Palace," answered Tom. "This is the place. Tony, you're the street guy — go and keep an eye on the boat. Take something to distract the guy. Anything. Lights. Noise. Whatever."

Tony jumped to the pavement. Giovanni glared at his nephew. "Where are you going? I know my way around a fire hose but this is a foreign city and we are on a mission to bring back *la Sindone*. Get back in here. We have holy work to do."

Tony reached up and guided Adnan down from his seat. "Adnan, you have any kind of a portable spotlight back here? And a portable megaphone?"

Adnan probed in a pile of hoses and hose reels, buckets, extinguishers, spare nozzles. He produced the biggest lamp and battery console Tom had ever seen. "Here's where you turn it on." Adnan touched a switch.

"Not yet!" screamed Tom. Adnan handed it to Tony.

"Megaphone? Don't know about that. How about this thing?" He handed Tony a three-feet-long funnel made out of stiff cardboard and stamped with the insignia of the Istanbul Fire Department, vintage perhaps 1938.

Tony jumped on the running board. "*Zio* Giovanni, you take care of these three." He gripped Giovanni's shoulders and held his face close. "I know what I'm doing. I live on the street. I know trouble when I see it. Mind your fire hose. And no funny stuff."

Giovanni fumed at Tony. "This is no time to be a comedian. This moment is no different than the great fire in the church; I am a firefighter, my mission is to save *la Sindone*."

Tom saw in Giovanni's face the old look that doubted youth's wisdom, the confidence that God above would guide the rig to the Shroud. He glanced at Rachel — she was picking up the megaphone.

"I'm going with Tony," Rachel shouted. "Macho man may get us all killed." Before Tom could object, she and Tony were off, running toward the boat. Tom followed them with the binoculars as they crawled along the rocks toward the end of the landing where the boat lay. They were within 20 yards of the boat when he saw Rachel suddenly push Tony to the ground. Tom could now see the three knights coming down to the landing. Cautiously inching their way down to the boat, they handed the suitcase to the guard on deck, who gave them an identical one. The knights retraced their steps — but turned toward Rachel and Tony. Tom gasped. And then the knights turned away from them and marched into the park — directly at him. And now it was very dark.

"What's that noise?" asked Yusuf. They looked up.

A helicopter circled over the parking lot. Very, very slowly, the pilot lowered the chopper down to the seaside park adjoining the parking lot where the fire rig trembled in the darkness. Tom spoke over the swish of the blades. "The rendezvous is under way."

CHAPTER 47

Some three kilometers away, a black Ford Otosan sedan bearing the Orthodox Patriarch, Cosmas, crawled along streets toward the Kennedy *Cadessi..* Inside, Cosmas fretted. Had Gregory and the Knight-Precursors already met? The sensation of being too late bristled like an exposed nerve inside him. His driver turned onto the *cadde* at Seraglio Point and finessed his way through the traffic.

***

Further west, At Ataturk International Airport, emergency aircraft touched down every two minutes, loaded with medicine, food and personnel. Emerging from one of the planes, Bruno Baumgartner flashed a press pass in front of two Red Crescent workers. "I'm the advance for a boatload of wheat and other staples from Athens, from colleagues of Gregory Samaras. I need to get to some lighthouse — near a park by the sea." The workers got the attention of a driver; he looked at Bruno and nodded. Within minutes the Red Crescent van was on the Kennedy *Cadessi.*

"The fucking Voice," Bruno kept muttering. The driver sped silently down the one open eastbound lane toward the Sultanahmet district, red light flashing in silence.

***

In Turin, after celebrating a solemn high mass in the cathedral, Michael Tucci agreed to make an appearance at the *Salone del Gusto* on the urging of a number of Piedmontese Catholics active in a food movement sponsored by the Banco Alimentare. The organization distributed food to the poor — free food contributed directly from small farms in the region.

Applause from dignitaries and schoolchildren rang in his ears as Michael Tucci blessed the crowd. He knew he didn't have time to do the Episcopal flip and sip routine for the cheering bambinos, but he didn't want to leave. And the two priestly secretaries, like children in a candy store, looked hungry. No sooner did the "amen" ring out from the crowd than Father Raffaelo's thick hands were deep into samples of pecorino cheese from Castel de Monte. Father Roberto was sampling a basmati rice dish from the foothills of the Himalayas. A solidly built matron brought Michael a dish made from the beans of Sorana; he ate while the cameras flashed. It was dizzying, this place; row after row of samples or product displays of meats, fruits, vegetables, cereals, pasta, bread, fish, mollusks and shellfish, sweets, chocolate, honey, jam, preserves, liqueurs, cheeses and dairy, spices, aromatic herbs, vinegar, teas, infusions.

Then he saw the booth offering olives from Turkey, with the handwritten sign saying "Back soon. Maybe." He started herding the two priests out the door toward the limo. It was at that moment he knew he had to get out of Turin, and soon, to a place of retreat and simple food. Next week, God willing. He looked at his two priests — both from peasant backgrounds, bless them — their faces happy, their mouths wet with the earth's bounty. Yes, Raffaelo and Roberto needed a vacation from him. He tugged on their black shirts and pushed them away from the last stall, still licking their fingers.

As Michael entered the car, he looked up to the roof of the adjacent building. He saw an evanescent figure sitting at the bubble wall, peering down in the darkness from six stories high, wrapped in smoke. He shuddered and sat at the edge of the seat, close to the window. From the front seat, the fathers burped contentedly. Father Raffaelo sped the car onto Via Nizza and Father Roberto waved down drivers, thrusting a crucifix in the face of the oncoming traffic. Michael pressed numbers on the cell phone, still looking at the figure on top of the roof. Somehow, the wispy little man up there personified the forces over which he, the man of God, had no control. "Hello. Cosmas. Hello, can you hear me? Are you there yet? Do you have police with you? No? Please — be careful."

CHAPTER 48

Gregory Samaras stepped down from the helicopter and knelt on the ground. The propeller blades revolving slowly above him created a halo cloud over the scene. "Eight hundred years have gone by and now, at the moment of need, we have seen the return of the Lord's Shroud. Alleluia, alleluia!" he shouted to the world rushing by. He leaned over and kissed tufts of grass. When he stood, he saw three skeletal men, emaciated from their discipline, he was sure, walking toward him unhindered along the *cadde,* like Jesus walking on water. He recognized Jean Baptiste. The bearded man he had met in Turin, with whom he had signed a contract for five million Euros, a man who frightened him with his intense and nonblinking gaze — the man was here, carrying a gleaming suitcase that reflected the riot of lights off the Kennedy *Cadessi.* Above them, the city was silhouetted by a halo of firelight.

Gregory bowed slightly to the three and spoke in French. *"Bienvenue à* Istanbul. We greet you and your precious weight." Close up, the French knights seemed grim, withdrawn, stolid — were they going to see things his way?

Jean Baptiste answered him solemnly. *"Merci, mon ami.* We carried *la Sindone* to the palace foundations where we saluted the site with incense and holy water and then recited the words of the ancient witness, 'In this chapel Christ rises again and *la Sindone* with the burial lines is the clear proof...still smelling fragrant of myrrh, defying decay, because it wrapped the mysterious, naked dead body after the passion.' Thank you for sharing your wealth of knowledge of the area with us."

Jean Baptiste came closer — inches away. "Behold, *la Sindone.* We are most privileged to have been part of your grand plan to bring *la Sindone* home. We, the Knight-Precursors of Christ the King, recognize you as a brother in our quest." The two others bowed to Gregory. Jean Baptiste held the suitcase in his arms. "Please open the vessel of the Lord's Shroud and see what God has brought to fruition."

His hands trembling, Gregory opened the latches on the suitcase. He recoiled when he touched the hard, harsh plastic container — so crass, so modern, so unlike the richly brocaded fabric that held *la*

Sindone in this very city a thousand years ago. Jean Baptiste removed a cloth covering the folded linen. Gregory, reverently, softly, caressed the linen.

"It cannot be removed. I'm sure you understand, Monsieur Samaras. The atmospheric conditions would…"

"I understand," Gregory grumbled. He was determined to examine the restoration work that had been done two years before, when a new backing cloth of raw linen had been sewn to the ancient linen, replacing the previous lining and the triangular patches sewn by the Poor Clare nuns of Chambéry in 1534.

In the dim blur of headlights from the *cadde,* he reached in and felt for the seam between the Shroud and the linen. Jean Baptiste yanked his hand away. "Do not be like the doubting apostle Thomas! Believe without touching *la Sindone*, Monsieur Samaras. Have you no faith?" Jean Baptiste was sweating, his motions jerky, his mouth locked in a tense grin. Gregory knew that the knight considered him only a devout Christian, one whose devotion to *la Sindone* was unquestionable. The knight did not know him as a wily, take-no-prisoners dealer in grain commodities, a man who would thrust his hands into a sack of grain and let the fine kernels run between his fingers before buying it. Gregory took nothing in business on faith. And this transaction was business.

What he felt had been all of one piece. There was no backing cloth, no seam — but he had only felt in one spot. This might be nothing more than an imperfection — but then it could be a copy. Gregory said nothing, betrayed no doubt. Jean Baptiste shone a flashlight on the faint outline of the holy face.

"It has withstood two thousand years and is still resilient. Our savior's Shroud seems happy to be here. Did not Jesus tell us there would be earthquakes as sinful earth foresees the last cataclysm? The Shroud is at home among earthquakes; the veil of the temple was rent in two at his death. And now the Holy Shroud is coming home, to Christ's home, and God is saying to us, 'Now the conditions for my return are being fulfilled — hurricanes, floods, natural disasters. The end is coming!'"

Gregory winced at the remark, "coming home." Where is *"Chez Christi"*? And he did not like being preached to about the last days. *La Sindone* was here to forestall the last days. Jean Baptiste laid the case on a blanket spread before Gregory by one of the knights. Gregory prostrated himself before it.

CHAPTER 49

Here was a scene for a modern Brueghel — in the background, the cacophony of honking horns, the burning smell of exhaust systems, the metallic sheen of cars crawling slowly by the park, their occupants' heads twisting grotesquely out the windows — men, women, children, the elderly, their faces streaked with sweat and dirt, ignorant of the unfolding drama. In the foreground — a simple, somewhat shabby park, three ascetic-looking men standing over a shiny suitcase; a fourth caught up in awe, face to the ground, kneeling in homage to the hard case's soft treasure; the pilot standing by the helicopter, its landing lights casting an otherworldly glow. Minutes passed, allowing the artist to capture the image before painting it. The artist was Giovanni Palmitessa.

On the ancient fire rig, Giovanni studied the scene as carefully as he had studied the florid paintings over the side altars in the Turin cathedral. Aching, sleepless, he was not distracted by the flood of fugitive automobiles in the background. He saw only the foreground scene. He had seen that shiny suitcase before. He had seen two of the three ascetics — the thieves. One of them lurked in the background, who just now extracted a pistol from under his shirt. And he had seen Gregory Samaras many, many times. He witnessed them all as figures in a painting. He held the power in his hands to scrub their images off the canvas before him. He knew that the jet stream of water from the ancient pumper had a couple of powerful spurts left in it. It would hurt and it would knock them down. And it could destroy *la Sindone*. Soak it, tear it, stain it, riddle it with holes. Too late for *pentimento*.

Santa Madonna, he was facing an old dilemma once again. If his colleague who rescued *la Sindone* in 1997 had collapsed in the midst of the flames, would he, Giovanni, have carried to safety his colleague — or the heavy container of *la Sindone*? To save Samaras' life, would he unleash a force that might damage *la Sindone*? Forever?

At his side, Yusuf blinked and whispered to Tom. "This is the grain merchant I have never seen." The three of them listened in the darkness, straining to hear the conversation over the pumper's steady hiss.

***

Jean Baptiste looked at his watch and spoke to the brothers. "It is time for us to go. Help Mr. Samaras to his feet."

Gregory rose without help. Jean Baptiste closed the cover and handed the suitcase to him. Gregory, his face reddening, kept his hands at his side.

"I take this matter most seriously, Jean Baptiste. You swear this is the true *Sindone?*"

"I swear; this is the true *Sindone.*" Jean Baptiste's body language, his abrupt and concealing mannerisms, the uneven vocal inflection of the double-dealer, convinced Gregory that it was a fraud. "After all we have sacrificed to bring it here, you question us? I'm sorry; we must leave you now. We will abide by the agreement to let you keep *la Sindone* for the prescribed period of time. And then it must be returned to Turin, as you have agreed. You are to keep it in a secured place of honor. And I will appreciate the balance of the payment."

"Something does not make sense..."

Jean Baptiste interrupted. "Sense? Monsieur Samaras, God's ways are not our ways. *La Sindone* is your responsibility now, to the church, to Christ the Lord. We have other precious relics to take to Jerusalem. As I say, I must have the money."

"Jean Baptiste, I had no reason to distrust you, but now..."

"We are the ones preparing the way of the Lord! Quickly, the payment. We must leave." Jean Baptiste's face was contorted now. "What makes you an unbeliever, like Thomas?" He glared at Gregory and shook unsteadily.

***

A kilometer east of the park, the black Ford sedan edged around a sharp curve where the road turned westward along the sea. "Almost there!" the driver shouted to the patriarch who was leaning forward from the backseat.

***

"The payment!" Jean Baptiste thrust his hand, palm up, at

Gregory.

Gregory Samaras picked up the case and pushed it into Jean Baptiste's chest. "Here, you bastard, take this worthless forgery along with you!" Jean Baptiste let it fall to the ground. The cover opened and a corner of the Shroud protruded out of the case. The knight with the handgun pointed it at the Greek.

"You will stay here. You will not leave this place until our boat has departed. You and your pilot are dead men if you make one false step." Jean Baptiste's words parted the thick pungent air like a sword.

"Jean Baptiste LaRoque, you are dead in spirit! This is not the true *Sindone*. You have betrayed me, you lying bastard! This is worthless! You have the true Shroud in your boat. You will go to Jerusalem with it. I should not have been so gullible to believe you. I warn you…"

"Your riches take you to hell!" Jean Baptiste screamed. The helicopter pilot lunged at him, but one of the brothers cracked him over the head with the butt of his pistol and the stunned man fell hard. The brother approached and held his gun close to Gregory's temple; Gregory took an envelope from his coat pocket and handed it to the bearded man. At that moment, he saw the patriarch's car.

The black Ford sedan swerved off the *cadde* and into the parking lot, its headlights illuminating the entire scene. "Hold whoever they are at gunpoint," Jean Baptiste ordered. A rifle was lying wrapped in a blanket in the grass nearby. The two brothers aimed, pointing rifle and pistol at the car. "Make sure the keys stay in the ignition!" The occupants of the car remained inside.

And then the ground shook furiously. Gregory looked up. He saw ancient boulders on the shoreline trembling. "The main shock is upon us. Pray god you have the true Shroud nearby. May it protect us all!" All was still for a moment. Then he saw it.

A spurting jet of water rose from the dark edge of the parking lot, arced across the pavement onto the grass and descended with full force into Jean Baptiste LaRoque. He was pushed back and knocked sprawling. Before the two brothers could shoot into the darkness, the mysterious source unleashed a volley at them; both went down hard; the pistol fell from the brother's hand into a puddle. The open suitcase, its contents exposed, lay on the ground in front of him, soaking up water.

Only he, Gregory, was still standing. He saw an ancient fire rig

160

creep slowly toward the park, the water jet still blasting the flailing knights, pushing them around like waterlogged sacks of wheat. A wet, bewildered Gregory Samaras cried out, "What if it is really....Oh God above, let this be a forgery! Oh, my God, let it be. I acted too imprudently." He knelt before the suitcase.

***

Tom and Yusuf sprinted toward the kneeling figure. As the rig ground forward into the park, the water hose snagged on a bench; the jet stream stopped momentarily. Giovanni slapped at the hose but in that split second one of the knights catapulted to his feet and knocked the sedan's two occupants to the ground with the rifle. He jumped behind the wheel. The engine started. Some 20 feet away, the head knight grabbed the soggy envelope and ran toward the car.

Tom and Yusuf were close enough to tackle him, but a shot rang out from the car and they fell to the ground. The bullet caromed off the rig, which Adnan was maneuvering seaward toward the landing. The bearded knight backed toward the car, his nostrils flaring, his muscles taut, a wild fury in his water-splattered face. That face — familiar. Long hair parted in the middle, falling to his shoulders. The bristling beard — where had Tom seen it? Of course — the image of the dead man of the Shroud. The figure in the farmhouse helicopter.

He watched the two knights barely able to shut the doors before the driver spun the car around toward the landing — only to confront the ancient fire rig, now positioned between the *Thaumaturgos* and the car. From the Ford's window a rifle poked out. Giovanni aimed again; a spurt of water through the open window doused the weapon. There was no going forward; the car lurched around and headed for the *cadde* — eastward, past the *Thaumaturgos* and its wondrous treasure.

CHAPTER 50

The *Thaumaturgos'* lone guard blinked against the ghostly panorama of an eerily red night sky. What an acrid stench of smoke and burning timbers! What a ghastly, fearful energy propelling a stream of cars, trucks and motorcycles out of the city! Maximim could not stop trembling. He was alone, armed with a weapon that seemed like a toy musket in the face of so much pandemonium, the earth shaking, the waves of the sea smashing over the breakwall and spraying him with an icy cold fury. Perhaps the Lord Jesus was coming to Istanbul now — not Jerusalem — here, this last night on earth. Had His Holy Shroud brought the Lord of Life here?

He tried to keep his balance, the rifle cutting into his shoulder blade. What was happening up there in the park? How would they ever make it across the sea to Asia and their destination if they could not even get out of Istanbul? He placed the gun on his other shoulder and started pacing. The mannequin elders scattered around the deck stared mournfully at him, making him jumpy.

At least Brother Jean Baptiste will be happy when he returns. Who else but he, Maximim, had fabricated the copy with perfection, had matched the original. There was no need to replicate the Holland cloth lining; the Shroud would never leave the suitcase. He waited to receive his brothers' accolades. And perhaps that of Jesus himself. This city looked like the end of the world. He needed to pee.

***

Crawling, slipping on the frothy rocks, Tony and Rachel closed in on the *Thaumaturgos*. It was easy to imagine themselves slipping, being washed away by the waves. They reached the landing and crawled along the breakwall, past the yacht and its transfixed occupant, until they reached the fingertip of the breakwall.

They could almost touch the restlessly heaving bow. The guard was looking off to the north, at the city and west, toward the park. They looked at each other. *"Subito,"* Tony whispered. Rachel flicked the switch and the spotlight caught the guard's back in its blinding beam. He wheeled and brought the gun up. "Who's there? Jean Baptiste?"

In his battered French, scooping down for as basso an effect as he could manage, Tony Mezzo Soprano raised the megaphone to his mouth and replied. "It is I, Michael. An angel of the Lord. *C'est moi, Saint Michel. Un ange du Seigneur.*" The sentinel hesitated.

Very, very slowly, the guard lowered the gun from his shoulder. He knelt down and crossed himself. God in heaven, Rachel thought. Could it be working?

"You, an angel of Jesus? I don't believe it!" Shaking, caught in the blazing light, the guard raised his rifle toward the unseen figure. Rachel knew that he could see only the blackness of sea and sky beyond them; he'd probably shoot wild.

"It is I." Tony's street vernacular was no vehicle for a divine message. "I am Michael, the warrior angel. Put that gun down!"

"It's only a Röhm TM TCR. Forgive me, divine one. I know Jesus' followers are not killers — only rubber bullets."

"Nevertheless, throw it into the sea." Tony's basso slid deeper on "sea." The guard kicked the rifle over the side of the boat. It clattered onto a slip and disappeared under the waves.

"Where is the Lord Jesus' Shroud?"

The guard staggered to his feet. He pointed first to the park. "Up there. No, down below. I have his true Shroud here. That one is a fake. Shall I bring it to you now? But we expected to leave it for Him in Jerusalem."

"Do not question the ways of the Lord! The Lord comes where and when he likes."

The guard appeared to be choking out his words. "Did it — did we — cause his return tonight?" Tony flinched and looked to Rachel for the answer. She flashed back on Tom's words. "These knights are a Christian cargo cult." She nodded yes.

"Yes. The Shroud! Hand it over!"

"Angel of the Lord, give me a sign that you are real. Let me see your wingspan…"

Tony squeezed Rachel's wrist. "Stall him; promise it after he gets the Shroud," she whispered.

"You will see it when I rise above you. The Lord's Shroud! Now!"

The man squinted into the light. Rachel feared this most — being stonewalled. A test of wills, wasting precious seconds. The guard heard his cell phone ringing. "It's Jean Baptiste. I must answer it." He backed unsteadily away from the source of the light and reached for the phone.

"Don't answer it! I, Michael, command you as the angel of your Lord and God!"

The guard gripped the phone, unsure. "Show me a sign."

***

The black Otosan sedan bore down at over 100 KPH on the eastbound *cadde* in the direction of the Galata Bridge. Jean Baptiste glared into the phalanx of headlights and punched the buttons on the cell phone. "Maximim! Answer the phone! Meet us across the bridge at the marina. Start the engine, get the boat out of there immediately!"

The sedan sped along the *cadde,* narrowly avoiding a batch of motor scooters trying to slip past stalled cars. "There's no answer. Nothing," Jean Baptiste screamed. "For the love of our dying savior, Maximim, answer the phone!" A newly built lighthouse loomed ahead. Beyond that, they could see Seraglio Point at the tip of the city.

"Look out!" shouted Jean Baptiste.

Ahead, a Red Crescent van was making a U-turn into their lane and accelerating directly toward their car. Jean Baptiste grabbed the wheel from Trophimus; the car swerved closer to the railing. There was nowhere to go. The brother braked. At that moment, the earth below Istanbul pushed up a final heave. The *cadde* trembled. The sedan skidded and fishtailed off the shoulder and burst over the guardrail. It brushed a tall light pole, smashing a hole in the right front headlight assembly and tearing off the panel.

Jean Baptiste held up his hand to the windshield; a huge boulder lay straight ahead, poised like a sentry at the top of a rocky escarpment wedged between the roadway and the sea. Jean Baptiste heard it punch the chassis. He smelled gas; the gas tank had ruptured.

The car exploded as it sailed into the sky and began a long flaming arc down into the waters where east and west met. The bodies of the three brother knights smashed against one other, their fists pounding against the car doors. "Save us, Lord; we perish!" screamed Trophimus.

Jean Baptiste whispered as he watched the dark water open up to swallow them, "I am sorry. I loved you three. *Pardonnez-moi.* "

***

"Look there!" Gripping a railing, the guard dropped the phone and pointed past the angelic visitor. "A sign!"

"I know that trick. Would you shoot an angel in the back?" Tony shouted. Rachel cringed at his question and spun around and saw it, a fireball disappearing into the sea.

"Merci! Your wings are of fire! I see and now I believe!" The guard backed on his knees toward the hold. Tony finally looked around. The angel of the Lord was shaking mightily.

Tony arched his back, took a deep breath and roared into the megaphone. "Yes, your sign, sir knight! Now go below and bring me His true Shroud, lay it on the deck and then return immediately below and get on your knees and pray until I return." Hands crossed over his chest, the guard rose and disappeared down the ladder. He returned within seconds, clutching the suitcase. He knelt on the deck, laid it down carefully, both hands still gripping it.

"Shall I open it for you, angel of the Lord?" The guard blessed himself and squinted into the light.

"No! I am not an invalid. Remain below until I return. What is your name?" Tony was pushing it too far — they were so close. Rachel squeezed his arm.

"Yes. Of course. I will. I am Maximim. Forgive my unbelief."

Tony whispered into the funnel. "I will forgive, Maximim. This time." When the man had ducked down the hold, Tony and Rachel stood and inched across the breakwall, expecting the fool to come to his senses at any moment, pop out of the hold and blast them to kingdom come with a real AK-47 stashed below — but nothing, nothing but the sound of the man chanting in Provençal. Tony swung his legs over the deck rail. He tiptoed to the suitcase.

"My God, who are those old ladies?" Rachel whispered, her eyes darting from one mannequin to the next. "Are they dead?"

Tony poked one of the mannequins. It flopped. "Store models." He picked up the suitcase, handed it to Rachel on the breakwall and jumped over the railing. She extinguished the light. They crossed the pavement and started walking toward the helicopter.

CHAPTER 51

In the park, Tom and Yusuf stared at the widening pool of burning fuel and its hissing, bubbling vortex where the car had disappeared. Tom managed a whisper. "God in heaven. I pray it is them."

Yusuf spoke softly. "Our Byzantine ancestors used to protect our city by hurling a firebomb — 'Greek fire,' it was called — over the great seawall that once stood behind us. The bomb burned on the surface of the sea and ignited the wooden hulls of the enemy ships. The enemy couldn't jump overboard when the ships had been hit because they would have burned to death in the sea. And so they burned to death in their boats. My friend, this time, Greek fire has conquered the French knights."

Tom looked down and saw the pistol still lying in the puddle of water. He picked it up, emptied the chamber and fingered the bullets. He looked at Yusuf. "Rubber bullets."

They walked back to where Gregory still knelt. Adnan had slowly, respectfully moved the sputtering rig close to Gregory and the patriarch and his driver. Gregory was bowing continuously before the Shroud, heavy tears falling on the linen. Looking past him, Tom saw the edge of a piercing white beam of light. "I'm going to the landing," Tom yelled. "Take care of Samaras." Yusuf blinked.

"Tony! Rachel! Are you..." Tom stopped and stared at the approaching figures. Rachel was carrying a sleek plastic case.

"Be still, unbeliever!" Tony brandished the speaking-trumpet. "What the hell was the fireball all about? Where's..."

Before Tom could answer, the Red Crescent van rolled into the parking lot. Bruno emerged from the backseat, bellowing in a coughing fit. Tom could see his color turn ghastly white when he recognized Yusuf. Tom ran toward them, but stopped to listen to the exchange.

Yusuf screamed, "What the hell are you doing here?" Bruno turned to get right back into the van. Yusuf grabbed his arm and held him.

"Bringing good news from the Red Cross — I mean, Crescent," Bruno stammered.

"What the hell are you doing in Istanbul?" Yusuf was shaking a fist in Bruno's face.

"I'm here to be of service to Gregory Samaras...and the people of Istanbul."

"Where were you taking him?" Yusuf shouted at the driver, who responded in Turkish.

"I brought him here to await a shipment of food he says is coming. We drove right by this park; I had no idea where the old lighthouse was; it's just ruins. I drove another kilometer to the new lighthouse, but there was no park there. I turned around to come back here — when the crazy guy in that black sedan..." His voice trailed off.

Yusuf smiled at Bruno. "That car belonged to our Greek patriarch, Mr. Baumgartner. You forced it off the road. You hold insurance, I hope."

The Red Crescent van, the helicopter, the old fire rig and a baffling cast of characters surrounded Tom. He helped the robed patriarch kneel down alongside Gregory. In thick English, Cosmas said, "Come here, everyone. My brother Gregory wants to thank you." Giovanni and Adnan, arms full of blankets, descended from the rig. Bruno, with Yusuf close behind, approached from the Red Crescent van.

"My friends. I am Cosmas, patriarch of the Greek Orthodox Church. The archbishop of Turin and I have spoken by telephone. You and I are to escort Gregory back to the cathedral of Saint George. We are to keep the Holy Shroud there for a time. Archbishop Tucci told me of your brave decision to come here. I thank you."

"This is not the Shroud," was all Gregory Samaras could sputter as he pointed at the damp cloth. Tom nudged Rachel; she handed her case to Tony, who walked over to his uncle and handed it to him. Giovanni held it reverently. He smiled.

Gregory looked up and saw Giovanni holding the suitcase, a twin to the one lying in front of him. Cosmas helped Gregory stand. Giovanni walked over and stood by the patriarch and handed the suitcase to Gregory. Speaking in his clear, direct Italian, he said, "A replacement, Signor Samaras. *Ecco la vera Sindone.*"

Gregory looked at him and then at Rachel. She nodded. Gregory opened the case and slowly fingered the seam between the backing and the linen inside. He smiled, looked at Giovanni and beckoned him. Giovanni, guardian of the Shroud, for the first time in his life, felt the soft folds of the holy garment. Tom came up alongside him, put an arm around his shoulder, and reached in to touch the garment; his fingers tingled to the touch.

Gregory replaced the cloth, closed the case and reverently passed it to the patriarch. Gregory opened his arms to Giovanni and the two men embraced. Gregory's body shook. Giovanni held him tightly and murmured, "*La Sacra Sindone*." Tom cherished the sight.

The patriarch raised his hand and blessed the group. His Italian was perfect. "Are we not witnesses? There have been no tremors since the Shroud came ashore. Blessed be God. Let us go to the cathedral." Gregory, smiling ecstatically, motioned to the helicopter pilot, now recovered. The pilot saluted and climbed into the cockpit. As the craft rose slowly above the group, Patriarch Cosmas' robes blew in the blast. Rachel held Tom's and Yusuf's arms. Gregory and Cosmas steadied themselves against the swirling wind.

Tony slapped Adnan and Giovanni on the back and they exchanged high fives on the rig. Adnan started the engine and led the way slowly toward the highway. The Red Crescent van, with the patriarch and his driver, Gregory, Yusuf, Rachel, Tom and Bruno inside, fell in behind.

The fire rig jerked to a stop, spun around and approached the landing. Tony sprang out, carrying the lit spotlight. Tom followed him and together they ran along the breakwall alongside the *Thaumaturgos*. It lay ghostlike, abandoned, socked around by waves. They climbed aboard, peered down the hatch and saw the kneeling Maximim in distress, holding his crotch with his free hand. Tom trained the pistol on him as Tony addressed Maximim.

"Come up, Sir Maximim. Your brother knights are dead. You are under arrest on suspicion of a crime of sacrilege. Come with me; we have a real gun. You can stand on the deck and pee." Maximim looked surprised to hear the angel voice again, now that of a no-nonsense enforcer, speaking in coarse Italian mixed with angelic French. He stared at Tony. He saw Tom standing alongside the former angel, holding a pistol.

"No. It was a trick?"

"*Avance!* You're holding your bladder; get up here now. *Pisse!*"

Maximim came up the ladder; he saw the vehicles; he did not see Jean Baptiste and the two brothers. "Is our great journey to prepare the Lord's way finished?"

"*Finito.*" Tony extinguished the spotlight. Maximim opened his fly and peed with the wind. When the man was done a minute or so later, Tony handed Tom the spotlight, pulled out some rope and bound Maximim's hands.

"This is your chance to interview the knight," said Tony. Tom had another scenario in mind; a jail cell, an hour to get inside their heads. This terrified, shaking youth on the deck of a rocking yacht was all that was left of them. The young man would be turned over to the small knot of police who were a kilometer away at the scene of the crash. In all the confusion, he might never see him again.

"*Pourquoi?* Why? Why have you done this?" Tom asked. Maximim looked at him sullenly. Tom grabbed his shirt and shook him. Maximim began speaking. Tom remembered the Provençal tongue Paul had recited in the Paris apartment. "Speak in French, damn you!" Tom shouted. Tony translated as best he could.

"We were called by John the Baptist in heaven to proclaim the coming of the Christ once again. He was in the world and the world knew him not. He came unto his own and his own received him not. Now he comes again into the world, unto his own people. We are his precursors! We walk through the waters of the sea which will close over the unbeliever. We live and die to make him return from death to life!"

Maximim said no more. They returned to the rig with their prisoner. They sat him down next to Giovanni, who slowly saluted him. Maximim broke down and wailed.

CHAPTER 52

The cortege of the fire rig and the Red Crescent van carrying the Holy Shroud into the city of its provenance drove onto the *cadde* and traveled eastward and then north, past the curve where the sedan had left long curling skidmarks. A policeman was directing eastbound traffic around the cluster of emergency vehicles near the broken guardrail; the van stopped and from the backseat the patriarch addressed one of the police. The officer whistled for help and a contingent circled the rig to remove the prisoner. Maximim stood, dazed. The police waved the procession on. Tom watched his one chance for an exclusive interview walk away.

Turning off the *cadde* before Seraglio Point and slowly traversing the streets of the city, the fire rig encountered small fires that burned along the way; they were swiftly doused by the sure hand of Giovanni on the hose. People were deserting the cots and chairs that littered the streets and prostrating themselves in impromptu prayer. Police and ambulance sirens still blared across the city, but another, more welcome, sound was heard. From Istanbul's minarets came brave calls to worship.

Rachel, holding Tom's hand, turned around to look at Bruno, who was nervously checking text messages in the third seat, Yusuf at his side.

"Won't you introduce us to your friend, Yusuf?

"He is Bruno Baumgartner," Yusuf said. "A reporter for *Der Welt-Wanderer*. He is telling our story to his readers back in Europe. And he is a spinning doctor!" He looked at Bruno. "Ja?"

Bruno smiled weakly. "Ja." Tom was trying not to laugh.

"Spin doctor," Rachel corrected him and bit her lip. "Bruno, I'm Rachel Cohen and this is Tom Ueland. I'm with the *Salone del Gusto*. Why don't you spin a story for us small growers?"

"I'm not taking any more clients," Bruno whispered. "Besides, I'm not the right person to represent your interests." He handed Rachel a business card.

The Cathedral of Saint George in the once largely Greek neighborhood of Fener was the symbolic center of orthodox Christianity in the east. A TV helicopter hovered over the approaching procession and caught in its landing lights the moment when Gregory and Cosmas emerged in the dark from the van and together carried the suitcase into the church. It was a scene that would be replayed again and again on TV across the globe in the days to come.

The others followed their host. Tom overheard Yusuf tell Rachel, "I have never been inside a Christian church."

"Get over it. They're everywhere, you know." Candles had been lighted, casting flickering shadows as they entered the nave. Directly in front of them was an ornate patriarchal throne that dominated the modest interior. Cosmas walked quickly to a locked door near the sanctuary, opened it and led the procession into a small vesting room.

Giovanni murmured something in Italian to Tony, who looked at Tom. "He wants to suggest we take the Shroud on the next Alitalia jet back to Turin. What is *la Sindone* of Torino doing in this oriental cathedral?"

"We are all the same, or so Michael thinks," said Tom. Giovanni's eyes misted when the Shroud had been locked into a heavy wooden vestment armoire. Cosmas led them out.

"You are all guests at my home. Please, come now, bathe, sleep. We will talk tomorrow." The patriarch shepherded them into his residence.

Yusuf stayed close to Bruno, nudging him as they walked. "If you are without enough beds, Patriarch Cosmas, I sleep with him." Yusuf grinned as the patriarch assigned rooms.

"We have many bedrooms here. Most beds have room for only one person," the patriarch replied. Bruno nodded and smiled weakly.

A half hour after everyone had taken very tepid baths, Tom crept to Rachel's room in the darkness. Snores were already pouring out from Giovanni's room. Tom crawled into her narrow bed. They giggled as they held each other and marveled at the palpable waves emanating from Giovanni's nasal passages. And Adnan down the hall was no silent sleeper himself. "Dueling banjos!" She whispered. Tom buried his face in the pillow at Rachel's apt description.

"Tom, we are not making love here! I'm seeing all of us here — yes, I'm in one of those minarets out there. I'm looking at this crowd in here — all these lives — all of them, almost lost. Just two days ago I was at the *Salone,* fighting the good fight for food. For farmers. For the land. Get me out of here!" She started a mock scream but bit her lip.

She sat up in the bed and lit a small candle. He was lying there, looking up at her. "And you, historian and writer, what will you say about all this? Write me out. I want nothing to do with the world of religious kooks. I was a nice simple secular girl who happened to be Jewish. Now I am in post-traumatic fucking stress over these…these zealots!" She was starting to shout.

Tom was stroking her hair. "I can't write you out. I thought about that when I looked into the face of that bearded man back in the park, when he hurdled me to get into the car. I've seen that face, Rachel. In the helicopter in the Camargue."

"Do you know anything about him?"

"We're about to find out."

CHAPTER 53

Rachel awoke early, slipped out of the residence and started walking. The streets were filled with people sleeping on top of their possessions; the city reeked of smoke. She remembered from Torah classes the story of Sodom and Gomorrah. She saw a solitary cab parked at a stand and asked the driver if he could find his way to the Neve Shalom synagogue. He agreed and after repeated wrong turns and blocked routes found it. He said he would wait; he was nervous.

Her parents had been members of Neve Shalom a half century before. She had never visited it in all her business trips to Istanbul. She found the synagogue closed. A year had passed since the November 2003 terrorist bombing. Walking up to the door, she let her mind drift back 500 years to the 15th century Ottoman rulers of Istanbul. They welcomed Spanish Jews fleeing the Spanish Inquisition — among them the Kohens. Running her hands over the synagogue door, she felt the presence of all those who had passed down life to her.

On the way back, she could feel herself stiffen as the cab neared Cosmas' residence. She had awoken that morning after a nightmare — Cosmas, a faceless inquisitor wrapped in a long linen cloth; she, the Jewess in the church docket forced to choose between conversion and death. Now, summoning what was left of her cosmopolitan bravura, she paid a generous tip to the cabby and knocked on the Christian door.

***

Tom, Tony and Bruno had just been aroused by a young priest banging on their doors and shouting "Let us bless the Lord" in Greek. "OK, OK," Tom whispered. "Whatever," Tony growled. *"Jawohl!"* shouted Bruno.

Patriarch Cosmas greeted the three late risers downstairs. "Giovanni and Gregory went next door to the cathedral to keep vigil — East and West dueling once again over the Shroud. I had to command them to come to breakfast. Your friend Yusuf ate early; Ramadan. And Miss Cohen went to visit her parents' old synagogue."

The visitors huddled together around a large dining room table, drinking strong coffee after the plates and the serving dishes had been removed. They grilled one another on what had happened and in what order, each correcting the previous witness. Tom wrote everything down, just to be sure. Only Bruno had been silent.

Cosmas sat at the head of the table, Gregory to his right. Gregory's face was beaming, a remarkable serenity shining there. Cosmas looked at him and spoke in Turkish. "You are happy, Gregory! Good." Gregory smiled dreamily. "But there are those here who will leave us shortly. And we must get everything out upon the table, as they say in America." He waved to Rachel as she entered and repeated his "upon the table" remark for her in English.

"What we also say in America is that if you are not at the table, you will be on the table," Rachel joked as she squeezed in next to Tom.

"You should be wary of her subtle shift of prepositions, Pastor. She's a street fighter."

"Ah. Well, then, everyone off the table. Let me start." Cosmas sipped his coffee and ventured forth in English. "Let me say that Michael now knows that Giovanni and Adnan here saved Gregory's life." Cheers and whistles erupted around the table. "And I will tell him how the true Shroud came into our hands through this man who calls himself Antonio Mezzo Soprano and you, Miss Cohen." More cheers.

Tony stood and bowed. "And tell him I borrowed his patron saint Michael to scare the shit…pardon, father — scare the suit of armor off the knight."

"But you sir, Mr. Baumgartner, how are you here?" the archbishop asked.

Bruno cleared his throat. "I'll speak in English if I may. My Greek is rusty. I'm not going to say I had anything to do with the heroics last night, your beatitude." Tom saw Bruno's face flush when he glanced at Yusuf, who rolled his eyes at Tom and Rachel. "Let me just say that I was sent here to be of assistance to Gregory Samaras."

At the mention of his name, Gregory grimaced at Bruno, who continued. "You don't know me, Mr. Samaras. I am a publicist. I write articles for a German newspaper. *Der Welt-Wanderer.* A Catholic newspaper. I also work as a consultant to a group of business people. And it was they who asked me to come here and offer their support to you and the people of Turkey. They have authorized me to promise that no request for food and medical assistance will be turned down. I...we...are here to lend a helping hand."

Yusuf wagged his finger at Bruno. "We don't need your helping hand filled with genetically modified wheat, corn, soybeans. No disaster can ever make it right enough to import Frankenstein-food into Turkey. Ever." Tom watched the three — Bruno, Gregory and Yusuf — their arms folded, their almost visible auras pushing and shoving.

"Gentlemen, before we all fall on one another's sharp words, let me share what my friend, Archbishop Tucci, has said to me." The patriarch selected his English words with care. Tony was translating for Giovanni. "Gregory, the plot to steal the Shroud from the church in Turin was your doing. It appears you did not intend for this 'borrowing' — your word — to be permanent. But it was wrong, all the same. You and I have been through history on many late nights. I had hoped it was just that, history. But these twenty-four hours have awakened the past from its deep sleep. And a drowsy giant is a dangerous giant, whether under the earth or out of the past."

"Your beatitude..." But Cosmas hushed him with a finger to his lips.

"Later, Gregory. The disposition of the Shroud comes later. Michael says that you are alive today only through the intervention of these good people here.   You were dealing with dangerous lunatics and convinced yourself that you could control them, just as you do your business. It is a great lesson in self-deception. Just as you have seen God's hand in the saving of the city through *la Sindone*, you should see God's hand in those who have saved your life and *la Sindone* itself. In particular, the good archbishop of Turin wants you to agree to the request of these people from the *Salone del Gusto*, or the Slow Food Movement, or whatever it is called. I think that is your duty."

Tom tried to feel what Yusuf had to be feeling — Gregory, the great tycoon of Istanbul sat there like a humble slave at the feet of a desert caliph. Cosmas looked directly at Yusuf. "The archbishop says you in particular, Yusuf, have a request."

"I do, sir." Yusuf cleared his throat. "That he sign the Declaration on GMOs."

"Your Beatitude, I don't think that this is a religious affair. I...I..." Gregory hesitated. "I acknowledge the hand of God in what has taken place. But as to feeding our people, you and I have discussed these radicals' demands in the past. They are un-Christian. We must feed the hungry."

Cosmas glanced at Yusuf. "Thank Allah they are not un-Islamic." Yusuf smiled. "We don't need to go over this again. You are alive today and *la Sindone* is safe because of these people. Tell them you will not allow these modified foods or seeds or whatever they are to enter our nation for at least ten years. Then we — or the next generation — can decide."

Gregory shrugged his shoulders and faced Yusuf. One could read the struggle on the tycoon's face — faith weighed against finance. He sighed deeply. "As you wish, Cosmas. I will sign the document."

Bruno squirmed in his chair. Cosmas looked at him. "So, it should not be a problem for your associates to honor the condition laid down by Mr. Aktug here. It seems simple enough, yes?"

Bruno slunk deeper. "Of course, your beatitude. I will relay this...this... rather unusual turn of events to them. They may have some problems with finding product..." His vocal strength suddenly ebbed.

Yusuf wagged a finger at him. "Product is not a problem, Herr Baumgartner. I'll have my peoples call your peoples."

Cosmas stood. "Now I would like a word in private with our Torinesi friends. Would you others wait for us in the parlor outside?" Bruno jumped to his feet. Yusuf threw his arm around Bruno's shoulder and chatting like an old friend escorted him out the door, followed by Gregory.

Adnan held out his arms to Giovanni. "Excuse me, my friend. I have work to do. Goodbye and be safe." Giovanni rose out of his chair, shuffled across the room and kissed Adnan on both cheeks. Their tears mixed and they pledged to meet again, soon, "before death extinguishes the fire in our hearts," said Adnan.

"*Grazie, Grazie tante, mio amico,*" Giovanni replied. When Adnan closed the door, Rachel, Tom, Tony and Giovanni pulled their chairs closer to Cosmas.

"And the Shroud?" Tom took another sip of the strongest coffee he had ever tasted. His head was throbbing. "When does it go back? How does it go back?" Tony finished translating for Giovanni. The old man was studying Cosmas.

The patriarch hesitated. "Michael says it stays."

"Who the hell is this Michael?" shouted Giovanni when Tony

176

had whispered the sentence in Italian to him.

"It's the archbishop." It took Giovanni a few seconds to make the connection to his own spiritual leader. He looked from face to face. He stared blankly at Cosmas.

"My friend, I know how you feel. I am sorry," Cosmas spoke in Italian. He put his hand on Giovanni's hand and continued in English. "I am as surprised as you all. My thought was to gain permission from Rome to keep it here for a brief period, perhaps a few months. We are not many, as you know, my friends, we Greek Orthodox. Perhaps a hundred thousand in this huge city of thirteen million people. We are not the glory that was Byzantium and will never be again, in spite of my friend Gregory's hopes. This church has limited resources; how are we to keep *la Sindone* as it should be kept? *Che pasticcio!* It is easier to resolve a dispute over grain than over God." There were polite, bewildered nods of sympathy.

"Your beatitude, what did our archbishop of Turin mean, 'It stays?'" Tony blurted out. "He must understand, I make my living taking tourists to the *Duomo* to see the Shroud. And my uncle here has devoted his life to the Shroud until this very moment, as you can see!"

"Capisco, mio amico. Your bishop has booked a flight back to Torino today for you all — even Mr. Baumgartner. He wants to explain his reasoning to you himself. I wish him good luck. Let me be frank. Archbishop Tucci wants to see an orthodox patriarch some day on the chair of Peter. For you, Miss Cohen, that means he wants an Orthodox patriarch — who among other doctrinal differences does not accept the pope as anyone other than a first among equals — to be the pope. He said to me, and I am quoting him here, 'This is a teachable moment.' I must say in all honesty, Antonio and Giovanni, your archbishop possesses a most byzantine mind." He smiled. Tony translated. Giovanni shook his head.

Tom knew he was observing a master politician even shrewder than Tucci. He twisted a spoon. "Something is not right about this story. When does the news hit? When do people find out what happened?"

Cosmas looked out the window. "The survivor, with the religious name of Maximim, has confessed everything. The car has been recovered and the bodies of the three. They have been identified and named by him. The police are trying to find next of kin."

"And one of them was a Jean Baptiste, yes?"

"Yes. Jean Baptiste LaRoque. The group's leader, according to the survivor."

"They never had a chance," Rachel said. "Those poor blind zealots."

"So. You must leave Istanbul now so you have a chance to rest before talking to the people carrying microphones and cameras. You should be with Michael, not here."

"Is Michael in trouble with the pope over all this?" asked Rachel. Cosmas looked down at the table. She went on. "I mean, we are all grown-ups here. Power is power, control is control. Is he in trouble?"

Cosmas looked as though he wanted to leave the room. He took a deep breath. "He has not shared his ecumenical scheme with the pope yet. Right now, it is much simpler being Orthodox than Roman, I can assure you!"

Tom tried to assess what the patriarch was saying. "So Archbishop Tucci will tell the Vatican he is going to let *la Sindone* stay in Istanbul until the Vatican invites the orthodox churches back into the fold and gives up all the 'supreme pontiff' stuff. And the pope will say 'never.' The Vatican owns *la Sindone* and will call Michael's bluff."

Giovanni poked his nephew on the shoulder. "What did he say?" Tony told him.

Cosmas leaned forward. "The Shroud of Christ, the last garment of the body of the Lord, in Archbishop Tucci's ecumenical mind, will heal and unify the broken body of the church, east still distant from west. And we of the east are riddled with division ourselves — bringing Russians, Armenians, Serbians and Greeks to the same table — *che pasticcio* again!" Cosmas did not smile. "And so the poor Church of Fener, where we Orthodox Greek Christians huddle together, will have to build the world's most sophisticated security system to protect the Shroud. Luckily, we have a benefactor." He looked toward the door where Gregory waited outside, then turned to Giovanni. "Giovanni, will you come back and train our tour guides? We will need your help."

When he understood what he was being asked, Giovanni sniffled and wiped his eyes. *"Si. Mi scusi,* Padre." He walked slowly out into the hallway, Tony at his side. Cosmas wiped his own eyes.

Alone there with Rachel, Tom asked Cosmas, "Pastor Cosmas, do you believe the Shroud saved Istanbul?"

Cosmas looked tired, worn out by the days and nights of rumbling earth, relentless panic and now this. "It is my turn to be byzantine. Look around you, friend. A main shock of only four point two. Istanbul became quiet when *la Sindone* came ashore; what does that tell you? On the other hand, the scriptures tell us that Yahweh would have spared Sodom if He could find ten righteous men in that city. He found only one. You are five; perhaps Yahweh felt five was enough to save our city; perhaps just one — Giovanni out there." He paused. "Thank you."

Rachel asked, "And if the pope calls you directly and demands the return of the Shroud against the wishes of the renegade priest in Turin, whom do you oblige?"

"Michael Tucci, of course," said the tired-looking patriarch, a genial smile masking the steely resolve. "We Orthodox don't like being, how can I say, ordered about by the first among equals. Excuse me. I must get ready for a meeting. Your airplane leaves in one hour; my driver is ready." He winked at her.

Outside, Yusuf's wife and children were waiting for him. They kissed him and hugged him and clung to him from head to toe. He introduced his wife to Rachel first and then to the others.

"He is a good man," Rachel said as she held the woman's hands.

"Hold a good life, Rachel." Yusuf said, embracing her.

"*Have* a good life! Don't throw your Berlitz book away, you sweet man." Rachel hugged Yusuf tightly.

Tom squeezed Yusuf's hand hard. "Thank you, Yusuf. Thank you."

"Gentile Tom, be good to her," Yusuf said.

One by one, Yusuf shook the men's hands, even Bruno's. He jumped into the family van and it disappeared down a small street. The patriarch's car pulled up. Giovanni and Tony shook the patriarch's hand without much emotion. Cosmas surprised them both with a fierce *abbraccio* and a whispered blessing.

After they had all piled in, Tom watched him waving them off, even blowing a kiss at Rachel. "I think he'd make a hell of a pope," she murmured.

Tom was staring out the window at the chaotic, churning streets of Istanbul — men, women, children, the old and the young, carrying boxes, bags, suitcases, lamps, pictures back to their homes. Merchants were setting up their stalls anywhere they could. Life went on.

"Wait a minute, wait a goddamn minute," he murmured to Rachel. "What Cosmas told us about Michael — that really meant he wanted the Shroud to come to Istanbul from the start. It was part of his great church unity scheme."

"Most assuredly, my dear," she whispered back.

"So — did the pastor of Turin himself turn the key over to the Knight-Precursors? And did he use us to make sure the Shroud was laid in Samaras' devout hands?"

CHAPTER 54

As the Alitalia jet rolled to a stop at the Turin airport, the five travelers had to be awakened by the cabin attendant. In the terminal, they were ushered out a side exit and were met by the Fathers Fiddle, discreetly dressed in civilian slacks and turtlenecks and driving an unmarked van.

Bruno, edging away from the others, waved to them as a limousine drove up near the van. "Stay in touch, *amici!* Greet my good friend Archbishop Ricci." They were too tired to explain to the Fathers Fiddle that "Ricci" was Tucci.

Michael had arranged for them to be taken to a hotel and there they slept another 15 hours. It was early morning when the desk clerk called the rooms and told them the archbishop's car would arrive in an hour. As they rode in silence to his residence, Rachel held out her hands to the three men. Yawning by turns, they grudgingly clasped hers. "My olive booth! Oh my god, the *Salone* is almost history!" Then she and Tom broke into "Istanbul was Constantinople." They rocked back and forth in the backseat as they sang. Giovanni smiled when Tony sang it in Italian.

Upon the group's arrival inside Michael's residence, Father Raffaelo and Father Roberto whooped and crushed the returning heroes with bear hugs. The two guided the group with fawning attention to the dining room where Alma the cook had concocted egg dishes and pancakes and sausages, all quickly devoured. The archbishop entered briskly. "Keep on eating, don't stand, don't stop!"

They all stopped and stood. He remained near the doorway and let his eyes move slowly from one to the other, then raised his arms in a touchdown signal as the cheers and whistles erupted. "My friends, you are safe. You are alive. That is my greatest joy!" He kissed each of them on both cheeks and hugged them.

"Now, we don't have much time. The press corps of every nation on the globe is awaiting an audience at the *Duomo*. Outside, the piazza is overflowing."

"Does that make you happy or terrified, Pastor?" Tom's inflection was just this side of baiting.

"Teachable moments are terrifying moments, yes?" Michael

smiled.

"They have something to teach us all," Tom replied stiffly. "Are we all prepared to learn? Even pastors?"

Michael nodded. "Yes, especially pastors."

"What do they know and what do you want us to say?" Tom looked around at his fellow eyewitnesses.

Rachel bit her nails, but her eyes said, "You are being really rude."

Michael spoke quietly. "Say nothing about the arrangements for the return of *la Sindone*. Keep the names of Paul and Genevieve out of it. They are our anonymous source. The French police have agreed to do the same. Say the police in Paris received the tip about the Knight-Precursors. Otherwise, tell the whole story." The archbishop looked at Tom. "And that applies to you as well, my friend. You are our Boswell, yes?"

"Ah, Pastor. Boswell I'm not. Somewhere between muckraker and paparazzo. Maybe the *New York Times* is interested. I'm going to write the story for somebody and I will leave nothing out. Nothing. Including things I don't yet know."

Michael, unflinching, did not take the bait. "I know. In good time, my friend. In good time. Until then, we are agreed?" He looked from face to face.

"*Zio* Giovanni feels betrayed by the decision to leave the Shroud in Istanbul," Tony blurted out. "He would like to say that here." There was no need to translate — Giovanni spilled out his deep disappointment in a torrent of Italian and then shrugged in resignation. *"Non capisco, padre. Non capisco."*

"*Capisco*, Giovanni. *Capisco. Va bene.*" He took Giovanni's arm and held it to his breast, then looked to the others. "Shall we go?" The archbishop was wearing his cassock and sash, the cassock outlined in purple piping. Tom had not seen him dressed this way. It made him seem distant, not the informal raconteur of only days earlier. There was something else about him; he looked tired, yes, but also conflicted; a purple-buttoned-down CEO of a transnational corporation. "One last thing; only Giovanni, Antonio and I will be on the stand in the square. They, after all, are the rescuers of the Shroud. I hope that is all right, you two."

"It's your show, Pastor." Tom joined Rachel behind the three Italians.

If Istanbul had pulsed with fear and trembling, Turin radiated giddy anticipation and delight over the news of the rescue. This day, Turin was to be found in the Piazza Castello. In the skies helicopters droned while below the camera flashes popped. The police escort for the archbishop arrived in the piazza outside the church against a backdrop of lights spinning and sirens wailing. Then the Fathers Fiddle went to work, bracing the backsides of police as they held the crowds back. The retinue threaded its way past the church, under the arches, through Piazzetta Reale and into Piazza Castello. Ahead, Tom saw a 15-foot-high stage erected between the equestrians Castor and Pollux, their heroic horses rearing back in homage. Piazza Castello was reverberating with wave after wave of 20,000 cheering, whistling, tootling echoes bouncing off the stately palazzos.

Once the group reached the platform of the stage, Michael was smiling, waving and blessing Torinesi and the out-of-town pilgrims and tourists. Tony raised his fists and swung his arms around. But when Giovanni waved his right arm straight up, the decibels became truly deafening. Rosaries were held up, images of *la Sindone* were floated high on poles and sticks. Down in the front row, Tom and Rachel never stopped gripping one another's hands.

"Sindone! Sindone! Sindone!" Twenty thousand voices chanted rhythmically. Michael stood in front of the microphone. The crowd noise subsided to a steady drone. "Today is a happy day for Turin and for the entire church. The Holy Shroud has been recovered." Shouts and cheers, then slowly, silence again. "We thank God for its rescue and pray for those whose lives were lost. And we thank this young man…" He pointed to Giovanni. Giovanni? A waterfall of laughter spilled over the piazza, followed by eddies of clapping, whistling and cheering as Giovanni bowed to the archbishop. "…We thank this young man, Antonio Palmitessa, and we thank his beloved uncle, our own brave fireman, Giovanni Palmitessa!" The waterfall surged.

"Giovanni *Papa!* Giovanni *Papa!"* By acclamation, *Zio* Giovanni was named pope. Michael, with impeccable stage presence, turned to Giovanni, extended an arm to him, brought him close to the microphone and placed an imaginary papal tiara on his balding pate. The piazza erupted with delight.

"Our beloved Shroud will be returned to our city in a manner fitting to its prominence." The piazza was quiet. Here was Michael's test. "For now, it is in the devoted hands of the Greek Orthodox Patriarch Cosmas, my friend and fellow bishop. It is being held in safekeeping in the Cathedral of Saint George, while that city recovers from its awful encounter with disaster. We Torinesi can do no less for Istanbul and its Christian, Jewish and Muslim citizens than to share *la Sindone* with them in an appeal to the One God to spare their great city." There was restrained applause.

"Sindone subito! Sindone subito! Sindone subito!" The *"Sindone* now!" chant was deafening. Michael stood by while Giovanni worked the crowd, punching his fist in the air at the *"subito"* before he saw Tony's discreet thumbs down. Again, the crowd hummed as the city's archbishop prepared to respond.

"It will return to us as quickly as possible. And it is my prayer and I hope it is all of ours that along with *la Sindone* will come the reunited heart of Orthodox and Roman Catholicism, the Christ of the east and the Christ of the west, He whose body bore the marks of suffering brought on by misunderstanding and religious hatred. Let us pray for the unity of all Christians as we await the return of the Shroud!"

There was a smattering of cheers and some catcalls. Tom gripped Rachel's arm. "He needs crowd control, this pastor. The sheep are restless now; if they ever found out his agenda..."

CHAPTER 55

The procession re-entered the *Duomo* under heavy security and intense scrutiny by the police. The returning heroes were quickly escorted to seats in the sanctuary to face an audience of TV crews and journalists under a sea of tall floodlights.

Cowering in a back pew of the church sat Bruno Baumgartner. He had wandered into the *Salone del Gusto*'s final day, alone, afraid to go outside lest he be picked off by a laser beam shot by the Voice from the rooftop of the Lingotto. Meandering among the booths, worming his way through 50,000 people, ignoring the rabid voice mails and text messages on his cell phone, Bruno watched the people go about their work — the people he had been working against these past months. *Mein Gott,* he thought. That Indonesian indigene in his loin cloth. The Polish matriarch in her colorful apron. The East Indian woman in her soft sari. The red-haired Irishman in his wool shirt. These were the enemy feared by the globe's biggest corporations? Then the sign at the Turkish olive booth. "Back soon. Maybe." Bruno shook his head, walked out of the convention center by a side exit, caught a trolley and rode it to the *Duomo* in time for the press conference.

He dialed the Voice and caught him in mid-shriek, cursing him for being AWOL and threatening to fire him if he did not "nail the archbishop to the cross." Bruno gradually turned down the volume on his phone until it silenced the screaming Voice at "dick — ," shut his notebook for the last time, stood, genuflected, blessed himself with holy water, left the church and set out for the glass bubble where the cancer-ridden mini-master of the universe held sway.

He fought through the crowded piazza and was about to get into a cab when someone gripped his shoulder from behind. He turned and recognized a reporter who was sitting in the church near him.

"What's your name again and who do you work for?" the man asked bluntly, in French.

"Bruno Baumgartner, for *Der Welt-Wanderer*." Bruno was annoyed.

"Of course and I am Marie of Romania, for the *Bucharest Bugler*." The reporter smiled lazily. "Listen, I'm with — a Paris magazine. The lawyer representing the last living Knight-Precursor has arranged for his client to sell us his story. I'll offer you five thousand Euros for anything you want to add."

"Not nearly enough." He climbed in, flicked the cab door shut and snarled at the cabby, confident he was anybody but Tony. "Lingotto."

Bruno had gone to turn in the tools of his trade. He was hanging them up, quitting this business. The nosy paparazzo from the Paris magazine in the piazza had made it easy for him. Scum of the fucking earth.

The Voice was screaming and snarling at him the moment he appeared in the bubble. "Dickhead! *Dumbkopf!* Dickhead! What the hell are we paying you for? This mess is now all yours; you broke it, you own it! Get back to Samaras immediately, talk him out of his promise to that control freak of a patriarch and let's get GMOs moving into Turkey. Schnell!" Bruno smiled. So, the boss wanted to keep him? He had some power. He was not an *untermensch* after all.

And then the Voice told him to wheel the chair back to the elevator; its battery had died. It was time to leave Turin, and he had a flight to catch to a meeting of all the corporate big shots in charge of dirty tricks, and by God, there would be hell to pay if Bruno did not redeem himself so the Voice could deliver on the contract! And so, *untermensch* again, Bruno wheeled the Voice out of the seat of darkness in the bubble down to the rooftop where a van awaited him.

He saw the man for what he was, a small, skeletal, nervous, chain-smoking, middle-aged *homunculus,* nothing more. His wheelchair was loaded with more appliances than a BMW. And 20 cartons of cigarettes. Bruno pushed the wheelchair past the lift alongside the van, toward the edge of the roof.

"Don't push me so close to the edge!" the Voice screamed at Bruno on the windswept autodrome atop the Lingotto Fiere. "Where are you going? I am not chopped liver! Back, dickhead!"

Bruno returned to the van and pushed the wheelchair onto the lift. He pressed the up button. The lift was at the car's floor level. He kept his thumb on the button.

"What are you doing, dickhead? Stop it so I can roll in!"

Bruno left the lift suspended, the Voice now a full five feet off the ground. "I could kill this motherfucker here and now," he murmured. He went around and got into the driver's seat, started the engine, put it in gear and drove slowly to the edge of the track.

"Where the hell are you going? Did you hear me, dickhead?"

"I heard you," he yelled back. He stopped at the edge of the roof, the chair vibrating back and forth over the guardrail. He could already anticipate the delicious sounds: dropping the brake on the lift, the Voice going overboard in his chair, the scream fading in a lovely Bernouli effect as the heavy weight dropped five stories to the pavement below, the crash resounding up seconds later. But he couldn't do it.

Frantic, the Voice was retrieving a pistol from the bowels of the chair. He pointed it at Bruno. Bruno slipped behind the chair; the Voice wailed in distress. Bruno picked up a carton of cigarettes and threw it over the edge. The Voice wailed again. Then another and another, smashing into the pavement below. He peered over the edge and saw some teenagers leaving the mall waiting for more to drop from the sky. The Voice was beginning to choke on his saliva, whimpering and waving the gun wildly in the air, shooting volleys down the track. Bruno laughed. "Try hitting this next carton of Marlboros with the gun; you win a prize, Herr Voice!" Bruno began walking toward the elevators. He turned once and saw the Voice trying to squirm around; the man was almost halfway in position to get a bead on Bruno. A *mensch* at last, Bruno shouted down the track at the trembling invalid, "I go to see Gregory Samaras. *Auf wiedersehen,* chief of the dickheads. If you only had a dick!" And then he was gone.

CHAPTER 56

The archbishop's entourage returned to his residence through the crowded streets of the Old City under police escort. Tony parked his very own Fiat inside the courtyard, directly under the Madonna's statue. "Hey, Rachel, Tom. You can't leave yet. There's a party at the trattoria: Giovanni Palmitessa, man of the hour."

Michael took Tom and Rachel by the arm and walked a few feet away. "You are my link to reality, you two. Tony here and *Zio* Giovanni are my own people. I love them as flesh and blood. I have legions of church and civil lawyers. But the church is about to close in on me. I need calm, clear voices from outside." He paused and smiled. "You are in demand; Genevieve called me and asked me to tell you she and Paul invite you to supper tomorrow night, in Paris. It appears our friends want to meet the lovely Rachel."

Tom braved what he felt as an especially sharp laser gaze of the priest. "Pastor, I think I want to know more about the Knight-Precursors; especially the one called Jean Baptiste."

The furrows on Michael's brow rippled and then smoothed out again. "Then I will see you — soon." Rachel threw her arms around him. Michael did not let her go, even after he drew back. "You have done more than I could have ever asked." He looked at Tom. "Oh, you lucky man. What must it be like? I confess envy. She is a beauty. Take her back to Minnesota. If she will go. *Allora, arrivederci.*" Michael wiped his eyes.

Back at the cab, Tom and Rachel watched Tony and Giovanni losing their shirts to those expert card players, the Fathers Fiddle. The two priests mussed Giovanni's hair and twisted Tony's arm until he yelled *"Zio!"* and all three laughed at Giovanni as he glared at the priests until Tony pushed him into the cab alongside Tom and Rachel.

A few blocks away, Trattoria di Gianna looked to Tom like an Italian family's idea of an ancient triumph for a returning Roman general. Tony's father had prepared a massive feast for his brother. His staff had decorated the street outside with banners celebrating the old man's exploits in Istanbul. An AP wire photo picture of Adnan's old fire engine had been blown up to the size of an enormous billboard. With the cathedral of Saint George in the background, it showed Giovanni standing on the running board, cradling the hose against his chest with one arm and waving a firefighter's helmet with the other. "Cowboy Giovanni!" the headline proclaimed.

Inside, the confetti hung so thickly from the rafters that the partygoers had to create paths through the jungle below to find each other. Platters of antipasti graced every table in the house. Lemon-flavored stuffed eggs. Fried baby artichokes. Stuffed mushrooms. Salads of roasted peppers, olives and fontina, a special Piedmont dish. Rice salads of all varieties, the rice cooked in a broth with white truffles. There were crunchy deep-fried toasts smothered with polenta and mozzarella cheese. Sweet pepper stews surrounded by bruschetta for dipping. The wine of Piedmont was being liberally poured into glasses as quickly as they could be washed in the kitchen and returned to service.

Tony pushed his way to Tom and Rachel, wine glass in hand, put his arms around them and started bawling and babbling. "Tell me about his wife," Rachel said.

"Giovanni misses his Catarina so deeply. She was never healthy. All their babies stillborn. In her old age, the cold winters started to affect her breathing. He regretted he never returned to Calabria with her when his fireman's pension started paying out. But the life in Turin was good and she demanded they remain here, especially when she saw how much he loved her city, the church and the families that grew around them. And so they stayed and the pneumonia she caught one cold winter carried her away."

Vittorio introduced the mayor of Turin, and the mayor, a rotund fellow with bulbous eyes, praised Giovanni for 45 minutes, hardly taking a breath. He presented Giovanni with a key to the city and a special medal containing a relic of Saint Florian, the patron saint of firefighters.

Tom saw Michael Tucci slip into the trattoria by a side door. Giovanni was choking up. "I will be honest with you all, as I have been all my life — mostly." Laughter. "When our *Sindone* was stolen and I found myself in the center of the search, I thought, 'I think this would be a wonderful movie. Yes, a movie. This is history being made and I have the story.' I told Antonio here to get in touch with Martin Scorsese. You laugh, but every one of you cowboys would have thought the same. Well, my nephew humored me along and the days went by, and then our archbishop called me in to help.

And after our young American friends here figured out what was happening with these thieves, I realized something. You don't get to be in the movies. You get to live a real movie if you open your eyes to what God above puts in front of you. You get to go to Istanbul. And don't let Antonio tell you anything else; it was I who said *'Andiamo!'* He was just my young assistant. See, already he's shaking his head no. Don't believe him.

"Giovanni Palmitessa made his own movie! I only wish my beloved Catarina were here to laugh at me with my big fire hose that nearly knocked me into Christ's kingdom and into her lap! *Mia cara* Catarina."

The handkerchiefs, the laughing crying eyes, the lifelong friendships and disagreements — one could lose all this in a heartbeat; time did really fly, not just anywhere, but past oneself. Tom felt it and knew Rachel did too. "I told you, Tom Ueland; I want what he's got. *Famiglia!*" she whispered. Red-eyed Tom Ueland was cheering wildly. Giovanni sat down and the applause went on. The archbishop, whose presence was by now the subject of approving whispers and pokes in one another's ribs, placed his arms around some grandchildren, his eyes moist.

Tony spoke next, first in Italian, then in English. Of course he got the laughs in Italian. But the feeling was there in both languages. He was never out of character. "The old man lies through his teeth. I set up the whole thing. But he gives a nice speech, yes? Don't let the old man fool you. I had lined up that seaplane in minutes. And I was a very convincing Michael Archangel!"

Tony led Tom and Rachel over to Giovanni, whose worn, ruddy face was covered with affectionate kisses and dabs of tissue. Giovanni held Rachel tightly for a minute and then took both of Tom's hands in his and pulled him close for an *abbraccio* and whispered in his ear. "Until *la Sindone* returns." And then he saluted Tom and Rachel. Tom saluted back. Tom turned and took Rachel's arm. The whole room was saluting the Americans. It was now clear that this gesture was both a symbol of gratitude and the pledge of the return of the Shroud. Michael left as quietly as he had arrived.

The cab ride to Rachel's hotel near Porta Nuova started quietly, until Rachel began needling the driver. "So when will you settle down and get married? You're not guaranteed perpetual youth, you know." She smiled at Tony's dreamy gaze reflected in the rearview mirror. Tom saw he was looking only at the road ahead.

"Life is still full of too much fun," Tony replied. "When I stop meeting Tom Uelands, that's when. Miles to go before I sleep. Robert Frosted?" He looked at Rachel and she winked.

When they reached the hotel, Tom leaned forward and touched the driver's shoulder. "We don't need a ride from here, driver. We can hoof it. Get out of here before you show some vulnerability." Outside, Rachel and Tom leaned into his open window. Tony was misty-eyed and hoarse.

"Best days of my life, *amici*. Best days of my life. And about Michael Tucci, don't be too hard on him, whatever you dig up." He was toying with the shift — low, neutral, low, neutral. Rachel kissed his left hand, which was dangling loosely outside the car door. Tom reached in and mussed his hair. And then low gear and clutch out.

Rachel and Tom watched him sail into traffic. An hour later, their train to Paris left Stazione Porta Nuova and they slept much of the way — the way leading to the identity of the fiery bearded man named Jean Baptiste.

CHAPTER 57

They found a room at a hotel on Boulevard Port Royal near the De Rosier apartment. For supper they had moussaka at a Greek restaurant near Rue Mouffetard.

Lingering over wine, she held her head in her hands. "My dear Tom, I have always wanted to be cosmopolitan rather than Jewish. Some people think they're the same. I don't. I have always thought it meant divorcing yourself from your ethnicity. The cool, detached, universal chick — not. Here I am. Jewish to the core."

"So you are thinking…"

"…How lucky I am; we'd have never met if my Sephardic ancestors had not chosen Turkey over Germany or Poland or Russia when they fled Spain in the fifteenth century. They might have ended up in France, running for their lives and not far enough to save them from the Nazis. And we'd have never met. Think about it."

She played with her knife. "Imagine the Spanish Jewish refugees sailing sadly, proudly, past the lovely côte d'azur on their way east to Istanbul where they are welcomed by the Muslim community. In fourteen hundred ninety-two, Columbus sailed the ocean blue. And Kohen sailed the wine-dark sea."

She paused, looking for the right words. "Can I make it with a cute Lutheran boy from the Midwest?" A young woman walked past outside, pushing her child in a stroller. Rachel studied her until she passed them. "In the final analysis, I just hope my inner Jew is compatible with your inner Lutheran."

"Rachel," he stopped her. She was hunching her arms around her shoulders. "You and I are meant to be together, a genetic, historic bond between this Lutheran and this Jew. Somewhere. I know it. But I fear it too."

Rachel took his hands. "You are a tweedy professor — so in your head, into your history, Tom. It's like we are all standing on continental plates that drift around — our drifting ancestors. Even long dead, they can still give you a jolt without warning. Enough with the hesitation waltz. You need kids. You should have been born Jewish. Stop being anal, come along with me, have a family. Roots. Of course the kids — we'd raise them Jewish. It comes through the mother. Then we'd let them choose, Jewish or Christian. *'Oy vey*

Maria.'" Tom grinned, then touched her arm.

She grabbed his hand and squeezed it hard. "OK. Fear. What are you afraid of?"

"I'm afraid one day I would just not come home to you," he said. "Like all those loved ones on Nine-Eleven. Life's slippery turns."

She blinked twice. "Come on! Life is someone you love, one day not coming home, not showing up, not knowing who you are, not waking up. Until then, you love someone, you come home, you show up, you know who I am, you keep on waking up. You take a chance."

She looked hard at him to see if he got it. "Talk about magical thinking. Professor, you are not doomed to repeat the past simply because you know it!"

They went home in a glow, undressed and jumped into bed. He snuggled closer and reached under the blanket to cup her breasts gently. He kissed and caressed her slowly and then slid down to her thigh. For long minutes he gave her pleasure until she stopped him and pulled him over her.

In the morning, when he opened his eyes, she was looking at him through tears. "The sex was great but oh my god the sadness!" Tom passed her a tissue and she wiped her eyes. *"Magnifique, mais mon dieu, la tristesse!"*

"Time to talk to the De Rosiers. Let's make the call."

CHAPTER 58

"Paul, it's Tom Ueland on the phone. They are in Paris!" Genevieve De Rosier motioned to her husband. "Come to our apartment at seven thirty. We're just heading out to the market. We are so anxious to meet your friend Rachel. Bring nothing. *D'accord. À bientôt."*

For the last two days they had slept heavily after days of anguish, waking to nightmares of what was yet to come. Cooking and cleaning their apartment assuaged grief — all afternoon, their apartment filled up with the scent of flowers from the market and the tangy smells of bouillabaisse. Paul set the table with their best silver, glassware and dishware. By the time the telephone rang that evening, they had masked their feelings as well as they could.

CHAPTER 59

"Mes amis, I would like you to meet Rachel Cohen. And, Rachel, may I introduce my friends Paul and Genevieve De Rosier."

"Oh, my darling, we have been waiting for you. I feel we know you already," Genevieve said. She kissed Tom and Rachel; Paul bowed.

Rachel said, "I am so happy to meet you both. About the Shroud, your instincts were so right. Who would have ever guessed that a harmless brotherhood of religious zealots, who had never given any inkling of really bizarre behavior, would become so obsessed..."

Genevieve said only, "Yes. Who?"

Paul took Rachel's arm to lead her into the apartment. He spoke after guiding her to the chair in the sunroom; he looked directly at her from a chair he placed within inches of her. "We were the rear guard; you were on the front lines, in the trenches." Abruptly, he switched the topic. "The Italians know their food, yes?"

Genevieve sat alongside Rachel. "Tom has told us of your passion to preserve locally grown foods. When I was younger what else was there? I am so proud of what you are doing. Food is becoming so homogenized. We French sometimes feel like voices crying in the wilderness of fast food."

Paul stood. "We'll just be a minute," said Genevieve. "Paul will get some wine and I have some little things to eat. Come, Paul." Paul looked confused, then followed her out. Rachel looked at Tom.

"She is so beautiful! Everything natural — no makeup, her skin as smooth as a young woman's — no facial surgery, it's all real. And the way she carries herself — regal, a goddess. But have you noticed their eyes? They've been crying for days. They are crying now. What's going on?"

"They know why we have come."

"OK. Why have we come?"

"For that I need a little wine — a lot of it."

On their return, Tom studied Paul and Genevieve — him carrying the wine, her a plate of hors d'oeuvres. Somber, hospitable, going through motions learned generations ago. Paul spoke with a shakiness Tom had not heard before. "Please, share this wine with us. A special occasion, a special bottle, vintage nineteen thirty-four

195

or thereabouts."

As Paul struggled with the cork, Genevieve lit a Gauloise. "We have just returned from Belgium. You must go there — Brussels, the Museum of Fine Arts, for Brueghel's *Fall of Icarus*. Tom, we spoke of it, yes?" He nodded, amazed at how pleading the question was; she seemed to be losing her composure over a painting.

"You know the genius of Brueghel is that he caught the moment when everything turns away from the disaster of the boy falling out of the sky. Auden sees the message as 'Life goes on, we all have places to go, things to do.' I think that is wrong; Brueghel painted the very moment just after the ploughman and the shepherd and the sailors saw the disaster — the moment they turned away in denial. Look at the ploughman, refusing to look again, the shepherd looking up but away. 'No, it did not happen!' they are thinking. 'We did not see that!'" Genevieve screamed the last sentence. It was quiet in the room. Tom was twisting his glass; Rachel sat transfixed. Paul shuffled his feet and slowly wound the corkscrew down. Genevieve cleared her throat and stood.

"And then we went to Ypres. There is a German World War I cemetery near there. Vladslo. Paul and I are very fond of it. In it are two beautiful sculptures, a kneeling man and woman, by the German artist, Käthe Kollwitz. *The Mourning Parents*. The sculptor's son was killed in nineteen fourteen, her grandson in World War II." Her voice cracked. "Her son is buried just in front of the statues. For these two parents, there is no turning away from, no denial of the disaster. They look at it, for eternity." Paul, shaking, pulled the cork out of the bottle and poured the wine. With effort he set the glasses in their hands. Genevieve snubbed out her cigarette. The hosts awkwardly raised their glasses together. Rachel and Tom raised theirs.

Paul toasted. "For the ultimate repose of the Shroud in Turin. For your own safe return from danger. For a resolution of the great schism our friend Michael Tucci seeks to heal..." He faltered.

Tom whispered, "And for you — the mourning parents."

CHAPTER 60

Tom held his glass steady. Neither of the couple looked at him after he spoke. Genevieve had closed her eyes. Trembling, in a trance, she raised her glass a little higher.

"And for our son, Philippe Jean De Rosier."

"Jean Baptiste LaRoque," Paul said, his voice cracking.

Rachel set her glass down. Tom could almost feel her thoughts jumbling, tumbling. "No way, no way, no way," she whispered.

Eyes closed, the old couple crumpled together as their tears fell. Rachel took Genevieve's wine glass and Tom held Paul's. A mantle clock tick-tocked a full minute before Genevieve opened her eyes. "You are correct, young Tom. No one knows except the two of you. And Inspector Toussaint."

Tom looked at Rachel. In her eyes he could see her replaying the scene of the fireball that flamed out of Istanbul over the coastline into the churning waters of the Sea of Marmara. In the burning car was the son of Paul and Genevieve De Rosier. Tom remembered whispering to Yusuf, "God in heaven. I pray it is them." Only when Tom saw the two of them tonight and looked at their faces was he sure that the man was the son of Paul and Genevieve De Rosier. His mother's handsome countenance. His father's awful fury.

"Who's helping you?" Tom asked.

Paul shrugged. Genevieve said, "Michael has been our rock. He has been our emissary with the Istanbul police. Here in Paris, Inspector Toussaint. The bodies are being returned to France to their next-of-kin. The one who survived will tell the story of our son, of that we are sure." There was a long silence, the space filled with sighs, with rustling of clothing against the upholstery, the squeaking of chair legs. Genevieve still shook. "We have selected a suit for his casket. Our little Philippe. We bury him tomorrow morning."

She wiped her eyes and looked at Tom. "You feel betrayed we did not tell you everything in the Camargue, yes?"

"No. I understand."

"We feel like the betrayers. Of Philippe. Oh we know...Our story was the truth, the truth we chose to reveal. I did work at the *Musée de* Camargue in the nineteen seventies. Philippe was a teenager. He grew to love the Camargue, its literature, its wildness, its desolation. He knew the territory well." Tom felt the weight of her eyes on him.

"Philippe went to seminary then. He was a very serious boy and emotionally fragile. They asked him to leave. He and a few other young men. I think they were worried about what the rector called 'particular friendships.' Homosexuality. That was not the problem. It was immaturity. They had all become inflamed with studying eschatology, the return of Christ, his judgment of humanity, everything that they had learned from their instructors in seminary. They had no perspective. Paul and I were dumbfounded. We had shared with him our dedication to the church but we did not know how to transmit a sense of balance, of the need to have his own life. He never had that balance. Never."

Paul held his wife's hand, caressed it and spoke haltingly. "After leaving seminary, he taught French literature in a Catholic school here in Paris, nearby, near the Grand Mosque. He lived alone in a small flat there. He was not interested in having a family. He became consumed with reaching the age of thirty-four — what he thought was the age of John the Baptist, the cousin of Jesus, when he was beheaded. He used to say, 'It is one of the numbers that define my life.' And when he reached it, he left home."

"When did you find him?" Rachel asked.

"Almost immediately after he left Paris. Inspector Toussaint found him. That good man spent every spare vacation day he had, scouring the backwaters of the Camargue. We knew our son was there, somewhere. Toussaint tracked him down, without Philippe ever knowing."

"But you never made contact with him?" Tom asked.

"Genevieve went back to the *Musée* for its twentieth anniversary and I accompanied her. Nineteen ninety-five. Nine years ago."

"You actually saw him?" asked Rachel.

"By chance, we met the monastery van on the road. We saw the driver. We were sure it was him behind the beard. He saw us for a split second and turned away. We could not restrain ourselves. We turned around and followed him to the farmhouse. The vault door was closed. He refused to see us." Genevieve's anguish was visible. "He shouted from the interior, 'I have forsaken you and your version of Christianity; I now follow Christ and prepare for His return and want nothing to do with you.' We went home, completely heartbroken. We found out about his order of brothers from pamphlets. Then, came the Internet. Their Web site. It was all there. 'To bring about the conditions for the return of Christ the King. To return to Jerusalem the things scattered throughout the world over two thousand years, things that were present at Christ's death.' They advertised, they begged for relics of the true cross. For bits of the veil of Veronica. And they prayed — this was on the Web site — that someday the church would return *la Sindone* to the church of the Holy Sepulchre in Jerusalem. Your evangelical Christians in America believe the Jews must return to Israel before Jesus can come again. Our son believed the Shroud must return to Jerusalem before Jesus can come again."

"Just when he tired of waiting for the church to give it up..." Paul's face flushed in anger. "...The order found a benefactor. I call him a malefactor!"

"Gregory Samaras," Tom said. "The man did not know whom he was dealing with, I assure you both."

Paul took a deep breath. "No matter. With his money they bought the computers we found in the farmhouse. They studied software, learned how to break into security codes. Disarm security systems. Access the most confidential files of the Turin cathedral. They learned to sail, to read the stars and nautical charts. They had been pilfering relics for years. And now, somehow, they had what they needed to take the Shroud and to bring it home."

Rachel cleared her throat. "Did Michael know?"

"We don't think so. Not until a week ago. We told him then. When you all were in Istanbul." She folded her hands and looked down. "With Philippe."

Paul drained his wineglass. "We may never know what Michael knew."

Tom cleared his throat. The sense of isolation in this couple in their grief was overwhelming. To be so ashamed of a son. To feel such failure as his parents. To wake up each day coping with the loss of their only child — year after year. No wonder Paul was a recluse. What could he say to them now about the freakish accident, the arc of the burning car down to the sea?

"I'm very, very sorry. He died quickly. Their car..."

Paul sat ramrod straight. Genevieve's words were a cry from the heart. "Icarus, falling into the sea, alone. Oh, Philippe."

For minutes they looked at one another. Tom finally took Genevieve's hand and said, "You've burned a lot of candles,

Genevieve. Pastor Tucci once told me you both knew about magical thinking. That's what brought me to Paris. Now I know how you know about it. The candle was all you had, the only visible link between you and your son. And why not trust the candle?"

She smiled weakly. "For all who would make a bad choice that day. You will come to his funeral tomorrow? At Sainte Elizabeth. Charles will be there. And Inspector Toussaint. Just the six of us." She dried her hands on an apron. "Come now. You must be very hungry." The scent of bouillabaisse drifted from the kitchen. Genevieve stood. "No appetite, no life. We decided this week to go on with our lives — at this late date, yes! Please, eat something."

Paul stood, apparently happy for the chance to play host. "And ask us anything. We are yours tonight — words of wisdom, words of failure, the past, the present, the future. You are the future." Paul's voice was hollow. He trailed Genevieve into the kitchen, where they exchanged some words in French. Tom and Rachel sat close, leaning into each other. Paul brought more wine. Genevieve carried in the steaming serving bowl. *"Allons! allons à table."* They walked to the dining room and sat down around the table. No sign of the cross, no blessing by their hosts. Just a bow of the head. Tom and Rachel did likewise.

By the time they had finished talking three hours later, the conversation had roamed across the 79 years of the De Rosiers' lives — Communism. Nazism. The holocaust. Post-war France. Camus. Sartre. The Catholic Church. Jewish-Christian relations. Terrorism. Religious fanaticism. Magical thinking. Love, marriage. Child rearing. Parental guilt. The United States and its culture and its arrogance; France and its culture and its arrogance. Tony Mezzo Soprano and Giovanni Palmitessa.

Not discussed, Michael Tucci.

By the time Tom and Rachel stood to leave, Paul and Genevieve were acting the gracious Parisian aristocrats again. They had allowed these young Americans into their heavy hearts for precious few minutes.

It was late, past midnight. Rachel embraced Genevieve and held her. Tom couldn't believe how fragile the old woman looked in her arms, a small child, she was so thin. Tom held Paul's hand only a moment, then let it go. Paul nodded to him, a nod that Tom knew meant feelings left unsaid. "One more thing," Paul said, hesitantly. He was shaking so — Rachel reached out to steady him. He was formulating a question.

"Michel de Certeau, the Jesuit I mentioned to you earlier this week. He wrote a book a few years back about the Ursuline nuns of Loudun, a village southwest of here, during the sixteen thirties. They were the subjects of a famous church trial. The poor women acted totally out of character, blaspheming and insulting the church. They were found by church authorities to be possessed by devils. They...It was mass hysteria, of course." He stopped. "My son was possessed by hysteria. But I need to know; would he have killed you?" Genevieve put her arm around her husband, and the couple waited, the question lingering in the air.

"They were armed. But the bullets were rubber. No."

"Good," Paul whispered. "Six o'clock then, this morning, Sainte Elizabeth." Genevieve led him back into the apartment, turning around to nod to the young couple to close the door behind them.

"Let's walk," Rachel said, once they were out on Rue Flatters. She led him down Rue Mouffetard, past dark shops and squares and fountains. They passed the façade of a Catholic school and Tom mused whether it was there that Philippe had taught. Over the Seine onto the Ile de la Cité, where their footsteps echoed alongside the great cathedral. At the memorial to the thousands of Jews deported from Paris in the war, they paused and held each other.

Tom whispered. "Dementia — the magic of the old; it's how we deny loss and death." On the bridge to the Ile Saint Louis, a lone violinist was playing softly. They dropped Euros into his violin case and danced slowly for a minute. They walked past closed shops and restaurants. Recrossing the Seine, they huddled together in the frigid darkness.

"They are like Abraham and Sarah in the Bible," Rachel said. "Nothing to do with death. Dementia comes after an angel walks up to your front door when you are in your nineties and tells you, 'You are going to have a child.' Yes! Can you imagine that? So Sarah laughed at him; what the hell else was she supposed to do? Dementia is caused by how carelessly God plays with our lives. You walked in there tonight and because of Istanbul you were the closest they ever got to their son in all these years. Oh, Tom."

CHAPTER 61

Giovanni could not believe it. La Prostrata — erect, on two feet. She looked like an ancient Mary Magdalene, standing at the foot of the huge cross on the other side of the nave — tiny, wizened, sorrowful, waving a bony, admonitory finger at him. Now she was limping toward him, pushing her way through the crush of people milling around the cathedral interior. There was no floor space on which to prostrate herself. Never had he seen such turbulence in San Giovanni. The Shroud in absentia was a greater draw than when it was there.

"You, Giovanni." He did not know her real name to answer her. The chatter of the pilgrims died down.

"Si. Signora?"

"You have betrayed the Torinesi! You have abandoned *la Sindone* to a den of thieves and infidels. Shame! *Vergogna!*"

Chiara approached to begin the usual ejection procedure. La Prostrata raised her hand, ready to smack her across the face.

"And you too, whore of Istanbul! Shame! *Vergogna!*" Chiara was dazed and looked at Giovanni. Scattered clapping echoed from around the church.

The rumors had taken root in the hearts of the faithful. The absent archbishop was being held in chains in the Vatican. *La Sindone* was enduring insults and sacrileges at the hands of the Muslim hordes in Turkey.

"You held *la Sindone* in your own hands and abandoned it. You could have returned it in honor. But you obeyed man rather than God, Tucci rather than our Savior! May you burn in hell!"

Giovanni took one arm, Chiara the other. La Prostrata went limp, her black dress and shawl dragging on the floor. Security guards closed in, picking up the woman by the legs and carrying her out to the piazza. She screamed all the way. A police van pulled up and the guards quickly hustled her inside.

"I will be good to that woman or go crazy myself," he muttered. But he looked at his hands and they were shaking. The shrill scream of her curse echoed in his brain.

CHAPTER 62

The concierge telephoned Tom and Rachel's *petite chambre* at 5:30. They dressed quickly, ordered a cab and arrived at the Church of Sainte Elizabeth just before six. No crowds, no cameras. Tom opened the front door cautiously, recalling the frenzied scene of the pummeling Brits there the week before. Rachel clung to his arm. Inside, a priest stood before a plain pinewood coffin. The cover was closed. Genevieve and Paul sat in the pew nearby. Next to Genevieve sat Inspector Toussaint. In the pew behind them sat Charles. Tom led Rachel to the third pew; Charles turned, saw Tom and shivered slightly, then smiled his Peter Lorre smile. *"Bonjour,"* he gasped.

The priest spoke entirely in French, reading without emotion from a book of prayers, looking up nervously from time to time. After 15 minutes, he nodded to Charles, who sprang from his pew and went to a small table near the coffin. On it stood a sprinkler, which he handed to the priest, who flung drops of blessed water across the casket while murmuring a prayer. When he finished, he took a censer which Charles had prepared and swung it back and forth, sending thick puffs of smoke around the little assembly. He then nodded to Genevieve, who stepped out of the pew and over to a candle stand where she lit a small candle, blessed herself and returned to Paul.

Tom watched the two of them stand shoulder to shoulder, the mourning parents. And then it was over. Charles and the priest flanked the casket; the mortician, who had been standing at the back of the church, now approached from the side. Genevieve turned to Tom and Rachel and spoke for the first time. "Philippe's body will be cremated today and interred later. Can you spend the day with us?"

Tom looked at Rachel. She nodded. "Of course," she whispered.

"We will take a train to the monastery of Taizé immediately. Michael is in seclusion there. He couldn't come to Paris for this. Too many eyes watching. Come, there is a cab waiting for us." She took Paul's hand and together they walked to the coffin and placed their hands on it. Paul thanked the priest, gave him an envelope and turned. Genevieve shook Charles' hand; the sacristan whispered something to her. Then they turned and walked out the door.

Taizé was an hour and half by TGV from Paris, plus a rental car ride from the train station out to the countryside. Paul asked Tom to drive the Renault sedan and sat in the passenger seat giving directions. All the way down, Rachel and Genevieve had chatted about fall fashions, the U.S. presidential election and the weather, which was a bright and cool November day. The ceremony in which they had said a stiff goodbye to their son was not mentioned. No one talked about why they were going to Taizé, the renowned ecumenical monastery near the Swiss border, for a late-in-life rendezvous with the archbishop of Turin.

"What are your plans?" Genevieve spoke loud enough for Tom to hear.

Rachel pressed her finger against the window. "Well, we're not great planners, you know? Tom's on sabbatical and I'm not due back to work for another two weeks. So here we are. This day is enough planning for us, Genevieve."

"Maybe we'll get married in Taizé," said Tom.

"Do they have rabbis at Taizé?" Rachel shot back.

"They have everything at Taizé!" Paul scowled, but soon broke into a grudging smile.

"Have you and Paul been there before?" she asked.

"We went once." Genevieve was looking out the window as she spoke. "Brother Roger's work of protecting Jewish refugees in Switzerland during the war was an inspiration to everyone. Many people went to the monastery, as we did, to get some kind of absolution for their own collaboration, their denial. It was as if they had rediscovered authentic Christianity. You will see." She looked at Tom. "About your plans. Yes, marry at Taizé! How fitting! We like you both. *Beaucoup.*"

Rachel turned to her. "I can't think of anyone I'd like for friends better." She leaned over and kissed Genevieve on the cheek.

"Merci très chère." Genevieve squeezed her hand.

Tom looked at Paul — OK, you old dapper dude — "Ditto for me." Paul managed a faux smile and nodded. Tom wanted to press his arm, but didn't.

The hills of Burgundy glowed under the early afternoon sun, now drifting behind the car as they drove into the fields of Taizé Monastery. Young backpackers were hiking along the road; minivans filled with young families rolled along up ahead on the hills, looking for parking in a vast field of cars. Tom found a freshly started row, parked and turned off the engine. Parents carried their children on their chests or in strollers — it was as if they were all going shopping. But they weren't. How disorienting this was. Gracefully blissful high school- and college-age kids held hands, drawn by the light that seemed to radiate out from the complex of buildings. They walked past hundreds of truck campers arranged as neatly as fresh models on a new-car sales lot. On a nearby hill, tent flaps snapped in the gentle breeze.

At a pavilion they fell into a line of visitors that stretched under a long canopy. A recorded chant played from speakers installed at one end of the tented area. There were at least 1,000 people waiting in line or seated at tables, eating soup and bread. And people spoke either in whispers or not at all. When they approached the serving tables, volunteers young and old, humanity in a continuum of skin tones and dress styles, served the food; heads turbaned or with caps turned any which way; bodies in shorts, veils, jackets, dresses, slacks, robes, jeans, a Harley Davidson t-shirt.

Rachel whispered to Tom, "I'd heard of this place but, of course, why would a smart-ass Jewish princess ever come here?"

After they ate, Paul approached a member of the community and asked to see Michael. The brother said something to Paul and walked away. He returned a few minutes later and led the four to a residence building, where he showed them into a reception room and asked them to wait. Michael Tucci appeared moments later.

CHAPTER 63

He looked dignified, even in a clerical open collar shirt over his black pants and shoes. A little more tired, a little thinner, than he was a week ago. But a fierceness in his gaze was new. Tom was sure Rachel saw it too. All four stood at once. Paul stood stiffly erect, head tilted back — the Christian knight, the bereaved parent, the jealous husband.

"Oh, so long it has been!" Michael came to Paul and embraced him gently. Paul was ramrod straight. He gripped Michael's arm and turned him toward his wife. Genevieve was crying softly; Paul gave his wife a handkerchief. Michael embraced her and she hugged him tightly. When Michael came to Rachel and Tom, he smiled, held each of them close. "My friends. Thank you for coming. It is my good fortune to see you both again." My god, the man was a smoothie, Tom thought. Suave.

The brother brought a tray with water and closed the door on them. Michael filled glasses and passed them around and then sat down with a small book in his lap. "I have had time to pray and reflect," he started. "The loss of your Philippe — could we somehow have saved him? I grieve for him and for your loss, my friends." Paul nodded; Genevieve trembled.

He looked at his guests. "We have much to talk about, but this will not be the time. I must return to Turin tonight. So, I will try to be honest. The pope wants answers."

"I thought the pope had all the answers," Rachel interjected. Paul and Genevieve laughed even as they held discretely shushing fingers to their lips.

Michael laughed with them, then stopped. "To some questions, he does not have answers. What drove young Philippe to such extremes; why have Paul and Genevieve suffered as they have; why has the Catholic Church been so often complicit with the worst devils of our nature; what is the real purpose of my life working in this church — I regret to inform you, Rachel, that he does not." Michael threw up his hands in mock despair like a game show contestant who falters at the big money question.

"Yet he wants an answer. Will the archbishop of Turin withdraw his request to the Vatican to allow the Holy Shroud to be shuttled every five years between the Cathedral of Saint John the Baptist in Turin and the Cathedral of Saint George in Istanbul, for a period that will continue as long as the schism between Rome and the Orthodox churches of the east?"

Tom loved this about the man, in spite of his deepening mistrust of the priest. A powerful dissenter in the face of authority. "And the answer is…"

"No." The fierceness again in Michael's eyes. Paul and Genevieve looked at him, tight-lipped. "For that is what I propose to have happen."

Rachel said, "Well that's that." Nervous laughter.

"And there is a second question they want answered. Will I cease my plans to write a pastoral letter outlining my request, in which I submit that the final disposition of the Shroud not be decided until reunification occurs — and an Orthodox patriarch sits on the throne of Peter — and the whole church, east and west, in full ecumenical council, sets a new course, recognizing the world we live in is Christian, Muslim, Hindu, Buddhist and on and on. And the answer to that question is also 'no.'"

Paul fidgeted with his shirtsleeve and frowned. "That's it? That's all?"

"Oui, mon ami. The Vatican wanted me to come to Rome for this retreat. I felt it was like asking the hen to retreat to the fox house. Is that how Americans say it? I chose Taizé, which did not make them happy, but which wonderfully cleared my mind."

Genevieve sighed. "What happens to our brave Martin Luther if he refuses to take down his pastoral letter from the doors of the *Duomo*?"

"I am no Martin Luther, my dear Genevieve. I am a dissenter, not a rebel. I accept the authority of the church, but not the authority of its practice. Most likely, I will be asked to accept a new assignment, probably in Rome."

"And then, Michael?"

"I will not accept. There, I would lose my faith."

"And then?"

"Retirement. Montepulciano may welcome me home again. I will become an embarrassment, another voice on the fringe calling for radical change. I may take up residence in Istanbul and lead tours of *la Sindone* in the Cathedral of Saint George — where, I assure you, it will remain! And I may ordain you a priest, Genevieve!"

"Michael, you are being ridiculous!"

"Oh, Genevieve, I am being idealistic — again. As you and Paul and I once were. 'To the streets, Young Christian Workers!' The Catholic Church has lost its hold on society just as it once did on the workers of France and Belgium and Italy. So let us go to Istanbul and restore the western church's good name. Let us come to understand what it is like to be a Christian in a Muslim world. That, I am convinced, will really clear our minds!"

"You don't need my permission, Michael. Go for it," Rachel said.

"I need your help then." Michael retrieved papers from a small briefcase, pulling off a paper clip and waving it in front of her. "Read this. It is the pastoral letter. Before I am forced to resign my seat, it will be published. Rachel, the metaphor I use in this little treatise is the seed. I will give credit to the Slow Food Movement somewhere in here. What I am saying is that the Roman Catholic Church has promoted one seed and one seed only as the standard for salvation. Spiritual monoculture, if you will. It is like a grain company demanding that all farmers on all lands use only its seed, genetically modified to fit all situations. But in the gospel parable of the man who sowed seed on all kinds of ground, the efficacy of the seed depended on the health of the soil, not on the power of the seed."

Paul shifted his feet. "You say you accept the authority of the church? This tract differs from relativism...how?" His voice swelled with a cross-examining tone.

"I am exploring its use of metaphors. To me, the metaphor is the land, not the word from on high. Call it biodiversity, Paul. The old metaphor built Christendom but identified it with Europe. The world has changed. *Vive la difference.* You and I will not live to see how much. But our young friends here..."

He turned back to Rachel and handed her the paper. "Here. It's in English. Your week at the *Salone del Gusto* was not entirely wasted. Please correct any errors."

Rachel paged through the sheaf of papers. "Michael, you are a rogue in shepherd's clothing."

Paul and Genevieve said nothing. Michael turned back to them and took their hands in his. All his lightness of touch sagged suddenly. "I don't expect you two to support me, my friends. We have too much history for that. But I need your permission to go ahead, suggesting the Shroud should rotate between Turin and

Istanbul."

"Our permission as Catholics?" Paul folded his arms.

"No. As my friends — still. It will keep alive the pain of losing your Philippe as long as you live. No matter how the transfer is carried out, no matter how much incense and procession, pageantry and incantations. The story of how Philippe Jean De Rosier brought the Shroud to Istanbul from Turin in the year of our Lord two thousand four will be told again and again. Starting perhaps tomorrow. Will you let me do that?"

Tom understood the full weight that the question pressed against this private, remote, guarded, high-security couple. He was asking them to give up what was left of their private old age. But wasn't that already gone with Philippe's death? Tom saw the priest wince; Genevieve was squeezing the stone on his ring into his finger.

"Maybe it's time. *C'est peut-être temps.*" Paul's voice was hoarse; he looked at his wife. "Maybe it's time." Tom memorized the image of the three of them, their aging hands grasping each other's. He addressed Michael.

"Tell your friends, I am writing the story as you speak — will you, Pastor?"

Michael took his hands away from the couple's hands. "I have told them." The priest's face flushed.

"It will be honest, Pastor. Our little talk about magic and religion. You said that religion uses magic to get its message across. Isn't that what schlepping the Shroud to Istanbul was all about? The precious relic is an amulet in your grand plan to unify the church. And you used us to make sure it happened. You used Philippe. Did you give away the key to him?"

Michael Tucci made a tent with his fingers and then spread his hands wide apart. "To the question, did I give the key to him — by no means. To the use of magic. Guilty. *Coupable.* Mea culpa. But I beg you to believe me. I did not see all this clearly at the start. It's clear now, isn't it? I deceived myself first and then you."

"I wanted to believe you — this is about denial, Pastor, not self-deception. Denying what's in front of your face. Denial and magical thinking — two sides of the coin." He inhaled deeply, then startled the shepherd and the French couple with his vehemence.

"Michael, you want history to remember you as a dissenter. Fine. But for God's sake, man, you are a shepherd! Those sheep out there in the piazza by your cathedral — you've got them running in circles. Herd them, will you? This Shroud is powerful medicine. Some of them are on the edge!"

A bell outside started to ring. Michael gripped Tom's arm, then released it. "Vespers; time to go."

Rachel held up her hands. "Actually, I want to say something." The others looked at her. "This is holy ground here. I want to sit Shiva for Philippe." She drew them all together in a circle in the center of the room.

"Yes," Michael replied. Rachel reached out her hands and the circle was joined. Quiet washed over the room.

"I've been sitting Shiva for my ancestors ever since Istanbul. So I am thinking about you, Michael. About dissent, delusion, deception, denial — whatever." She took a breath. "Did you know Philippe?"

"I baptized him."

"Did you ever see him again? When he had grown up? When he joined the Camargue community?" Tom looked straight at Michael. His facial muscles were twitching. When he did not answer, Paul and Genevieve grew restless. Tom studied Rachel; what was she getting at? And why wasn't Michael answering?

"Michael?" Genevieve asked. Michael looked at her and then Paul.

"Perhaps nine years ago, I was about to begin mass one day in the cathedral. The bells were ringing outside the church; the choir began to sing. My associate, Father Roberto, told me that a man, very thin and pale, demanded to speak with me in the sacristy. I saw him; he looked disheveled, like a homeless person. I beckoned to the man to come closer. He was dressed in a wrinkled black suit, a frayed white shirt. He said his name was Philippe Jean De Rosier. I recognized him then."

Paul shook his head in disbelief. Genevieve's body sagged; Tom held her around the waist. Michael's voice was muffled. "He said he knew that I was a friend once with his parents; they had spoken about me to him. He had been in the seminary but had been dismissed. I invited him to have breakfast with me after mass. He said no, he had to go. But that he would return for my answer. I asked him, to what question? He said...he said...

"He said he knew I was once in love with his mother. That we had had an affair lasting years. One summer in the village of Saintes Maries de la Mer, he had spied on us. He knew. He wanted money to keep the whole affair out of the newspapers. He said he suspected he was really my...my child. He said the money would be used for a holy purpose, to return the holy things to Jerusalem. If I did not get him the money, he would divulge the story." He paused. "There was no key given, Tom."

The sounds of sighs, inhaling, exhaling, old lungs grasping for oxygen. "And then, Michael, what did you say to him?" Rachel asked.

"Rachel, I don't..."

It was Genevieve who interrupted him. "Yes, Michael. You must."

"I said I had never had an affair with his mother. I loved her and I loved his father. That he was his father's son. That the only time his mother and I had ever held each other happened when she slipped and I caught her to stop her fall. That day in Saintes Maries de la Mer." His voice weakened; he cleared his throat.

"I said he would have this falsehood on his conscience if he went ahead and did what he threatened to do. I told him he needed help. He laughed."

"Did you give him money?" Rachel asked.

"I did."

"Enough to keep him quiet?"

"No. Enough to let him know that I still loved his parents and that I knew he was living in poverty."

"And that's why you let slip their names to Tom this week. Yes? You intuited that Philippe was somehow involved in the theft of the Shroud. Tom could re-establish your relationship. It was not because he could talk to them about magical thinking."

"I did not know for sure that Philippe was involved. Tom could help..."

"And you never told Paul and Genevieve of Philippe's extortion attempt?"

"I did not. That would have been too much to bear. I buried it. And I knew that Philippe was full of rage; I waited for the story to appear. It never did."

"Because Gregory Samaras entered the scene shortly thereafter. Money was no problem then."

"I didn't know that then. We all know now."

"And you did not tell them this past week. Why?"

"I did not want to open an old wound."

211

"The wound of love."

"Yes."

"Which is what?"

Michael's hands flailed the air, aimlessly. When he spoke, it was a hoarse whisper. "That his seeing my love for his mother may have given him a key — to a life in which Philippe Jean De Rosier became Jean Baptiste LaRoque."

"Well, I think nothing, not high office, not human weakness, not denial, not illness, should destroy the love you all once had. Life is more than religion and faith and rules, your precious church unity — even more than my precious biodiversity. Life is this place we're in. Taizé. The basics. Beyond all the Shrouds of all the holy people in the world."

Genevieve held out her arms to Michael and embraced him. Paul laid a hand awkwardly on his shoulder. Tom and Rachel walked to the edge of the room and looked out the window. Outside, the brothers of Taizé were processing to the chapel. In the window's reflection, Tom could see the three elderly friends behind them, caressing each other's faces, gripping each other's hands. He gathered a strand of Rachel's hair and whispered into her ear. "I always thought I was the hunter and you were the gatherer. Foolish man. I was gathering a story. You were hunting the truth."

Tears brimmed in her eyes. "How terrible that a son must die to bring these three back together," she whispered back. "But, oh Tom, how fortunate for them that the Shroud was stolen."

Michael led them out minutes later, across the hillside past the great canopy to the church — a simple structure for sure, but set against the rolling countryside, it loomed like Chartres. Inside, a row of pilgrims in the back made room for them. In the center of the room, the brothers sat in a circle around the lectern, surrounded by row after circling row of pilgrims. One of the brothers, a man in his eighties, Tom estimated, opened a book and prepared to read. Tom watched the brother look directly at Michael Tucci and then start reading. "The Lord is my shepherd. I shall not want…"

When the singing, chanting, laughing and praying ended an hour later, the monks started their recession down the aisle. The dignified old brother held up a finger to ask the brothers to pause at the row where Michael and the others stood. Tom watched as Michael knelt down and the monk laid his hands on his head. Next to the priest, Rachel was still scribbling on Michael's draft. They went outside where a car was waiting for Michael; he embraced his friends, collected his pastoral letter from Rachel and was gone.

The sun was losing its bloom. Tom thought that whatever hand painted the evening sky had artfully arranged billowing clouds just above the horizon, bright golden, red and pale blue. Hundreds of pilgrims — those who had been inside and others who with crying babies at the breast listened from the outside — returned to their tents or cars in silence, a silence that lingered on in the Renault back to the little town and on the TGV all the way to Paris. The two couples said goodnight at the cabstand and agreed to meet for breakfast. Michael's story would break quickly and they knew they would need each other in the morning.

CHAPTER 64

For Giovanni Palmitessa, the Savoy Chapel, now empty of its precious *Sindone,* was the empty tomb of Jesus in Jerusalem two thousand years ago. Here he was, keeping watch over the glass wall beyond which had reposed the savior's burial Shroud. He remembered the gospel story about the women followers of Jesus, confused, abandoned by the apostles, yet still hoping, as they kept watch over the empty tomb. He fingered his firefighters pin and read again the notice on the white sheet of paper fixed to the wall. The text was in six different languages. "*La Sacra Sindone* has been recovered. Pray for its safe and timely return." It was signed by Archbishop Michael Tucci. The same Michael, successor to the apostles, whose instruction to the Istanbul patriarch was "*La Sindone* stays." The same Michael who had returned only yesterday to his flock in Turin. *Deo gratias,* thought Giovanni.

Chiara tapped his shoulder. "There's a visitor; give him a tour." Giovanni looked down the nave to where a pale, sickly, ghostly little man was maneuvering an electric wheelchair up the side aisle toward them. He was talking to himself, waving his free arm wildly in the air.

"Where the hell is this piece of miraculous dry goods? Who's in charge here?" The man's words, spoken in English, reverberated around the nave, punctuated by severe bouts of coughing. Giovanni was amazed the man's vocal cords had that much power. He seemed collapsed inward, from wizened appendages to shallow lungs, a truly compacted piece of skin and bones. But on he came; Chiara hid behind a pillar.

"Well? What the hell are you looking at? Where's Bruno the dickhead? Where is the god…"

Giovanni didn't understand the English but he caught the hostility full force in his stomach. *"Silenzio! Siete nel Duomo."* Undaunted, the man drove his machine right into the kneeler in front of the glass wall. The wheelchair bounced back.

"Bugger the kneeler, dickhead. I can't see past it!" Giovanni moved the kneeler to the side. Before he could turn around, the skeletal rider throttled the chair at full power into the glass wall. The thick pane trembled but stood, uncracked. Aroused to the danger,

Giovanni charged the wheelchair, held tight the man's flailing arms, reached into the controls and turned off the starter key. The man's fury rose up and congealed on his lips, a thin line of white foam. He stood.

"Dick…" The man's voice stopped in mid-syllable. He looked down at his legs. He screamed, "My God, I am standing! *Mein Gott, Bruno!* I am standing!"

Before Giovanni could usher the man and his machine out the door, as he had done so compassionately for years for the poor deranged La Prostrata, the man turned and, gripping each pew as he went, scuttled to the front door of the church and was gone. The wheelchair, nestled against the glass and exuding a thin film of smoke residue, felt human to Giovanni, happy to be rid of its burden. Patting it gently, Giovanni told Chiara to go downstairs to the chief of security and ask about what to do with it.

He went to the candle stand in the nearby chapel. He always lit two candles; one for Catarina, one for Antonio. He worried every day about his nephew, and many nights as well. The boy was in his 30s and unmarried. That was not normal. He knew that Antonio loved making deals, that he was busy putting together a taxi empire and running an Internet café called "Duca de URL," that he would do anything for his *Zio* Giovanni, that he had time for everybody. But he had not settled down. And he never talked about young women he was interested in. That was not normal. He did not know what the silence meant. It was Antonio's life and none of his business. But he worried.

"Per mio nepoto," he whispered.

He lit a third candle. *"Per Padre Michaelo."* Giovanni felt like a conspirator, unfaithful to his calling to protect the Shroud. But he had decided. He would line up with the archbishop, now that he was back in Turin. Michael Tucci was a good man, a man who was lonely in his job, but honest. He was like Giovanni. And whatever his motive was in ordering the Shroud to be left behind in that oriental cathedral in Istanbul, so be it. Giovanni was with him. It was a step Catarina would have agreed with. She would have said no relic is worth breaking off from those who are holy people. And Michael Tucci was one of the holy people, or as holy as people ever get on this earth.

And then a fourth candle. *"Per La Prostrata."* The crazy lady.

CHAPTER 65

Outside the *Duomo*, the story was breaking. Tom and Rachel had just stepped off a plane at the Turin airport along with Paul and Genevieve. Tom found a taxi to take them to a hotel.

Michael Tucci had given his pastoral letter to *La Stampa* and the *New York Times*. Tom read aloud from the *Herald Tribune* at a sidewalk café near their hotel. It contained one quote. "Are you starting a separation in the church?" a reporter had asked Tucci. "No. I am ending one."

The reporter commented on the story in a sidebar. "The letter's title *'La Nostra Colpa'* is one whose significance no Catholic over 50 can miss. For those under 50, it is an allusion to the old confession of personal sins from the Tridentine mass. *'Colpa Mia'* is now *'Colpa Nostra.'* The prelate's point is this, this cleavage between east and west is the fault under the church, as real a fault as that which lies below Istanbul, with as harmful an effect in the spiritual realm as earthquakes had been to Turkey, except, mercifully, this time. After that introduction, the metaphor switches to the land, the earth and the seed, with which humankind rebuilds society after a calamity.

"The theologically suspect propositions and the shocking declaration that *la Sindone* will remain in Istanbul for five years is making headlines across the world. The Vatican has no comment, either on the text or the fate of its author, except to say that the Congregation for the Faith is studying the archbishop's letter and will discuss with him what is essentially a church matter." Tom turned to an inside page.

"No pink slip yet," Rachel said. There was a full page of photos of red-faced, outraged men, women and children parading back and forth around the archbishop's residence, wielding signs demanding the return of *la Sindone* and the resignation of Michael Tucci.

"You better get busy writing your inside story," she said.

"Look here, there's a rally to protest the pastoral letter on the steps of the *Duomo* this morning at ten, organized by a Catholic group called *La Tromba del Difensore,* the Defender's Trumpet...speeches by prominent theologians and lay leaders...a petition is to be circulated to demand the resignation of the archbishop and the return of *la Sindone*...an organizer estimates the crowd will be in the hundreds of thousands. Hey, let's go. Part of the story. We'll check in with Paul and Genevieve later."

An hour earlier they had sent the Paris couple on their way to Michael's residence; they would all get in touch with each other that afternoon. Tom had been calling Tony Mezzo Soprano's cell phone with no luck ever since they had arrived. Not a good sign. They had taken a cab to Trattoria di Gianna; Giovanni's cronies said he was probably at the church.

They caught a cab that brought them close to the *Duomo*. They jumped out at the first sign of a roadblock and pushed their way into the piazza. Tom climbed up on a street barrier and estimated the crowd at no more than 2,000. They looked for someone they might know. Even Bruno Baumgartner.

Huge banners showing the face of the dead Christ were fluttering in the winds that blew around the *Duomo* steps. The speakers were fiery, mostly older men, but now and then a stern maternal figure; mostly lay people, but now and then a bearded friar or monk.

"Look!" Rachel had climbed up on a mound near the old Roman wall that adjoined the piazza. She pointed at a figure pushing his way out the doors of the *Duomo*, walking through a cordon of police surrounding the speaker's podium. For some reason, the police let the figure pass, even though it appeared he was not part of the program. "It's Giovanni!"

Giovanni Palmitessa pushed his way to the podium and grabbed the microphone. The burly organizer, head of the Defender's Trumpet group, grabbed it back. Giovanni punched him in the face and the trumpeter fell into the arms of an acolyte. Giovanni faced the crowd, which had on first sight applauded him as an old friend of the Shroud, but now fell silent. Tom and Rachel caught a few words but the primitive sound system mushed his voice. It was clear that whatever Giovanni was saying, the crowd was not liking it, and catcalls and whistles and boos began to rise up like bursts of firecrackers. Giovanni was kindling the rage of a mighty big adversary and had no fire hose this time. Tom guessed he had to be defending Michael Tucci. Rachel gripped Tom's arm.

"There's Tony!" Rachel yelled. Tony was edging his way toward the podium from the steps. Then he was pushing people out of his way, frantically.

"These people are crazy! Look at her — I recognize her!" Tom yelled back. An old woman was approaching the podium from the side opposite Tony, hair askew, dressed in a ratty, patched coat. She was moving silently, but purposefully, unseen by the police who were watching the crowd. Rachel and Tom heard Tony yell, *"Zio, Zio!* La Prostrata!"* They saw him lunge at Giovanni, trying to break through the police cordon. Giovanni turned to look at Tony.

At that moment, Tom saw the woman slip through the cordon. He screamed, "Tony — knife!" The woman was removing a kitchen knife from under her coat. She plunged it into Giovanni's neck. He slumped, bleeding heavily, fell down at the top of the steps and lay there motionless.

When Tom and Rachel finally reached the steps, pushing and shoving their way through the stampede to get out of the square, they found a sobbing Tony hunched over Giovanni as medics worked to stop the bleeding. Time was condensed into timelessness — the police pushing back the crowds, Giovanni's last shallow breaths, Tony's sobs and bloody shirt, the square emptying out except for a few hundred old women kneeling at a distance. Policemen carried the crazy lady to a van as she fingered her well-worn and blood-stained beads. The ambulance carrying Giovanni and Tony screamed away. Then the square was quiet. Tom and Rachel wandered in a daze, circling around the podium, hugging, crying. He reached for his cell phone.

CHAPTER 66

Just blocks away, at the residence of the archbishop, Michael, Genevieve and Paul sat in the reception room under the yellowing photograph of the three of them in younger years. Looking at it, they had laughed and told stories that one or both of the others had forgotten. When their laughter ended, they would look up at the picture again, communing silently with their memories.

"What will Rome do now?" asked Paul.

"I have heard they intend to send a flotilla of Swiss Guards to Istanbul to storm the cathedral and return *la Sindone*."

Genevieve was not amused with Michael's attempt to be lighthearted. "Michael, this is not a moment..." she snapped.

"My dear, I have not been summoned yet. Soon. *Bientôt.*" She cupped her wrinkled hands in dismay at his nonchalant answer.

"You must come to Paris."

"Of course. I will have more leisure — *bientôt.*"

"I mean, to live there." She looked at Paul, who nodded.

"Yes. You can stay with us until..."

Michael cut him off. "Until you tire of another mouth to feed." Genevieve shook her head in disagreement. Michael reached into his coat pocket and retrieved a letter. "I have been invited to give a series of lectures at the Sorbonne. Room and board is included. Can you put up with a heretic at your doorstep?"

"With this heretic — yes!" she smiled. "We will hide you under a sofa. All of us are too old to be a threat to anyone, I think. Yes! We will take the heretic for long walks through the Jardin de Luxembourg. We will share food and wine together on Rue Mouffetard close by. We will go to concerts and operas and lectures and..." Genevieve felt her heart pounding. Her face flushed. "I talk like a schoolgirl."

The door to the room opened. Father Raffaelo signaled awkwardly to the archbishop. *"Excusez moi."* Michael stood and left the room. The sound of a distant ambulance siren pierced the silence.

"Am I talking too much, Paul?" She sat back in the chair and rested her head.

"I like to hear you talk as you do now. It has been a long time. We have become heavy, grave. Michael has made us light again.

219

Keep talking!"
The door opened. Michael stumbled in. Genevieve stood and took a step toward him. "What is it? Michael, what is wrong?"
"It's Giovanni. He's been stabbed. At a rally. He's dying."

***

"Giovanni Palmitessa died on the emergency room operating table yesterday afternoon," *La Stampa* reported the next day. "His attacker was identified as a mentally ill resident of a Turin group home. She had been to the Cathedral daily, for years. She knew Giovanni. He had been good to her, parishioners testified. They considered her harmless; deranged, but harmless."

CHAPTER 67

The next three days Tom, with Rachel always at his side, watched as Turin kept vigil for the dead Giovanni. His body reposed in an open casket in the nave of the cathedral. He was laid out in his signature corkscrew tie and flower-patterned shirt, the firefighters pin on his lapel catching the glow of a score of flanking candles in the dark aisle. Whatever animosity had fueled the fatal rally had now converted to solemn grief for the old firefighter. Tom and Rachel stayed close to Tony as legions of family members stood near the casket while the people of Torino filed by.

Tom saw, in a back pew, Michael Tucci kneeling alone, for hours on end. He looked like a stranger in his own city. Only Father Raffaelo and Father Roberto stood by him, stoic, faces tear-stained.

Giovanni's funeral was big — it overflowed and filled the piazza outside. Video screens outside the church transmitted the flickering images of the funeral liturgy. The honorary pallbearers numbered in the hundreds, the firefighters of Turin and many police. Giovanni's fellow tour guides had an entire section of pews reserved for themselves; red-eyed Chiara, his colleague, led them in a droning recitation of the rosary just before the service began.

In front of the side chapel where the Shroud had once rested, a delegation from Istanbul had bravely weathered the bruised feelings of Turin to attend the funeral. The delegation was led by the patriarch of Istanbul and Gregory Samaras. Grief was written on the deep lines of the two men's faces. Tom wrote furiously, absorbing the event's pain and trying to make sense of its searing irony.

He and Rachel found themselves working their way up a side aisle where they could see everything. They saw Paul and Genevieve seated in a pew and were about to crowd in with them when they spotted Bruno Baumgartner next to Gregory Samaras. "What is he doing here?" she whispered. Tom shrugged his shoulders. Another day, another surprise. He was taking notes on a pad damp with tears, when he was nudged hard in the back. Yusuf Aktug was grinning at him.

"What are a Jew, a Lutheran and a Muslim doing in this place, huh, infidels?" He snapped his eyes back and forth at the huge assembly. "Only for Giovanni would I be here. Ah, Giovanni."

"What's Bruno up to?" Rachel jabbed him back in the ribs.

"Haven't you heard? He's working for us now. I mean for Samaras. Samaras is going to announce the beginning of an east-west dialogue center to make peace between Muslims, Jews, the Orthodox and you western Christians. He told me the name, The Archbishop Tucci Center for East-West Dialogue. I tell you, dear Rachel and gentle Tom, make friends with those in top places!" Chiara, the guide, shook her rosary like a rattle and shushed him.

Michael Tucci presided over the ceremony with austere grace. "*Santo* Giovanni Palmitessa da Torino, *priez pour nous!*" he said softly, his whisper amplified across the church and out to the piazza. "The knife was meant for me. But he placed his body in danger, as he always did. *Caro* Giovanni." He repeated it in Italian, laid his hands on the coffin, started to turn to the altar and then spun back to face the congregation and the television cameras.

Tom watched Michael Tucci closely. What a political animal this churchman was. Noble, yes, brave, yes — but all politics, all the time. Every act was calculated, a gesture, a tactic, a manipulation. Taking time to meet with him and Rachel. Sharing the names of the De Rosiers. Blessing the mission to Istanbul. Seducing them into a plan that was not yet a plan even in his own mind. Every movement sent a signal that he knew he was making history, changing the story's ending, cementing his place in chapters yet to be written. That's what it was, this simpatico between the two of them. A celebrity and his paparazzo. They both had shares in magical thinking.

"I have been thought by some to be heretical, or sympathetic to heresy." Michael spoke tentatively, switching back and forth from English to Italian. There was a murmur in the church, many heads nodding yes, others shaking no. "There is a heresy I am fond of, I confess. Patripassionism. A belief in the third century of our Common Era that when Jesus suffered and died, God the Father suffered and died. And rose. And even more; that when any of us suffers, God the Father suffers. And even more; that when a bird falls from the sky — the Father falls as well.

"I believe that God the Father must have felt something when Giovanni fell. We call God a loving father. I know of no loving father who does not suffer when his child suffers." He touched the casket. "Oh, Giovanni, you never had a child of your own. In this you and I are brothers. But you were a father, a hundred more times

222

than I ever could be. You had passion! It was a gift from your Father in heaven. Now go to Him and comfort Him and his Son. Tell them a joke. Tell them things will improve, this mess we have made of our world. Show them this burial cloth on your casket, your own Holy Shroud — thank him who taught us to be brothers and sisters in a world in which there is no East and West, no Christian and Jew and Muslim, no male and female."

Tearful sighs swept the church. "They love it, Giovanni's homecoming," said Rachel.

Tom stopped writing and gripped her arm. "God, I love heresies." She smiled and dabbed her cheeks.

They watched the archbishop lead Tony to the podium. Tony Mezzo Soprano started reading but crumpled his notes. "I have no words of my own today to praise my *Zio* Giovanni. Only his last words. 'No movie, Antonio. Something better. I believe.'" Michael led him back to the pews.

At the greeting of peace, Michael embraced all of Giovanni's family members and a good number of the firefighters and civic officials. He walked over to the pew where Gregory and the Greek patriarch were standing. In full view of the people of Turin and the television cameras, he greeted and warmly embraced the two leaders and the entire Istanbul delegation.

At the communion rite, the patriarch distributed blessed wafers brought from Istanbul, while the rest of the congregation received communion from Torinesi clergy and laity both inside and outside the church. Tom and Rachel joined the procession of Istanbullus and when they stood before Cosmas, Tom asked for his blessing on Rachel and himself. The patriarch beamed as he laid his hand on their heads. "He was the one just man Istanbul needed, that Giovanni. I would take his body over the Shroud."

Tom and Rachel followed Michael out the door. He was accompanied by teary-eyed Father Raffaelo and stoic Father Roberto and wedged his way through the nave out to the steps of the *Duomo*, where hundreds stood in line in the morning sun, waiting for communion. Michael took up a station at the very spot where Giovanni Palmitessa had been stabbed and began distributing the wafers. *"Il Corpo di* Christ," he intoned again and again and again.

Tom wrote, "Even a church formula is a personal mantra to Michael Tucci." He crammed his notebook in his pocket as he heard the helicopters droning overhead. There were other paparazzi up there, snooping for celebrities and snapping photos in the sky. Rachel shook his arm and led him through the crowd of mourners in the piazza — the same faces of people he had seen that first Monday when the theft of the Shroud had been announced. She stopped when they reached the old Roman wall, a ruin of timeless dignity in the hurly-burly of the piazza.

"Every two years we will come back for the *Salone del Gusto.* Promise?" She asked.

"I promise."

"Every time we return, we will come and rub this wall." She reached out and pushed her palm along the rough, ancient stones. Tom put his hand atop hers. "Promise?"

"I promise."

"And we will say together, oh, something profound, like, 'Yes, the earth moves under our feet, but we're still here.' Or maybe, 'Still here after all these years.' Until the last one alive dies. OK?"

Hands covered with flaky stone dust, they turned back toward the steps of the *Duomo.* Michael and all his acolytes had returned inside. Police were preparing a path for the funeral cortege to leave the piazza. Tom and Rachel watched a battered old steam pumper fire truck chug toward them on Via Settembre XX. Ramrod straight behind the steering wheel was old Adnan, from Istanbul. He carefully backed the pumper up against the base of the steps just as the casket was being carried outside by six firemen, followed by the Palmitessa families, an endless stream of firefighters in uniform, the citizens of Turin and the denizens of Trattoria di Gianna. The casket was gently pushed into the back of the rig. Adnan tugged a rope attached to a bell on the pumper chassis. The bell clanged in muffled cadence as mourners made the sign of the cross in the jammed piazza. The journey to the cemetery began.

Leaning against the old wall, Tom and Rachel waved to ancient Adnan, tolling the bell, bearing away the body of his old friend. "OK?" she asked again, insistently.

"OK," he whispered, one hand in hers, the other at his brow, in salute.

EPILOGUE

Levi Paul Cohen-Ueland, European correspondent for the *New York Times*, filed this story on October 15, 2054. "In this year one thousand years after the great separation between Rome and Constantinople, a new pope has been elected in Rome. The new pontiff has taken the name of John, after the great Saint John Chrysostom of the Eastern Church. 'John' had been the new pope's name when he was the Orthodox patriarch of Constantinople for the past 12 years. In that position he has been instrumental in leading the drive for the end of the long separation between east and west, a work which has taken almost 50 years to complete, much of it through the efforts of the Archbishop Tucci Center for East-West Dialogue. At the First Council of Istanbul, held in 2049, church differences on ancient questions like the relation of God the Son to the Holy Spirit, or the Immaculate Conception of Mary, had either been resolved or relegated to theological think tanks. Mandatory celibacy for clergy was made voluntary in the west and the autonomy of patriarchates was recognized under the nominal primacy of the Bishop of Rome. The First Vatican Council's pronouncement on papal infallibility was "contextualized" — in effect it was shelved, "back-burnered."

"The celebrations in Rome have been of a kind never before seen here. A full force of patriarchs from almost every Orthodox branch in Christianity sat in their places not as observers but as brother bishops, splendidly robed and speaking in many tongues. The election brought a nervously ecumenical spirit to the shocked civil servants of the Vatican; the inauguration of this eastern rite pope has totally disoriented Rome.

"A mirror celebration was held in Istanbul yesterday. Istanbul, its minarets and mosques bright in the sunlight off the Bosphorus, welcomed the pope as it never had the patriarch. Turkey's former minister of agriculture, Yusuf Aktug, was the official host, although confined now to a wheelchair. The aged widow of Gregory Samaras was at Yusuf's side for part of the ceremony. The government of Turkey was jubilant in its welcome, even though newspaper editorials, Internet blogs and the chambers of political discourse were filled with arguments over how to steer the ship of state through these new uncharted waters. A Roman pope in Istanbul? A new Constantinian order? There were snide comments that the Knight-Precursors of Christ the King were having their way after all, that the world was rewinding back to Constantine's fourth century on its way to the first.

"But the real action takes place over these two days in the north of Italy, in Turin. It is the beginning of the five-year period for the Shroud to be at the *Duomo*, the church of Saint John the Baptist. The line flowing into the doors snakes all the way from Piazza Castello. Bells are ringing throughout the city for the entire two-day papal inauguration period."

Levi stood waiting inside the Turin cathedral. He was watching an old man, one of 20 tour guides escorting the endless lines of pilgrims through the church. The guides led groups of 100 and alternated in Italian and English. Levi stood near an elderly American couple, attended by their grown children — his siblings — and grandchildren and a few fresh-cheeked infant great-grandchildren. They made their way together down the aisle when the old guide motioned them forward. Levi was dazzled by the vases of flowers on every altar, on the floor, in the sanctuary and especially around the Savoy Chapel. The guide snapped his fingers to command Levi's wandering attention.

"In the year nine forty-four the image of Edessa was transferred to Constantinople, where, the historical record tells us, for the first time *la Sindone* of the Lord is to be found. The crusader Robert de Clari wrote that during the sack of Constantinople, *la Sindone*, on which the image of Our Lord could be seen, disappeared from the city in twelve oh four."

The guide stopped and shook a bony finger at the old man at the center of this large family. "You there, old man, pay attention." The old man smiled at him and gave the old guide a shaky but smart salute.

"Now, in the last decade of the last century, nineteen ninety-three, *la Sindone* is temporarily placed behind the high altar, ahead of us, while the chapel of Guarinl was restored. Then, four years later, just before *la Sindone* is scheduled to be returned to that chapel, a fire breaks out — the chapel is gutted. Thank God *la Sindone* is still behind the high altar, where it is also threatened by the fire; it is saved by the brave firemen of Torino. And my sainted uncle was one of them that day.

"In the year two thousand four, a terrible crime took place. Religious fanatics stole the Shroud from its reliquary and reversed the route it had taken to come here. They escaped with it over the sea to old Constantinople." He paused and warbled a few bars of music. "'Now Istanbul. Once Constantinople.'" He rocked unsteadily on his feet and winked at the old woman. "A terrible crime. But *Santo* Giovanni Palmitessa and, yes, I, his nephew, went to Istanbul and saved *la Sindone* from being lost forever. And I see two of you in this group who were also there and gave us some assistance." Again, the wink at the elderly couple. Their children clapped. Levi felt very proud.

"Then a few weeks later, Saint Giovanni Palmitessa was stabbed as he spoke on the very steps of this church, defending his archbishop's vision of bringing the churches together." Levi saw his parents' eyes glisten.

"Out of that sad act came a good ending. Ever since then, the Shroud has gone back and forth, like the pendulum of a clock, between our two cities, saying the time is now, calling the churches together. My uncle gave his life for that noble union. And today it has come to pass. It is a happy fault, no? Since then, miracles have taken place in his name. So last year the church declared my old *Zio* Giovanni a saint. *Zio* Giovanni would have been the first one to laugh at the idea. We should all laugh. Laughter softens all sorrow. Thank you for coming today. It is wonderful to see all you beautiful ladies here. God bless you all!"

The applause rose and echoed through the church.

The elderly couple and their brood stayed with the guide near the chapel after the rest of the group was ushered out. Other new contingents of pilgrims were shuffling toward the chapel on their three-minute tour. English and Italian commentaries blended together in a kind of hushed Esperanto up and down the aisles.

"Tony Mezzo Soprano!" The old American man's voice trembled. The old guide's shining eyes cast a sly look at him; the two men hugged and held one other up.

Levi watched his mother, Rachel, pull at the guide's cheek. "Still charming the women, I see." She wrapped herself around him as steadily as she could. A horde of camera flashes lit up the church and a sacristan at the altar turned to enforce the no-pictures rule, but stopped. Ancient tears flowed. Rachel mussed Tony's thinning hairs. The laughter of the group was also violating the no-talking rule. The sacristan could only shrug his shoulders.

Levi's father, Tom, grasped Tony by the collar. "I have a question, Tony. We have seen each other almost every two years for the last fifty years. For the *Salone del Gusto*. For too many funerals to remember. And every time we meet, there are stories about somebody cured from cancer or restored to health after a stroke or throwing away one of these crutches here."

Levi looked over at a wall of photographs of dazed, happy people, images surrounded by canes and walkers and crutches, a wall of testimonials that almost threatened to overshadow the prominence of the Savoy Chapel across the nave from it. At the very top of the heap of thanks was a set of keys attached to a yellowing faded note from a man who said he had been cured of cancer by Giovanni in 2004. Levi fingered it gently. "Here's an extra set of keys. I am donating the wheelchair to your church. Send me a receipt; its value is 4,325 American. Thanks." He wrote the inscription down in his notebook.

"So what I want to know is, did you pay those people to say they had been cured by Giovanni?" asked Tom.

The wounded-looking guide chuckled. The grown children of the pilgrim couple had crowded together around him. He took one of the infants in his arms and smiled through teeth that still seemed mostly his own. "Did Tony Mezzo Soprano engage in the crime of simony? Buy a holy thing? Tomasino, what a nasty thing to say about your old friend. And I am sorry to say, no, I never thought to do so. *Santo Zio* Giovanni would have enjoyed that."

Near the wall of mementoes stood a statue of *Santo* Giovanni Palmitessa, staring back at the group with the innocently threatening mien of Marlon Brando's Godfather. He was dressed in a rumpled suit and aiming a fire hose at trouble somewhere. "Ah yes, the man himself," Tom croaked to Levi. He saluted the statue. Rachel blew a kiss to it. Levi and the adult children applauded. The small ones stared in wonder at the collage of crutches impressed upon the wall.

"I think it was my book that convinced the church to make him a saint," said Tom.

"No, it was the movie," Tony shot back.

"It was the opera," Rachel chimed in.

"It was my Bar Mitzvah commentary," Levi said, effectively terminating the biennial ritual of conflicting claims.

The grandchildren were fussing. Tony stretched to his full

height, much shorter than in his youth. Holding his arms wide, he looked at the generations begot by Tom and Rachel Cohen-Ueland. "Miracles? These are the miracles! These are the miracles! So many! From such a quiet Lutheran boy! We will need my entire fleet to take us to Trattoria di Gianna."

Out on the church steps, Levi watched an endless line of limos and cabs stream into the piazza. Emblazoned on the doors was the trademark "Mezzo Soprano Limo/Taxi *Servizio.*" They were lined up across the piazza near the old Roman wall. The entire Cohen-Ueland brood left the church, dodged a tram as they crossed the piazza and processed to the wall. Levi and the others surrounded Tom and Rachel, the two of them caressing the stones, kissing for the cameras and whispering something to each other. Nobody ever asked what.

THE END

Other Dagger titles available from Second Wind Publishing:

Staccato
Deborah J Ledford
Performed against the backdrop of the Great Smoky Mountains of North Carolina, Staccato transports readers to a behind-the-scenes glimpse of professional musicians, the psychological twists and turns of its characters, and in the end, retribution that crashes in a crescendo of notes played at the literary pace of a maestro's staccato.

False Positive
J J Dare
A tale of murder, war, espionage and vast conspiracy. Joe Daniels, thought he had at last escaped his brutal past. His placid world begins to unwind when his lovely wife Beanie is involved in an inexplicable accident that leaves her changed in every way; then ghosts from his past begin to emerge.

White Lies
Brad Stratton
Julie Dempsey was sending $5000 a month to someone in Idaho . . . before she disappeared. Derek, her lover, wants to know where she has gone, so he has hired an L.A. detective—Michael Chambers: ironic, bright, and not to be underestimated by anybody, including the thugs who want him dead.

Made in the USA
Charleston, SC
05 January 2013